Fire Heart

FIRE ISLAND SERIES
BOOK TWO

ALEXANDRA BANKS

For more information, or to book an event, contact:

alexandrabanksauthor@gmail.com

Book design by Alexandra Banks

Cover design by Haya Designs

ISBN (ebook): 978-1-7641949-2-1

ISBN (paperback): 978-1-7641949-3-8

ISBN (hardcover): 978-1-7641949–45

First Edition: September 2025

Also by Alexandra Banks

Rosewood Ranch Series

Tough Love

Heart & Hope

Saving Grace

True North

Fire Island Series

Tender Heart

Fire Heart

For the hearts who fight.

Author's Note

TW –

Non-consensual scenes.

Mature, explicit intimate scenes.

Coarse language & violence.

The location and topographies of the places in this story have been fictionalized. They may not accurately represent actual location and terrain.

Fire Heart
PLAYLIST

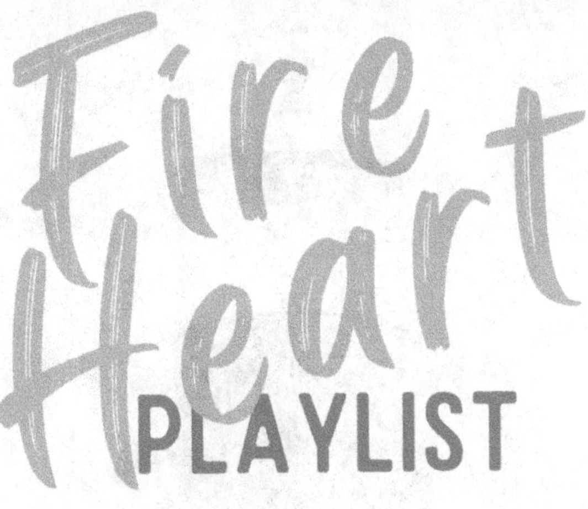

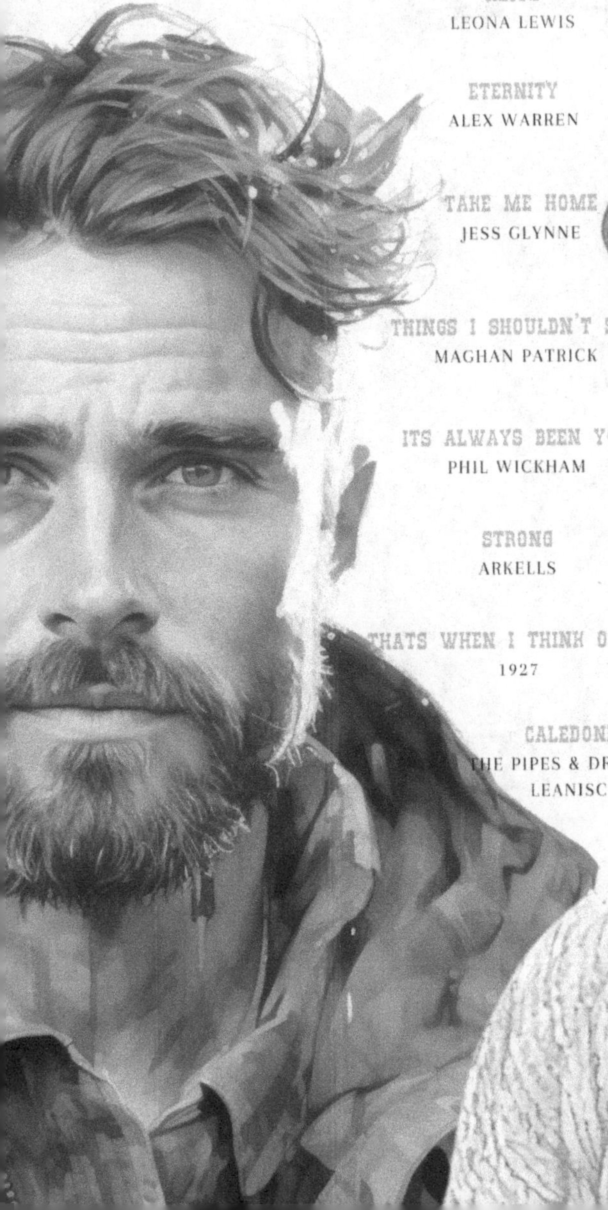

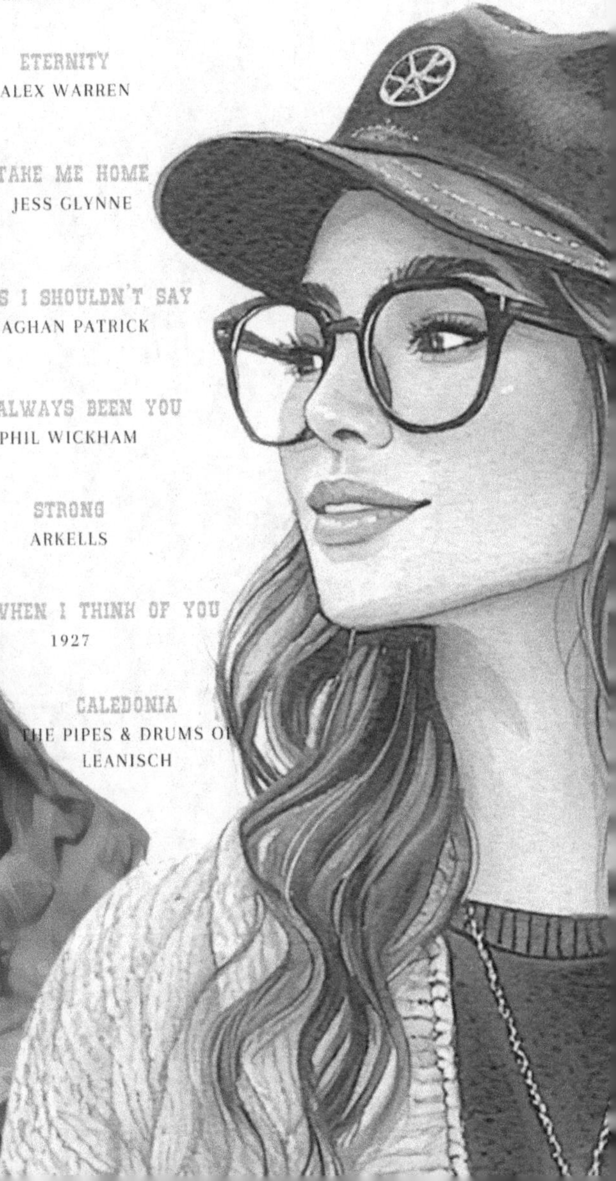

ALIVE
LEONA LEWIS

ETERNITY
ALEX WARREN

TAKE ME HOME
JESS GLYNNE

THINGS I SHOULDN'T SAY
MAGHAN PATRICK

ITS ALWAYS BEEN YOU
PHIL WICKHAM

STRONG
ARKELLS

THATS WHEN I THINK OF YOU
1927

CALEDONIA
THE PIPES & DRUMS OF
LEANISCH

Fire Heart

One

EVIE

The generator hums beside me, rattling the chain and cuffs attaching me to its bulky body with every vibration. Leaning against the cool wall of the basement, I close my eyes, trying my best to ward off the panic that comes around every few hours when I remember how I got here.

Wrestling with the fact that . . . Cal isn't.

He isn't here.

Firefly, I assume, is still run aground on the eastern side. She won't stay there if the swell rises or a storm rolls in. The small, dank space I've been a prisoner in for the past week offers no comfort. The nights are a little cool. The days long.

But I prefer my isolation to the three times a day *he* comes down, armed with a tangled mess of threats, feigned kindness, and scraps of the food Cal worked tirelessly to grow and harvest.

Emotion rolls a boulder into my throat.

I break down every time I think of the man I shared this lighthouse with for the past nine months. The one who, by all counts, is most likely gone.

If I have learned a thing from history, it's that it repeats itself. Against all hope. Silent tears streak a well-worn path over my cheeks, dripping off my jaw. They splatter onto the concrete underneath, darkening the hard surface with their small, round pools.

"Where are you, Callum?" I sob.

I want to scream out for him, but my voice is still hoarse from the first three days of doing that. When I got no response, I tried for Emmett.

Still, that produced nothing.

Guilt and shame wore me down to silence.

The small wooden door to the generator room cracks open, and the blinding midday sun bursts through as the crack widens. I dip my head into my arm to save my eyes.

"Time to eat, Butterfly." The slim, tall figure of T enters. He bends, placing a tray at my feet. "Any time you want to come upstairs, all you have to do is promise not to run away."

I will do *no such thing*.

I've promised a man something before. I couldn't keep it, and I love him.

Loved.

My face cracks with the uncontrollable wobble of my chin.

"Butterfly, no more tears for him. It's you and me now," T says, squatting a few feet from where I sit. A few feet away, because last time I lashed out.

And I will do it again.

"There is *no* you and me." I seethe, tears flinging from my cheeks as I lurch forward until I hit the end of the chains.

There is no meek-and-mild girl here anymore.

Cal got what he wished for.

If only he'd been around to see it. If only he was the one to feel the benefits of the months of him guiding me back out of the dark place I'd crawled into. To find my fire for life.

My fire, period.

Emotion tries to steal my face again, and I tamp it back down.

T doesn't get my tears.

They will never be for him.

As if reading my thoughts, he moves closer, holding out a hand, the way you would to a dangerous animal—injured, but dangerous nonetheless.

"Butte—"

"Don't call me that!"

His face hardens, eyes mad. "Eve." He rises and steps forward. "You have one more day, then you will be coming upstairs with me. If you are still thinking of running, forget about it. I've secured the lighthouse. A spot for you at the very top. There is no other way out but with me."

He slides a hand into the pocket of his jeans, producing a set of keys.

He's locking me away in the tower and throwing away the key.

Literally.

Without another word, he turns on his ridiculous loafer-clad heel and leaves me to my misery in the basement.

The food sits at my side for the next few hours. A potato and a small bowl of something that looks like lumpy stew. If I eat, I have to relieve myself.

The first time with the bucket was humiliating enough to want to avoid it at all costs. I'm guessing my tower prison will also have a bucket.

Maybe chains . . .

Maybe not.

No way down, and the light oscillating all night long, stealing my sleep.

The light . . .

If I can sabotage the generator, the lantern room will

have no power. No power means no light. No light would surely prompt someone to come out to the island, wouldn't it?

Gosh, I'd even be happy to see Errol at this point.

The old diesel machine runs twenty-four-seven, surely it will run out of gas soon enough. The exhaust is vented out of the basement by large piping. I guess I would be either high as a kite or dead from carbon monoxide poisoning by now if it wasn't.

I scan the old engine for something to break, tamper with, or . . .

Then I see it.

The kill switch for the machine. A toggle in the center of the aged beast. If I can just—

Shuffling forward, I reach out, fingers straining for the small metal flip switch. The machine hums against my shoulder as I contort myself, gaining inch by inch.

My fingers swipe past the tiny lever, not affecting it at all. "Dammit."

The metal around my wrists bites as I push harder, shoulders curled in and chin tucked to my chest, desperate to reach.

The cool, hard switch brushes over my finger. I groan, willing my body into a pliable, boneless form. The generator rumbles against my right side. Holding my breath as if that will wring out the last of my bones' resistance, I take one last pass at the switch.

Metal hits the pad of my middle finger. And . . . it gives. Falling with my hand.

The hum fades out, and the small generator room stills with the silence.

I jerk back up, shuffling away from the machine like I'm about to be busted. Like the noise I barely heard in nine months living upstairs will suddenly be missed. My wrists burn from the force of straining against my bonds. I rub them the best I can. The chain rattles as I soothe the angry red skin with a wince.

Now I just need the light to stay out until someone notices tonight.

Fingers crossed.

Nightfall descends and the waters outside are dark.

So far, so good.

I attempt a bite of cold potato, my belly aching from emptiness from the days I've refused to eat. The mouthful is bland but not unwelcome. I swallow it down and pluck up the small enamel mug of water accompanying the food. Not trusting the contents of the stew, I push the tray away and lean against the wall.

Come on, Emmett. See the dark little island.

Please realize something is wrong.

Please.

"What did you do?" A voice hisses through the silent darkness. I jolt from a restless sleep to look up at a hunched grey figure looming over me.

T.

"What did you break? You think this is a game, Butterfly?" He leaves my space, checking the generator over.

No. No, the failed light was my only hope.

I sit up, holding my breath. Praying he doesn't find the toggle. Doesn't know how to restart it.

He squats, tapping his phone before light streams through the small room, illuminating the old generator. He runs a hand over its many parts before flicking the toggle up and cranking the old diesel over. It groans to life.

I huff out a sob.

The small, defeated noise is drowned out by the reverberating rumble of the machine. I slump back to the stone floor, curling in on myself.

That's it.

My hope, snuffed out. Unlike the long, bright beam I'm sure is now swinging around the top of my entrapment. Something slides over the rough floor.

The tray of food. A fist grabs my hair, tugging me from my protective position.

"Ahhh. Stop!" I scramble to my knees as he hauls me up by my hair. "Ow, please, I'm sorry!"

"Get up! NOW!"

I wobble to my feet, trying to curl away from him, keeping my head against his fist. Gasping, I sway on my feet as I search his pale eyes in the dim light.

"Please." I try for a thread of humanity. "Please, let me go home."

He leans in closer, a rough hand sliding around my arm, too tight. His fist releases my hair, but he pulls me close. "You *are* home."

My chin wobbles.

His breath hits my face. His nose almost touching my own.

Repelled, I cower with a whimper.

He shakes my arm, rattling me in the process. "There is nothing else left for you now, Eve."

"I don't believe you," I whisper, sucking back the sob wanting out of my throat.

"Why would I lie to you, Butterfly? I love you."

"You're a psycho. Who does this? This is not love. Nothing like it."

"My methods may not be conventional, but my motives are as pure as it gets."

I—

I can't respond.

We stand too close, breathing into each other in the dark. Lost between hopelessness and rage, I'm frozen. He searches my face with those pale eyes I have grown to hate.

This man I hate.

Heat slithers down my spine, and I shudder at the proximity.

He sniffs, tossing his head to the side before hauling me by the arm toward the spot where my bonds are tied down. He unlocks the chains, then releases them from the handcuffs.

Where he stole them from, who knows.

With the cuffs remaining on my wrists, T drags me from the generator room. Closing the door, he mutes the hum of the old machine as the light above us swings around and into the night.

The cool ocean breeze plays with my messy hair. I stand rigid, taking in the sight of the island I've been shut away from for days. The grassy area that meets the beach. The tree line marking the border of the forest I love. The shacks . . .

The—

Greenhouse.

A sob tangles in my throat, transforming into a boulder blocking my airway.

Cal.

Callum.

Above, the night's dark blanket is studded with brilliant white stars. Their shimmering points unwavering. The moon, slowly rising in the east, is a giant orange pocked globe. She's magnificent.

And Cal isn't here to sit and watch her rise with me.

Cal isn't here.

"Inside." His voice breaks, as if the beauty of this place is a stark reminder of his black fucking heart.

Reluctantly, I move toward the front door. It's hanging open. When I step over the threshold, what I find takes my breath away. Everything is trashed.

What the hell?

The furniture is turned over, books scattered over the floor. It's like someone raided it, looking for something. Or had a monster meltdown.

"What happened?" I utter.

"Eyes on the stairwell," T grinds out.

With his hand shoving me up the twisting treads, I take the steps one at a time. When I reach the first floor, I expect our room to look much the same as the living area. To my surprise, it's untouched.

"You'll be back in your bed soon enough, my

precious girl," T whispers, his hot breath hitting my neck. I wince, tugging forward in his grip.

"Not with you," I hiss.

His grip tightens. "You're mine, Butterfly. I have waited long enough. Been more than patient. You will give me what I want."

We ascend the stairs to the lantern room. I focus on each tread to stave off the rising panic. When he leans past me and shoves the door open, I stop in my tracks.

Rough hands smack into my back, and I stagger into the once-pristine lantern room.

Now, the glass enclosure is boarded halfway up, only letting the beam skim over the top. Way past my head height. The lamp rotates blindingly, and I raise my hands to protect my face.

"I thought of smashing this old giant. To take the last piece of him in this place." T glances at the light before it comes around.

I spin back, horror etched all over my face.

The door slams. Something on the other side rattles like a lock being clicked shut.

Then another.

Fists pounding against the wooden door, I slide to my knees. The wail that leaves me carries on the breeze, echoing over the Atlantic.

firefly

CALLUM

B*l—ee—p*
B-ee-p
Beep.
Beep.
Beep.

Light cuts through the slit of my cracked-open eyelid. Blinding me. I raise a hand to shield myself, but something snags, sending a sting through the back of my right hand. The tight surface beneath me crunches.

I—

Something covers my legs and chest, holding me in place.

I'm trapped?

Forcing my eyes open, white nothingness swallows my vision. I slam my eyes shut. Flinging them open again, I make out the light-grey blind over a window, the sectioned popcorn-textured white ceiling.

Beep.

I turn my head toward the screech.

My mouth is full of sand. My head feels like a swollen balloon. Gripping the edge of the plastic mattress, I pull myself up. Dizziness sinks heavy behind my eyes. Groaning, I hold firm on the bedrail as I sit up.

What the hell?

I sway on my seat. My mouth waters, and bile rises.

"Fu-uck."

Boat.

The dark waters of early morning.

The guy on the half-sunk vessel.

The thwack of hardness connecting with my skull.

Panic for something I can't place settles low in my gut, edging my nerves something fierce.

Greyish blurs roll in, stealing the context of each piece of memory rushing me like a freight train.

A rescue gone wrong?

I reach for my head and find a bandage wrapped around it. The pulse point at the tender spot on the back of my head thrums to life as I brush my fingertips over the material. A dressing over my temple snags my middle finger as I let my hand fall. With a little pressure over it, I can feel the telltale bump of stitches.

The hell?

I lean to one side, lifting the blanket. All that covers my body is a hospital gown. "Christ."

The simple movement sends my head spinning. My stomach lurches upward. I panic, searching the small hospital room for something t—

Grabbing the small bowl on the bedside table, I lose my stomach.

The door chooses this moment to open, and Iris breezes in like it's the goddamn country club.

"Oh, you're awake!" She's by my side a second later, handing me a cloth, removing the bowl, and setting it on the bedside. Green eyes level with mine. "How are you feeling?"

I give her the foulest look I can muster, and she tilts her head. The happiness drains from her face as her eyes tighten and she forces a wobbly smile. "You scared me, Cal. If Em hadn't go—"

Her face breaks.

"Wha—what happened?" I croak.

Apparently, that's the wrong thing to say. She sobs before she can tamp down the emotion.

"Em found you in a capsized boat. The both of you almost drowned, him trying to get you out."

"Is he okay?"

Em. Emmett.

Guilt drowns out the next words I want to say. Did the man on board survive?

Did Emmett have to save us both?

"I'm just happy you're both safe now." Iris slides her hand inside mine, dropping onto the side of the bed. "But there's someth—"

The door whooshes open and a white-coat-clad man strides in, a nurse close behind.

"McCreary, you got lucky." He holds a tablet up, tapping on the screen, not looking at me. I see nothing in this town's changed. "A pretty bad concussion. How are you feeling today?" Still, he doesn't look at me.

"Nauseous. Why do I have stitches?"

Now he looks up. "There was some damage to your temporal bone. A small plate was secured to patch it back up. The drain came out yesterday. No swelling. A good outcome. The stitches can come out in a few days. Like I said, lucky."

The stone-faced doctor stares me down.

I don't have the energy to put up a fight, so I lie down and close my eyes.

"Jamieson, can I speak to you outside?" Iris says, her voice far too saccharine. I suppress the smile that comes with the knowledge of what she's going to do next.

"Of course." He shuffles outside. The nurse stays, checking over the tubes sunk into my veins. Her gaze swings over the bandage and dressing on my head.

As the door swooshes closed, I watch through the large window as Iris spins back on the doctor. Her finger pokes his chest and her brows drop, the fiery little sister I've always loved serving Jamieson his own ass. It's entertaining. Watching my favorite person in her element.

Where would we be without Irry?

I, for one, am willing to let her take the reins on this one. Relaxing into the bed, I let the soft warmth pull me into its embrace. A sting pinches my cock—the tip, to be more precise—and I grunt, jerking off the pillow.

"The hell?" I grind out, hands pulling at the blankets.

"Easy. You have a catheter. The discomfort should go away when we remove it. As soon as you are back on your feet." The nurse offers a soft smile.

A catheter.

Fuck me. The thought of any woman handling me, surprisingly, has no effect. I drop the blankets, and she sets them right before asking me my meal preferences for the day. Nothing she rattles off the list sounds entirely appealing, so I go with traditional choices. Fish and vegetables. Meatballs and spaghetti.

At least I won't need her to feed me . . .

The bursting flavor of fresh tomato floods my senses.

Odd.

I don't have time to analyze the thought as the nurse goes about her hourly observations. When she's done taking my temperature, blood pressure, and so on, she reminds me where the nurse call button is and how to operate the television in the room via the corded remote to my left.

"Ah, thanks," I grunt at her back as she leaves me to my solitude.

She's gone without a word, and my focus drifts to where I last saw Irry. But the window is now empty. No scolded doctor. No feisty little sister.

The man is an island.

And the island is the man.

But who is taking care of the lighthouse?

"That's it, good." The young, tall rake of a guy to my right nods, a hopeful smile plastered over his face.

I repeat the motions he set for me. Tests, all of them. My mobility—the subject of this inquisition. So far, so good. I've walked up and down the rails with no assistance. Passed every reflex test.

Next, the mental assessment.

And as I turn back to find Iris leaning on the door-frame, a resting place close to my own heart, something in my gut flips. Like I should be the one leaning, doing the watching . . .

"Shouldn't you be at the café?" I call toward the redhead holding up the doorjamb.

She pushes off and moves to where I stand in the clothes she brought me. "Nope. Paige has it covered."

"Who?" *What?* Did I lose my memory on that sorry excuse for a boat?

Iris sighs. "She's new, started this week. Paige, you know her, Errol's granddaughter."

"Good lord, Irry. Dancing with the devil now, are we?"

She huffs a laugh. "Yeah, well. She's a good kid, works hard. Is taking a break before she starts college in a year or two."

"You paying her?" I raise an eyebrow.

"Of course." She slaps my arm. Skinny guy snaps his head up from his tablet, and Iris meets his stare with a glare. "Toughen up, bud."

"Montgomery, this is my sister, Iris."

Monty, the nickname I gave him two minutes ago, looks more afraid than enthusiastic about meeting my little sister.

"I was looking to take in a boarder in my spare room above the café, too, help pay for the new Fresnel, but no bites yet." She shrugs the handbag on her shoulder up, eyes studying my face. For a reaction? When she finds none, she looks around the physical therapy room like she might discover something I can't see.

I don't say a word, and she turns back with the fake smile she's been giving people since the day our parents died. "Anyhoo, I'd better be getting back. I dropped your phone and a change of clothes on your bed. Text me when you get your results, will you?"

What's that all about?

She's back to looking down at Monty. Poor guy's face is crimson, his eyes trained onto the screen.

"Yep, should be all good here," I say.

Iris nods. Her smile is soft, but it doesn't reach her eyes the way it usually does. Like something is up, and she's not telling me what it is.

She's . . . worried.

I rack my brain for what could be wrong. But apart from me being away from the lighthouse, I can't grasp what could have her looking like she's passing a kidney stone every time she comes to visit.

"Bye, Irry," I call out as she crosses the threshold.

She turns back and waves before disappearing.

"Right, well." Monty slips into view. "I'll take you back for your next evaluation."

"Sure," I say, following him back to my room.

He nods, holding the door open, and I walk in, feeling more like a child than a grown-ass man who kept himself alive for the past twenty years on a literal island.

Damn.

It's as if I'm just waiting for the penny to drop. And I hate it.

My skin's too tight.

A soft knock pops through the still silence of my room.

"Come in," I offer without looking at the door.

Jamieson enters, tail appropriately between his legs. I see he's been properly reprimanded by my little sister. Serves him right. So much for being a professional. I know I haven't been the town's favorite since Ava, but hell, he's one of the few doctors we have. That ought to count for something.

He gestures for me to sit, so I sit on the side of the bed as he pulls the only chair in the room closer. "Right, so you've done really well on the physical assessments. We just have to check your mental capacity now."

I give him a glower, and he shakes his head. "You two are peas in a pod. But, Callum, I can't clear you to leave until I've assessed the impact of the concussion on your mental functioning."

With a sigh, I say, "Go on then."

"Okay, what year is it?"

"2022."

Not missing a beat, he says, "Okay, next. Who is the president?"

"Joe."

"How old are you?"

"Just turned forty."

Jamieson looks up from the tablet, his face blank. "Right, and what's the last thing you remember before the accident?"

"I . . ."

"Take your time."

"The greenhouse. I finished the extension that houses the back end, for herbs and edible flowers."

"That's fine, thank you. Give me a minute." He rises and leaves the room.

I wait as he moves to the nurse's station. Surprise fills the nurse's face as he speaks to her, and she grabs the phone receiver and turns to make a call.

Jamieson returns, shutting the door behind him, and sits back down. "We've called Iris back. There's some things we need to confirm with her. If that's okay with you?"

"Ah, sure. Is there something wrong?"

"A few small discrepancies. If we can pinpoint them, we can evaluate the impact better."

"So, there is something wrong."

"Look, Callum, brain injuries are a very individual thing. What's normal for one person can be detrimental to another. Someone who knows you as well as Iris will help shed some light on the assessment is all."

He pats my shoulder like he's my best fucking friend, giving me the most pathetic smile I've ever seen scrawl its way across a man's face. He leaves me to the silence he broke before his mind-bending stupidity.

Hope Iris hands him his ass twice when she gets here.

Fuck me.

Then I realize he never told me if I passed.

Three

EVIE

The Fresnel's light sweeps over my curled-up, shivering body as the day's first rays of warmth splinter through the sky. I hold my eyes shut tight.

Thank god.

The cuffs around my wrists rattle against the wooden floor with every shiver. A rhythmic, endless tune of captivity. I hope T rotted in the bed he laid in last night. Hope his deranged mind snapped and he—

The locks on the opposite side of the lantern room door clunk against the timber.

No such luck, apparently.

I push once to sit up, then again to move up against the far wall. As if that will save me. The door opens, and the gangly, pale man gripping a tray of food creeps closer, rounding the lamp's base as he bends, sliding the tray toward me.

"Good morning, Butte—Eve."

I don't take my eyes off him. I'm not stupid enough to be distracted by the food my aching stomach is desperate for.

He squats. "Eat something, then . . . Did you want to come downstairs? You look cold. We could snuggle in the bed for a while. Til the sun warms up the day."

My heart ratchets up speed as he sweeps a bony hand ending in long nails through his oily hair.

"No thank you," I grind out.

"Eve." He shuffles forward. I inch away. "You're cold. This doesn't have to be hard, precious girl."

"Don't you dare call me that!" Rage flies through my veins, searing every inch.

His jaw clenches. Hurt flickers through his pale-blue eyes before he snatches up the tray. He places a cup of water from it onto the lamp base and stalks for the door. "Hard way it is, Eve."

The door slams.

The locks snap shut.

Thirst finds me the second my body calms down. I stagger to my feet and grab the cup, draining it in a heartbeat. It runs down my chin and neck. I sink back to the floor and pull my knees to my chest.

"Fuck you, T. Or whatever your name is."

As the sun starts to warm the room and my weary bones thaw, I feel the buzzing. The heaviness of a wet blanket draped over my entire body claims me, pulling me down.

What on earth?

I slide down the wall and lie on the floor. The buzz turns to fuzziness, dragging my eyelids down.

He—

He drugged me.

Panic explodes throughout my insides, flying up and hitting the wet blanket still descending over me. I claw at the floor as a strangled noise escapes my lips. I jerk, fighting the pull.

As the sunlight finds the base of the lamp and fractures the light around the round room, a whimper tumbles from my throat and the brilliance succumbs to darkness.

Everything bobs. Something digs into my stomach.

My hair hangs around my face . . .

The floor moves in my line of sight.

It swells and dips.

The thing digging into my stomach groans as hands —not mine—tighten around the back of my thighs.

Blood rushes to my head.

Upside dow—

Steps tread, one after the other.

Downward.

Gasping for air, I slip back into the darkness.

The pillow under my head is soft. A luxury that's like a dream. I roll over, and Cal's scent folds in around me. I snuggle closer to his warmth. For a moment, I wonder about the nightmare I'd been having. T had found me. I was in the lantern room. I was cold. Scared. And Cal was—

I jerk from sleep, and a scream rips through me.

Large, bony hands push me back into the mattress, holding me down. "Shhh. It's only a dream. Go back to sleep."

I shake my head, my eyes focusing in the dim light.

I turn my head to find stars outside through a round opening. Then, the small desk that sits under the window in the room where I've sat for the last nine months.

I'm in Cal's room.

With T.

With . . .

I struggle against his hold. "Get off me!"

"No, no. Eve, this is how it's meant to be. Calm down."

"What did you do!? Where is he?" I spit at him.

He clenches his jaw. "He. Is. Gone. Forget him."

"No! No . . ." I wail. I struggle against his bruising grip. He moves over top of me, and I freeze.

"Calm. Down. You'll see, soon enough, I'm who you are meant to be with."

I search his face, tampering back the sobs that slam into the stone blocking my airway. And it hits me—if I cooperate, I might have a chance to escape. Or run. At least.

So, I nod. It's a shallow, indecisive gesture.

He smiles.

And I *hate* it.

Bile rises, burning my insides.

"I'm going to let you go now. Okay?"

I nod again with more certainty.

"I love you, Eve. You make me feel everything with your stories and your words, and I know that's what I want in my life. Always. I want you always."

A tear slips down my temple as I force myself to not react. To not scream, not fight back. He runs a hand down my arm. Goosebumps trail down it, sending a sickening heat down my spine.

"See, your body understands who I am."

It most certainly does not.

"Trust me Eve, I will only take what is mine."

What is *his* . . .

A bullet, perhaps?

The long blade of a broadsword . . . ?

Not me. *Never* me.

"It will be better with me. You will see."

"What will be better?" I manage to utter.

His gaze drops to my breasts, then lower, trailing over my stomach. I tamp down the need to cry out. Instead, I whimper and force a nod. I need him to think I'm bending. That I'm coming around.

But he will never have me.

Will not.

One thin finger touches down on my stomach, over the shirt I'm wearing—the shirt I left New York in days ago. It is filthy. "We should get you cleaned up, before."

Before?

Oh god.

I need to play this smart. Or he will win.

And that is absolutely not happening.

I shiver in the warm shower. The man standing inches away from the shower curtain is breathing heavily. I scrub my skin relentlessly, as if by peeling away the layers of my skin I can erase the devil inside this bathroom.

It's late.

I woke up an hour ago. And the memory of that one second where I thought things had gone back to the way I wish they were, with Cal and me tangled in the sheets, burns. Holding myself together—barely—I manage to clean my body. Every part of me is purified, set for *him* to defile. Hot tears run down my cheeks.

If I am going to do this, I'm going to have at least a scrap of dignity.

I set my shoulders back and sniff the sobs down.

"Almost done?" T says.

"Yes," I utter.

The curtain shifts to one side. I cover myself the best I can.

"Out, Eve."

I step out of the tub, still holding one arm over my chest and the other hand over my groin. He hands me a towel and waits, eyes wild. Anticipating the split second

I will have to remove my hands and expose myself to grab the towel.

I grind my molars shut and reach for the towel, sacrificing my breasts.

His mouth falls open, his breaths coming in quick, short pants.

My chin wobbles, but I stand tall. If I can affect some sort of control over him, I'm going to use it to my advantage.

No matter the cost, I am going to get off this island.

"On the bed. Let me look at you."

"No." The word leaves my mouth before my strategic mind can intercept.

"Now, Butterfly."

The front of his black sweatpants is tented.

The thought of what the material hides makes me ill, but I manage to say, "Fine, where do you want me?"

He nods to the bed, and I drop the towel. I swear he groans behind me.

This is going to be easier than I thought.

If only I can find the line between his need and protecting myself.

I lie. T moves in, pulling the cuffs from his pocket.

"No—" I shoot my hands up, and he catches my wrist.

No, stop.

The cuff strangles my wrists before he attaches the

other end to the cast-iron bedpost. He pushes me onto the mattress.

Fuck.

"Now." He traces his knuckles across my jawline before dragging his gaze to mine. "This is progress."

"If you call chaining up a woman progress, you have a few things to assess, T," I hiss.

"Timothy."

"What?"

"My name is Timothy. And you are going to open those gorgeous thighs for me while I show you what you do to me." He tracks a finger over my temple, pushing a stray, damp strand of hair behind my ear.

With a sickening touch gliding over my skin, he walks down the side of the bed and widens my legs.

I gasp for a useful lungful as tears burn behind my eyes.

He sits on the chair at the desk, facing me. As his gaze drifts over my bare body, goosebumps flood my skin, and he moans, closing his eyes. With an erratic shake of his head, he stands, pulling the chair further back before sitting at the end of the bed. His focus is solely on my wide-open legs, my pussy now bare for him.

I tug on the cuff above my head.

Metal bites my wrists, burning the skin.

My legs tremble.

He rises, his palms against the soles of my feet as he shoves my legs open even further.

My chest tightens, sending my head spinning. I pant out strangled sobs before schooling my composure.

"You want to see what you do to me, looking like this?" Timothy hisses.

Frozen in the position he put me in, I stare as his hand dives into his sweats, and he pulls out his cock.

It's red and veiny. Bent to one side, the tip smaller than the base.

It's revolting.

He studies my reaction, as if looking for some sort of affirmation. He starts to stroke it with one hand, and I look away.

"Hey! Eyes on me."

Closing my eyes, I force my head to turn back before letting them open again.

"Good. Now, say my name."

I turn my head.

I. Will. Not.

"Say my name, or it goes in that pretty mouth of yours."

My mouth gapes in horror.

"Fi—fine. Timothy," I choke out.

He hums, closing his eyes, his hand tightening around his cock. "Keep saying it," he rasps.

"Timothy," I breathe.

I hate myself. Over three fucking syllables.

But I need him to think I'm coming around to his delusional fantasy, so I keep going.

"Tim-o-thy," I mewl this time, and his eyes fall shut.

"Fuck, Butterfly."

"Open your eyes and look at me," I whisper.

His eyelids snap open, his pale, insidious eyes burning into mine.

"Lower," I say, moving on the bed, setting my breasts bouncing. Cal would tell me to take what I wanted, to ask—no, demand—what I want. So, I'll use the skill he taught me.

But no memories of Callum McCreary will puncture this sordid space. This scene will be one I lock away in the deepest depths of my mind, never to be seen again.

For now, I need to seduce the man.

The oldest trick in the book. The oldest because it's too easy. And that's powerful. In this moment, *I* am in control.

I have what he wants, and I'll be using that fact to my advantage.

His face pulls into something painful, his hand pumping faster. It's not that I want to give this man any kind of pleasure. That's not what this is. This is my ticket to a long enough leash so I can break free.

Widening my legs just a little further as my heart

thunders in its empty cavity and my limbs shake, I say, "Lower, Timothy. Look how wet you've made me."

Almost choking on the stone forming in my airway, I force myself to stay the course, to stay still long enough to reel him in.

The ache of my pussy runs indignant heat through every inch of me, flushing my face. Arousal non-concordance. That's what they call it when your body responds to sexual situations, regardless of where your mind is at. I've used it in my books, and now I'm living the horrendous moment my main characters have suffered through. I am, in fact, wet. But not for the man in front of me.

I'm living for each hour now. That pivotal moment where I come into my own. When life's training wheels come off. I get to own this. I'm living for . . .

My freedom.

That sends blood thundering through my body.

I'm high on that control.

He jerks forward, collapsing over the end of the bed as he comes in his own hand.

I'm done being scared of this pathetic excuse of a man.

Checkmate.

firefly

Four

CALLUM

"What do you mean, it's 2025?" I stare at my little sister like *she's* the one who's lost her mind.

I've lost three whole years. The restlessness in my gut that flip-flopped into existence like a dying fish when I woke up here flares back to life.

Dammit.

I mean, it's not like anything ever changes in my life, but hell. The ass-faced Jamieson stands on one side of my hospital bed, Iris on the other. Em hovers outside, worry etched over his face.

"Do you remember your lodger, the one who came to stay for nine months?" Iris asks, her face strung on the marionette strings of tentative hopefulness.

Sorry, little sis, nada. Not a damn thing.

"Who?" I ask, and her face falls. God, you could see that one movement from Mars.

"What about the Fresnel? It needs replacing?" Iris prompts.

"Yeah, well, thought it could have lasted another year or two."

Iris raises an eyebrow.

"Oh yeah, I guess it's time is up, then."

"So," Jamieson starts, "from what we can gather, your memory's been affected. You have lost the last three years, give or take, a few months."

"Will it come back?" I ask, brows dropping as my gut sinks.

"That depends. Everyone is different. With time, most of it should return. It can come back in bits and pieces or all at once. Sometimes another traumatic event will spur the old memories back into existence. But it doesn't mean you go out chasing thrills to get your memories back." His face turns harsh. As if my history of doing stupid shit in this town is not history at all.

"Don't get your panties in a knot, Jamieson, no intentions of any such thing. I just want to go home to my island and get back to my days of solitude."

Iris shifts on her feet. "About that."

Jamieson leans in. "You will need to have someone with you for the first few months. Just in case."

"In case what?"

"Relapse, a sudden loss of motor skills, or acute dementia after the fact." Jamieson is looking at Iris when he says this. I grind my molars and tug the blankets from my legs.

Over the devil's frozen carcass am I being babysat. Iris has other things to do. *Better* things to do.

"Nope, ain't happening."

"Callum McCreary, you sit down right now, or so help me god I will give you one on the other side to match." Iris's wild green eyes bore into mine.

With a twitch of my lip and a low, heady groan, I sink onto the mattress. I refuse to climb back under the sheet and hide away from the world.

"I can't release you unless you have someone to stay with you for the next few months. Sorry, bud, hospital protocol." Jamieson looks at me as he says this, like somehow we're now friends.

Fuck you, *bud*.

"Fine," I breathe. "I'll stay at the café with Iris. But you'll be getting the bill when she loses her shit and cracks me a new one."

Jamieson has the audacity to laugh, like I'm being dramatic.

Fucker.

"He'll be fine with me. Thank you. Can I take him home this afternoon?"

"I don't see why not. Be a few hours before the last

set of rounds and he gets discharged. Then he's free to go."

"I'm right here," I drawl.

Iris pecks my cheek before heading for the door. "Text when you're ready, Cal."

The room falls into silence as they leave, and I sit on the chair, not wanting to be the vulnerable pleb in the bed, as I wrangle with the reality of losing three years of my life.

It's not like anything significant would have happened in the last three years. Each day on Fire Island is a carbon copy of the one before it. Lighthouse, garden, chop wood, eat, sleep, and repeat.

Three months of being holed up in Iris's tiny-ass café quarters is going to drive me nuts.

She'll be worse than a damn prison warden, if I know my little sister.

Maybe I can convince the warden to let me wander the docks aimlessly. At least the sunshine and the salty sea air will settle this unnerved restlessness that's been bearing down on me since my eyes opened in this cool, clinical white room.

That's all a man needs. Sunshine, fresh air in his lungs, and a purpose.

The first two are easy. And the sooner I get better, the sooner I can get back to my purpose. The lighthouse. Hope Em's been taking care of the old girl.

As I look over the items Iris left on my bed, I pluck up my phone to check the messages. One from Em from a few weeks ago. About a boat going missing. Another from Iris looking for someone called Eve at the festival. Must be one of her friends. She has so many.

The docs do their afternoon rounds, and they hand me the discharge papers, double-checking Iris is collecting me and coddling me for the next few months. They arrange for me to visit outpatient or my GP to get the stitches out and a follow-up scan. Agreeing, I watch as they mutter between themselves before moving on to the next poor sod trapped in this place.

I send Irry a text to come get me the hell out of here.

Iris stands in the doorway of the guest room, my bag in her hand, her lips rolling together. "You sure you don't want to take my room?"

"Why? It smells like you. Ew, girl germs." I throw her my best grin. The bandage around my head shifts.

"Okay, if you say so." She steps out of the way and waves an arm, as if welcoming me to the too-small room with its tiny excuse for a bed. I walk in, taking in my cozy confinement—the view out the window, the chair by the door with throw blankets, the bed that's made up with a light blue cover and too many fucking pillows.

"If you need anything, I'm downstairs, okay?" She drops my bag by the door and closes it as she leaves. I've traded one small room for another.

At least this one comes with better company.

I sigh, dropping onto the side of the bed. I rub my head, tugging off the bandage. I leave the dressing, since the stitches would most likely gross Irry out. I run my hands through my hair. I would love to talk to Em. He's been suspiciously absent since I woke up. I pull out my phone and flick him a text.

When nothing shoots back right away, I assume he's out on shift. I toss my phone onto the bedside and lie on the bed. The pillow is soft, and I slide my hands under my head. Tired from a day of waiting and doctor talk, I roll over and close my eyes.

Inhaling, a familiar scent floods my senses. It's almost feminine.

My eyes snap open.

I sit up, chest heaving.

And I have absolutely no idea why . . .

Is this what happens with a brain injury? Random scents and sensations are going to set me off at any time now? Until I get my three years' worth of memories back?

Dammit.

Tightness claims my airway, and I rub the space over my heart, fully expecting an ache to bloom. I sit up and hang my head, letting it fall into my hands. What am I going to do if I can't get them back?

What am I missing?

Iris won't offer up anything useful—I quizzed her on the way home in the car. She said Jamieson told her not to try to fill the void with her version of events, that I have to remember them on my own accord.

Fucking great.

That could take a lifetime.

All the while I feel like I'm operating at half speed. Half capacity.

Running my hands through my messy hair, my palm shoves across the stitches. I wince.

Dammit.

I can't take this. I can't sit around doing *nothing*.

I walk downstairs and into the café. It's bustling with afternoon and after-school patrons. Iris is busy talking to a couple on the far side of the café. I take that as my opportunity to slip out the door.

I make it all but two feet before the door when I hear, "Callum McCreary, where the hell do you think you're going?"

I turn back to find my sister, one hand on a popped hip, pot of coffee gripped in the other. The brows she's raised almost meet her hairline. "Hmmm?"

"Fresh air," I mutter, turning back to the door.

"You have ten minutes before I send Em after you!" she calls to my back as the door closes behind me.

A little wobbly on my feet, I head for the marina. The cobbled street feels familiar. It's reassuring to be sure of even the most basic things. I cross the parking lot and slip down the steps to the walkway. Boats bob in their slips, masts swaying in the ocean breeze.

I make my way toward Firefly's slip, only to find it empty when I eventually make it there. She must be at the island.

Remembering Emmett hauled my sorry ass onto shore for medical help, that makes sense. I sit on the dock and dangle my legs over the water. Hands gripping the edge, I gaze around the marina I have lived in and out of for the last twenty years.

Slow, steady footsteps plod to where I sit.

I'd know that easy gait anywhere.

Em.

I don't look up. I can't.

I know I'm only still here because of him. He slaps a hand on my shoulder as he sits by my side. "The warden let you out, hey?"

I chuckle, but it's strained.

A stone grows in my throat when I rustle up the courage, the gratitude, to look at the man who's been my brother for decades. His grounding dark eyes find me, full of kindness and worry.

"Guess you're never gonna let me live *this* particular rescue down," I manage to rasp.

Em simply looks out into the water.

"Iris would've had my head on a rusty platter if I came back in without you, Cal."

Now, the half chuckle, half sob, grinds its way up my throat.

Fuck me.

He nudges my shoulder with his. "The lengths we go to stay on her good side."

A laugh overcomes my emotion, and we laugh together at the thought of the little boss lady who rules our lives with a manicured iron fist.

We wouldn't have it any other way.

"I'm serious, Cal. There's no way I was coming home without you, bud."

It's all I can do to nod.

"Geez, can you imagine my life if I did? I mean, my balls would go first. Irry is ruthless, man."

I crack up, hysteria taking over at the thought of those two. When the laughter peters out, Em's amusement fades, and he continues, "Besides, that old lamp only runs for you, temperamental thing it is. It was acting up two nights ago. Seemed fine last night, but I'll keep an eye on her for you."

Now I turn to study his meaning. "What'd you mean, acting up?"

"Blinking in and out, but she settled. Shining through the night shift. Guess it was just a glitch. But I got to tell you something." Emmett stares out at the water.

"Well?"

"I was there the day before she started acting up. To check on things, you know. And the house . . . it's trashed."

"Who the hell would do that?"

Em gives me what I assume is a meaningful look, but I don't get the underlying sentiment.

"I didn't find anyone there. Just the mess. If they were there, they were either long gone or heard me coming and hid. Don't know why they'd do that."

I frown, wondering what kind of person crosses the water to a man's isolated island to mess things up and leave. Probably fucking Errol. Lord knows he holds a grudge as long as the prehistoric era. Guess he thought it was deserved.

Maybe. Maybe not.

"Was Firefly there?" I ask, realizing he would know where she is.

"Nope. Found her adrift a couple days back to the south. One of the passing shipping lane vessels called it in. But—"

He tugs his cap from his head as he runs a hand

through his hair. "She must have run aground at one point. There's damage and sand lodged into her side. I limped her home, just. She's in the dry dock. One of the maintenance guys is fixing her up as a favor."

"Don't want any favors, Em."

"For me, not you. Besides, that's a technicality. You have bigger concerns. The Restoration Society has questioned your capabilities after the accident, and along with them hell-bent on making Fire Island redundant, you and Irry have one hell of a fight on your hands to keep her up and running."

"Dammit. I knew they were iffy about the whole situation, but I really thought the heritage and safety of folks would win out there."

Em shifts on his seat, crossing his legs as he runs the brim of his cap through his fingers. "You remember anything from the last year?"

I snap my gaze to his.

His face is twisted with worry, but something else wars with it.

Like there's more at stake than just me.

The lighthouse?

Did something happen to the lamp?

"Nothing yet," I say. It's the truth.

"Sure. It's just that I didn't find *anyone* on your island when I went over, Cal. *Nobody* was there."

Nobody else on my island is the status quo. What is he blithering about?

Five

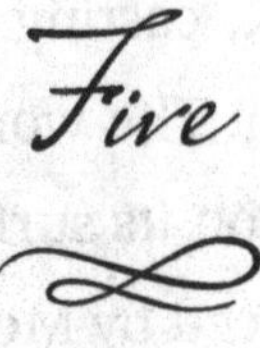

EVIE

Big plans. Should have known they would go sideways at the first opportunity. After gaining an inch toward my freedom, Timothy threw Rapunzel back in the tower after he had his way, gawking at me through his release. And threw away the key, so to speak.

He hasn't returned since the wee hours of the morning.

Apparently, my powers of seduction are a little rusty. Instead of the freedom—or at least a longer leash—I thought I would gain, I'm back in the lantern room, watching yet another sunset in captivity.

All I feel is dirty. Filthy from his gaze. Like I need to scrub myself clean with a wire brush and shed these layers of myself to the tub floor. As the ever-reliable whir and click of the lamp come on, I shield my eyes and reposition to face away from the retina-burning blazing light.

The breeze tangles through my hair as the light sweeps across my back, casting its iridescent brilliance over the Atlantic Ocean. The world is such an enormous place. I'm barely a blip on its surface. One that will come and go, never to be noticed by Mother Nature.

Noticed.

Who would notice a light shining?

Who would notice one that doesn't?

The watchhouse? The shipping lanes to the east of Fire Island . . .

Crawling, I hunt for some way to shut the lamp off. The chain to my cuffed hands drags as I crawl my way along the floor. Timothy said he wouldn't take the last piece of Cal . . . Because it would be missed?

Not by me.

He meant the Coast Guard would realize it's not coming on.

That's it, my chance to signal for help. Or at the very least, to get someone—anyone—to come out here.

With both hands, I pry open the base, looking for something to break, snap, bend, or undo.

All I find is a bunch of wires.

Wires that no doubt run straight to the generator, and all that voltage.

Shit.

Knowing my luck, I'll pull the wrong one and electrocute myself.

No thank you, I want to live. I want to leave this island on my own two feet, my heart beating safely in my chest.

The light sweeps around again—its timing never fails.

The lamp, in all its shimmering glory, oscillates on her axis like the queen she is. The heart of this lighthouse. The last connection I have to Cal. The one thing he had to ground his life and give him meaning over the last twenty painful years.

She swings around, shining right through me.

Sometimes, the queen must be sacrificed to save the maiden. One life for another.

One soul for another.

What about the vessels relying on her tonight? If they run aground and people are in jeopardy because of me?

No. Evie.

I can't think like that.

Besides, not anymore. Technology and safety protocols would make it unlikely . . .

I drop back to the floor, scrambling toward the maintenance cupboard. I fling it open and hunt for the heaviest, longest thing I can find. The thing that will do the most damage. May as well keep it after, too, in case I need to defend myself.

I pull out bunches of rags and brushes.

Nope.

Tossing the contents of the cupboard behind me, I send my bound hands into the dim cavity, hunting for whatever is left inside.

My fingers brush over a tin surface.

Hope blooms like a forest flower after much-needed rain. I grab a small handle, sliding the box forward. A toolbox.

Yes!

Oh my god, yes.

I flip the lid open. To my delight, a host of heavy metal tools sit in the bottom. Screwdrivers, pliers, and . . . a wrench.

A long, heavy, solid wrench.

Perfect.

Shoving the cupboard contents back and shutting the door, I stand, shielding my eyes as the lamp swings back round, the wrench firmly gripped with both hands.

Lowering my hands, I shift on my feet.

I can do this.

I can smash the last piece of the man I love to smithereens.

To save myself.

He would be telling me to do it. If he was here, he

would growl, *"Do it already, mo nighean. What are you waiting for?"*

That thought has me caving in on myself. God, I miss him.

And . . . I can't do it.

I can't.

Sinking to the floor, I cradle the tool to my chest. Tears burn and swell. I let them fall, rocking on my seat. The lamp turns overhead, never wavering.

I hide my face in my hands, letting the wrench clatter to the floor.

I have to.

I have to.

I have to do this.

With a raw scream, I push to my feet, swiping the wrench from the floor. Waiting until her back is turned, her light penetrating deep into the Atlantic, I rush her from behind. I slam the bulky, destructive head of the tool into the planes of glass that make up her crown. It cracks but doesn't shatter.

She swings around, as if turning back to face her opponent.

I duck my head, shielding my eyes. And when she is careless enough to show me her back again, I smash down hard. Glass splinters, showering across the wooden floor.

I swing again, the heady craze of something manic

taking over. I bring the wrench down, over and over, into the heart of her shining body.

The tinkle of raining glass exploding under the weight of my attack fills the air.

The light flickers as I reach her heart and destroy it in one final, deadly swing. The long, bright beam dies, fluttering out like the desperate wings of a butterfly taking its last breaths.

Fitting.

As the coastline fades into darkness, I stand, the metal handle hanging between my fingers. Tears pouring over my cheeks. Blood thundering through my head. Breaths burning through my too-small lungs.

The queen is dead.

The heart and soul of Fire Island is obliterated.

Now, I wait.

The smallest sliver of hope is coaxed to life as the gravity of what I've done settles in.

Glass shards and chunks of lamp cover most of the floor. I shove as much as I can to the side with the wrench. I make a clean path to the cupboard and pluck out a brush and sweep the glass in a pile to one side. Kneeling by the remnants of what I've done, I bow my head.

A gesture of sadness. My sorrow over losing the last piece of Cal. The fraction of hope I cling to like my life preserver with her gone. And she absolutely is.

Timothy may not frighten me like he used to, but he is still in control. And I have no idea how to take that back without a fight.

One I'm not sure I'd be able to win.

"Sorry, Cal," I whisper to the pile of glass, contemplating what I've done, and what I might still have to do. As if Callum can hear me, the wind whips through the lantern room, tugging at my clothes, sweeping over my wet cheeks, and drying my tears.

"Get up!" Bony fingers sink like vicious talons around my upper arm, ripping me from sleep and up off the floor. "You did this!"

I scramble to my feet, shoving my glasses up my nose. "Get your hands off me!" I try to pull away from his hold, but he's stronger than he looks. He shakes me, his face so close his breath hits my cheek. I lean away.

The door is open. He drags me toward the stairs, not looking back. I glance over my shoulder at the wrench on the floor that had been inches from my fingers. The one now out of reach. The morning sunlight washes the small room in its golden glow. But it disappears as I stumble down the stairwell, dragged behind the hysterical man in front of me.

"You have no idea what you've done." Timothy shakes his head. "Now we have to move on. We were supposed to have time. This is all your fault. Why do you keep screwing things up?" He stops on the tread below me, looking up, his jaw clenched, anger lining his pale eyes.

From this vantage point, I could lash out. Knock him backward down the stairs. I brace against the railing and—

"Stupid bitch." He drags me downward, and it takes all I have to not topple down the metal stairs myself. My feet wobble under shaky legs as I descend. The cuffs binding me press into my skin, scraping along the knobby bone of my wrist. We reach the living room, and I stall out just past the last tread, taking in the trashed home.

I saw it last time he dragged me through here. Now, with the lamp destroyed, it feels as if Timothy is right—this is all my fault.

With a firm grip still on the chain between my hands, Timothy crosses the living room, grabbing a backpack and a few items.

It's then I hear the hum of a boat.

A big boat.

The Coast Guard boat?

Em . . .

"Emmett!"

The second the first syllable passes my lips, Timothy swings around. The back of his hand slams into my cheek.

Ringing starts in my ears. My head spins as I sway on my feet. Copper blooms in my mouth, and I swallow metallic liquid down.

"Shut the hell up," he hisses, slipping a hand into the side of the backpack, producing a handgun.

I gasp, cowering as he wields it in my face.

"You don't make a sound." His face is feral, livid mania sinking his wide eyes into their sockets.

I nod, biting down hard on my bottom lip. I barely register the burn as more copper laces through my mouth. Checking outside is still clear through the cracked-open front door, he pushes through, the tip of his gun now stabbing into my ribs.

I try and fail to hold in a whimper when I see the Coast Guard boat closing in on the jetty.

From here, I can see someone aboard, but their back is turned. Timothy pulls me toward the forest tree line. No . . .

"Emmett," I gasp. The name barely passes my lips before fading out.

Desperation claws at my insides. Rendering me almost mute.

Timothy glances at the jetty before his glare lands on me. "Keep your mouth shut, you stupid fucking slut." Then, as if talking to himself, he mutters, "Another one to take down. How many will she have before she has me . . . God, he said she was ours."

I stare at the side of his face, horror lancing through me, impaling my senses.

He's not just a stalker, he's lost it.

Who is *he*?

Caught up in some fantasy where he's the chosen one, and I'm the prize. Everyone else is simply another obstacle for him to eliminate.

I feign a limp, trying to slow us down. To give Emmett time to see me. To see us.

To realize I'm here, and I never left. That I need his help.

The gun reaffirms its position at my ribs, and I close my gaping mouth.

Emmett . . . he's so close.

Em finally disembarks, carrying a load in his arms, as Timothy pulls me into the forest past the tree line. Sobs tumble from me in bouts of despair.

I want to scream for Em. I want to turn on this weedy, sick little man and tear him to pieces. But amidst my panic, I simply hover, frozen.

Unable to do either.

firefly

CALLUM

Errol stares at me like the enemy I am from *his table* at the café. I return the glare tenfold but lose it as his granddaughter delivers my breakfast.

She beams at me. With pretty brown eyes, a splatter of freckles over her cheeks, and wavy brown hair, she's the much prettier spitting image of her grandfather. Or at least, the version of him thirty years ago.

"Thanks," I grunt before shoveling a hearty helping of scrambled eggs into my mouth. Better the eggs stuff my mouth full before something I'll regret slips out.

"See you tip, you lousy ingrate," Errol says from behind the paper he now holds up like a goddamn shield.

Chicken shit. Come over here and say that.

"I tip everyone the same. Knock it off, asshole."

A gruff sound halfway between a laugh and a grunt slips around the paper in his hands. Ignoring him, I continue my breakfast. Iris makes a mean plate of eggs, bacon, and hash, and I am going to take my damn time savoring it. Regardless of Grandpa Grump across the room. He's probably here to make sure no McCreary treats his kin badly. Lord knows that's what the entire town expects now.

Some grudges never die.

"How's the eggs?" a sweet voice says from my side.

I look up to the brown eyes and freckles, back again.

"Good," I say, pushing another mouthful in.

"Great!" She spins on her heel and wanders around, checking in on the other patrons.

About time Irry has someone to help out. Paige seems to enjoy the work, and if the response she's getting from other diners is anything to go by, she's good at it. One of those people-person types. How the hell someone as sweet as her spawned from the descendants of Errol's loins beats me.

"Finish up. We have to get to Rockland for a meeting with the Restoration folks." Iris stands on the opposite side of my table, arms crossed.

"We?" I scrape the last of my breakfast onto my fork, shoving it into my mouth.

"Yes, we. Hurry up, being late is not the impression I want to make after they turned us down last time."

The shortest meeting in the history of meetings, that one was. We walked in, stated our case for the island, for the lighthouse, and they said no further permission would be granted.

Just like that.

I don't know what going a second time will do that the first didn't. But I'm not one to argue with my sister. Hell, if they knew what was good for them, they wouldn't, either.

Iris has a quick word with Paige before grabbing her bag from behind the counter, picking up her phone from by the register, and sliding her sunglasses onto her face.

The woman means business.

The old croaks at the Restoration Society should be scared.

I wander to the counter and grab a coffee to go before Iris ushers me out the door.

"You sure Paige will be okay without you?" I ask.

Iris stalks down the sidewalk to her permanent parking spot, where her Jeep Wrangler waits. The small white vehicle has been hers since she was old enough to have a license and make her first down payment. To say my little sister had her life in order long before I did is the understatement of the century.

I open the door and squeeze my large frame into the

small passenger seat. She tosses her bag on my lap and drops into the driver's seat.

"The meeting is with the Restoration Society and the mayor. If anyone has a little sway with those useless haggards past their expiration date, it's the mayor." Iris pays me a glance, the same pitiful smile I saw back at the hospital stuck over her face again.

"Sure, Irry. Whatever."

The Jeep pulls away from the curb and she frowns. "Whatever?"

I stare out the window. I haven't felt this helpless since Ava. And this pity party Iris is throwing me is grating on my damn nerves. "If they decommission her, I'll start again somewhere else."

"Like hell you will. When are you going to fight for this, Cal?"

"I did. They said no." The small, quaint homes of Bay Shore sail past as I stare out the window.

"When's the last time you fought for something you wanted—I mean, *really* wanted?"

Now, I turn to look at her.

"What'd you mean?"

There's some underlying issue here. I'm certain there is. The look of disbelief on my little sister's face takes me by surprise.

"You let her go, just like that?" Iris's face flattens like she's holding back something upsetting.

"*She* is a hunk of cement in the middle of the Atlantic, Irry. I'm not happy about losing my home, either, or my way of life, but recent events have kind of put things into perspective."

Iris snaps her focus to the road ahead, her hands tightening around the steering wheel. She shakes her head, resetting her composure.

Four hours later, we arrive in Rockland. Iris has been stewing beside me the entire way, and after her statement about me letting things go, she hasn't said a damn word.

Now I'm worried.

Not talking is not my sister's style.

Something is eating her, big time.

"Spill it, Irry. Now, or I'm calling Em."

She shifts the car into park and sighs, letting her head thump backward on the head rest. "I can't."

"Yes, you can. We don't have secrets, remember?"

She huffs a laugh and turns her head to look at me. "Maybe later. Let's get inside before they think we're not coming."

She gathers her things and is out of the car before I can object.

We enter the large, overstated grand building housing the Rockland Restoration Society. Iris leads the way to the reception desk.

"Iris and Callum McCreary for Mr. Mullins, please."

The receptionist looks up. "Of course, Mrs. McCreary, have a seat. He won't be long. The mayor is already inside."

"It's Miss McCreary, and since when were they starting without us?" Iris snaps back.

"I—Oh. Please . . . Take a seat?"

Iris growls, turning her back on the woman. I sit on the long, cold bench seat, and she drops by my side.

"Don't slaughter the messenger, Irry. First impressions and all."

She pulls a face and settles in, bag in her lap, pushing her sunglasses up into her fiery hair.

"I know this is close to home for you, but don't burn any bridges on my account." I shove her shoulder with mine. She forces a smile. This whole situation is taking a toll on her. She's usually much more composed than this.

Her bag vibrates.

She dives a hand inside and tugs out her cell.

The screen is lit up with an incoming call.

Livvy.

Odd. We haven't spoken to her for months. Or, at least in 2022 we hadn't . . . Maybe they talk more now?

Iris glances at me and rejects the call.

"Why'd you do that for?"

"Oh, it's probably nothing. I'll call her back after."

She bounces a leg, her red flat shoe scuffing the old tile with every harried movement. A door down the hallway opens, and the large man we spoke to last time waves us in.

My sister takes off like a shot, and I amble after her.

"Iris. Lovely to see you again," Mullins says, a hand on his oversized gut and a radiant smile on his face.

"Sure. Hi," she replies, disappearing inside.

"McCreary. Good to see you in one piece, lad."

Sweet Jesus.

The man must be barely ten years older than me. "Lad" is a bit on the nose.

"Mullins, living the life, I see."

With a rough chuckle, he follows me into the office and closes the door before rounding the desk and dropping into an enormous plush leather office chair.

"You had some further concerns regarding the Fire Island services?" he says to Iris.

"Yes, we would like to appeal the last decision regarding the lighthouse."

The mayor, who has stayed silent until now, raises a hand. "Before we get into the logistics and finances one more time," he glances to Iris, "I want to commend Callum on a brave attempted rescue. How are you holding up, son?"

God, another one.

Attempted. That's a low blow.

"Fine," I say.

This small office is starting to feel like a trap. The

mayor, the bait. The McCrearys, the prey. The fallout, my lighthouse. The predator sits behind his shiny desk with his big gut and cushy damn chair.

Less lighthouse means more budget for other projects he wants to back.

Hell, Irry was right, these assholes are playing us.

"The lighthouse not only saves lives and is a part of our heritage, it's a permanent feature of the coastline, drawn into maps, waypoints for vessels. It is also my brother's home. Surely you can understand that?" Iris leans forward, talking to Mullins.

Who responds by steepling his hands over his stomach. "I understand you have a sentimental attachment to the island and the lighthouse, but that doesn't justify the expense of keeping it operational. Let alone the maintenance it desperately needs to remain active."

"I understand it costs money to run and maintain, I'm not arguing that. But it's a required coastline feature. Not a static communal installation like a memorial or such. You must see this?" Iris says.

"It's outdated. It's practically redundant, Miss McCreary."

Iris sighs.

I have nothing useful to add that would appeal to Mullins, so I keep quiet.

The mayor leans forward. "Bay Shore would like to thank you for years of service on Fire Island, Callum."

"No!" Iris stands. She moves toward the door, stalking away before pacing in a circle. "Cal, out. Now."

"Iris," I growl.

She implores me with fiery eyes I can't refuse. With a sigh, I rise and leave the room. She closes the door and turns back to the men, the door slipping open an inch.

"You don't get it. You are not simply decommissioning an old hunk of concrete and windows, not even a shitty old lamp. You are decommissioning a man and his purpose. Aft—" She hauls in air, the inhale so rough I hear it from the hallway. "You are kicking a man when he's down, after all he's done for the seafaring people of this coast."

Murmurs hum for a moment before Mullins clears his throat. "We can suspend the shutdown for another few years. But the lamp that's currently in use will have to do. There is no budget for a new Fresnel, nor would the board approve a replacement this late in the game."

"You've got to be—" Iris starts.

"Iris, this is a good deal," the mayor says calmly. "Please talk it over with Callum."

I swear I hear my little sister curse them out under her breath before the office door flies open and she strides out. She slams it, storming down the hall and throws me a glance that tells me all I need to know. I feel like the bad kid outside the principal's office whose mother went ten rounds to save their ass.

Or something pretty damn close.

"Irry, wait up!" I take off after her.

She slows down and I take her elbow. "Thanks, I think?"

She stops now and lays her hand on my shoulder. "I'm sorry, Cal." Her chin wobbles. She's out of sorts over this. I know our family has lived on and worked that island for decades, but it's just that—an island.

Her bag—no, her phone—buzzes again.

With a sigh, she slides it out.

"I better take this, wait for me outside?" She offers a small, sad smile.

"Take your time." I walk through the front doors and drop onto the seat outside.

Iris taps the screen and accepts the call, turning away from me. I make out a few phrases before letting my attention wander to my surroundings.

"... I tried, Em. Nothing, again. She's not answering." Iris's voice ratchets up a notch.

I still, listening when I know I shouldn't.

She's nodding, but a hand rises to cover her mouth.

"Livvy tried her, too. She got the same as me. No answer. I have a bad feeling about this, Em. Nobody knows where she is."

Iris turns, and her gaze meets mine. Surprise floods her face before something like regret sinks over her features.

"Shit. I gotta go."

She pushes through the door, scanning my face as she stops in front of me. I look up and notice—for the first time since we left this morning—the dark circles under her eyes. The fatigue weighing her pretty face down.

"Who's missing, Irry?"

Seven

EVIE

"Do you have any idea where you're going?" I snap as the damp earth under my bare feet slips again.

Timothy pays me no heed, just as he hasn't since we cleared the tree line, simply tugging on the bonds around my wrists. By my estimate, we are around halfway into the forest. In twenty to thirty minutes, we should reach the fishing hut.

My stomach growls.

I haven't eaten since the night before last when he drugged me.

Not willing to experience another scuzzy jerk-off scene of Timothy's, I have opted against food or drink. A decision that weighs heavier and heavier with every passing hour.

My head thumps from dehydration.

My mouth is so parched the Sahara is damp in comparison.

Every step I take, my limbs shake with fatigue and the weakness hunger brings. I stumble over a fallen branch, and my knees hit the muddy ground. Arms suspended above my head, his grip unwavering, I whimper at the burn around my reddened, tender wrists.

"Get up." He stands close. Too close.

Soulless pale eyes glare down at me.

"Please, just let me go. We can forget this ever happened. We've both made mistakes. Consider the score even and we go our separate ways . . . Please, Timothy." A sob spills out after my plea.

He leans down. The barrel of his pistol brushes my temple, dragging the sweat-drenched hair from my face. "No."

"I—if I give you myself, will you let me go?" The words are acid on my tongue. Bile rises in the aftermath of the thought of giving myself over to this insane man.

His head tilts a fraction. "Also, no."

The sickest, most rabid grin splits his face. He chuckles for a moment before reeling me to my feet. "Fucking slut. If I'd known how desperate you are for cock, I wouldn't have spent six fucking years on you." He steps into my space. "You are MINE!"

I cower at the last word. The rage lacing his tone

sends shivers down my spine. I stand rigid with fear as he traces the tip of the gun over my lips. His hot, foul breath hits my face, and I swallow the sob that wants out. He grabs a handful of my hair and tugs my head back. "I will have you as many times as I want. I didn't wait six years for a taste, Butterfly. I will have it all. And you will never escape us." He drags my glasses down my nose until they teeter over the tip and fall onto the muddy ground. "Much better. Now, move."

His iron grip in my hair doesn't budge. I scramble beside him through the trees as fire consumes my scalp. My throat closes, overwhelmed by the emotion of never being free of this hideous human being. My once-perfect vision, albeit a little smudged, has been replaced with blurs of green and brown, the occasional object coming into clearer view as I pass each tree in a near miss.

"Please . . . slow down," I utter, pain twisting my face and contorting the words.

He doesn't relent. The pace stays too fast, the grip in my hair too tight.

After twenty minutes of me staggering at his side to keep up and him marching through the trees like a man possessed, we reach the fishing hut.

Cal's fishing hut.

My heart lurches at the sight.

The flood of beautiful, happy memories and one sad moment at the end catches me off guard.

"Oh Cal," I whimper.

Timothy spins back on his heels. He's in my face instantly. "Never, EVER, say that name in my presence again." He is almost on top of me. His fist in my hair falls away, only to grip my neck, his fingers curling into my airway.

"O-okay," I splutter.

"Ever!" His lip twitches. He's shaking, like he's as exhausted as I am.

If only.

Without another word, he pushes me through the warped front door to the hut. I stumble and sink to the floor, and his grip fails. With no time to scurry away or attack, he crouches over me and releases one wrist, securing it on the leg of the cast-iron stove to the left.

Fuck.

He stands, shoving the gun into the front of his pants. "Don't try anything."

He's out the door, disappearing south before I can reply. I sit, straining to listen for his movements, only to hear him talking softly, then the sound of something clicking.

He comes back through the door, sliding a phone into his back pocket. *Good luck getting service out here, buddy.* His pocket lights up, the shine of the lit screen barely visible through his sweats.

He sits at the table and pulls out his phone again,

running a hand through his greasy brown hair. Tapping the message, he nods and sends a reply back.

Dammit.

Just my luck, *he* gets service out here.

Of course he does.

"Where are we going next?" I say quietly.

He ducks his head, studying my face as he replies, "None of your business."

"I beg to differ, since you are taking me there against my will."

He bolts off the chair and is squatting in front of me a heartbeat later. "I said, none of your business, Butterfly." He moves to stand but decides against it as he turns back and closes in on me. I press my back into the stove. The harsh metal grates against my spine. "Just know that you will never see this place again."

My face wobbles with emotions set to betray my facade of composure.

"That makes you sad, precious girl? Good, you deserve some punishment for all the trouble you've put me through."

He coughs, and spit lands on my cheek. Refusing to gag, I harden my features to stone, not giving him a fucking inch.

"You won't get away with this. People will know I'm missing. My editor—"

"She won't bother to track down a writer who can't

stick to a deadline to save herself. And those so-called friends of yours in the city weren't plussed when you never called or emailed from the lighthouse for nine months. No one is going to miss you, Butterfly. Not one person."

My chin wobbles, and I bite back a sob.

Softening just the slightest, he tracks a grubby finger over my jaw. "You're better off with me, you'll come to see that."

I rip my chin away from his touch. "Over my dead body."

Resting on his heels, he slides the gun from the front of his sweats. He points it at my forehead and smiles, like the fucking Joker. "That would be too easy. Besides, I don't have any intention of living without you."

Right. Because torturing someone and keeping them in captivity is love.

His kind of love.

The drone of a boat wakes me from a restless, pointless sleep. I jerk awake, the back of my head smashing into the stove door.

Fuck.

I groan before my consciousness can catch up to my current situation and shut it down.

Timothy is on his feet a second later, gathering his things. He tucks the gun into the front of his sweats again as he shoulders the backpack and moves toward me. Bending down, he unlocks the cuff from the leg of the stove. Pulling me to my feet, he secures the metal bracelet around my wrist once again.

"Our ride is here." He tugs me along at his side.

"No!" I struggle against his grip. "I'm not going anywhere with you."

"Move, Eve."

"I—I . . . need to pee, please." I tense up on the spot, trying desperately to hold my ground.

He looks around the old shack. The tin bucket Cal and I used for our hunting trip sits by the door. He swipes it up and pushes it into my chest. "You have one minute."

Without a word, he walks outside and shuts the door, guarding it. I really do need to pee, but I also needed to buy some time to find the small knives I hid in the cupboard last time I was here. I place the bucket in front of the cupboard and tug my jeans and panties down. As I relieve myself into the old bucket, I slide my hands to the side into the small, weathered cupboard and feel for the old, rusted knives.

"Hurry up, thirty seconds," he grunts from outside.

"Okay."

My fingers find the handle of the larger knife. I grab it. As I pull my jeans back up, I slide it into the waistband at my spine.

Eve - 1

T - 0

Now, I need the courage to use it.

Finishing up, I make sure the knife is secure before walking to the door and knocking softly. It opens, a hand grabbing for the chain between my cuffs. The gun is in his hand as we walk for the southern end of the island toward the hum of a boat engine. Toward god knows where.

A small cruiser bobs in the water off the rocky shoreline to the east. The water must be deeper here, because the boat hovers by the rocks, like a makeshift jetty.

Timothy hauls me toward it like the ground's on fire. I struggle through the dense sand. When we reach the boat, a plank is resting on the rocks. We board, and Timothy turns back, crowding me as he removes the cuffs. "Our little secret."

He rubs a sweaty, grimy hand over my swollen wrist before we board the boat proper.

"Sit the fuck down," a big man around the same age as us says as he slips from the captain's chair. A rough grip takes my chin, forcing it upward. Something deadly emanates from him.

"Here she is," Timothy says with a smile, like he's pleased with himself. *Oh god.*

I want to scream, but the way new guy's gaze runs down my body and the look he gives his friend tell me all I need to know. I thought being abducted by a psycho fan was bad . . . Now he has backup that's just as depraved as he is, by the look on his face. And huge.

Exhausted, I shake where I stand. Thirst burns, making my every breath an effort.

So I sink to my seat and cower against the side of the boat.

The big guy smirks. "Looks like she's given up already. That's no fun, T."

Timothy shoots him a hard look. "Hands off, the last one was yours."

He stands over Timothy. "Watch your mouth. Time to make ourselves scarce, the fucking Coast Guard is out here."

I lift my head. The words register, just.

Em . . .

"Emmett," I breathe.

I need to push through one more time. I search the cabin for some sort of escape. Everything is so blurry. I need a weapon. A—

The cupboard to the left of the captain's chair is open. Inside, the yellow EPIRB attached to the inner wall flashes.

Bingo.

The memory of the afternoon Cal and I were stranded on Firefly floods back in.

"They get wet," Cal said.

"Like when you sink?" I had asked, and he responded, "Something like that."

I can't sink a boat, but I can jump overboard.

Cal always told potential rescues to attach the EPIRB to their person.

I need to get closer to that cupboard.

"Water," I gasp.

Timothy turns back from where he stands by the other guy's side.

"Please, I need water." I hold my hands up in a plea.

"Water, you idiot, she's no use dead," the big guy mutters, not looking back.

I rise, unsteady on my feet, and make my way to the cabin. Timothy goes to the cupboard beside the one I need and opens it. A small built-in fridge fills the space. Bottles of water and beer are stocked there. He plucks out a bottle and tosses it at me. It grazes my fingertips and falls to the floor. Dropping to the ground, I take my time assessing the detachable face of the EPIRB.

Two push buttons, one on either side, are what release it.

Good to know.

Now all I have to do is wait until they fall asleep . . .

And hope like hell they don't take shifts staying watch overnight. I plead with the heavens that we aren't out of Emmett's jurisdiction when I make my move.

Big guy is on watch.

Fuck my luck six ways to Sunday.

On the other hand, maybe my powers of seduction will work a little better on him?

Who am I kidding, the thought is as ridiculous as it sounds.

Still, I sit up on the small bunk at the rear of the boat and clear my throat. Looking around as I pad toward the cabin, I see we are literally in the middle of nowhere in the ocean.

"Bad dream, sweetheart?" he drawls in a bitter tone, raking his gaze over my body.

You have no idea.

"A little," I whisper, looking up from under my lashes.

A crooked smirk blooms over his face. The dark hair, nothing like Timothy's, is mussed like he's been running his hands through it. He holds a bottle.

Beer.

Maybe my luck isn't so bad, after all.

"May I have one?" I ask, using my most innocent tone.

He raises the bottle to his lips and chugs the last few frothy mouthfuls down. "No."

I repress the shudder that starts at the base of my spine.

"They're in here?" I ask, pointing at the fridge.

"I said no," he says, his gaze dragging over my body again, this time landing on my chest.

Fear sparks deep in my core, lighting every inch of my nerves.

I need him distracted. "Do you have anything to eat?"

He studies me for a beat before rolling off the seat and heading for a backpack hanging on the wall of the cabin. I duck down, thumbing the two buttons on the EPIRB. It slides off easily, and I tuck it down the back of my pants. Dislodging the knife . . .

Cool metal wedges its way down my right jean leg.

Fuck.

He turns back. "Chips or crac—"

I stand up, straight, holding my breath. My stance suspicious.

"What are you up to, girlie?" He raises an eyebrow.

"I—ah, really need to go to the bathroom."

He runs his narrowed glare over my face.

The knife slips, hitting the floor.

Fuck. No.

"Sneaky little bitch, hey." He closes in, swiping the rusted blade from the deck. He presses it to my throat. "You wanna play, slut?"

I shake my head. *No.*

Crowding me against the wall of the cabin, his hot, beer-laced breath hits my face as he presses his hard body against mine. The EPIRB digs into my back. I wince. He pulls back and lowers the knife. The blade drags down my top, tugging the flimsy material past my breasts, exposing my lacy bra.

He growls, tilting his head like a madman.

I tug my top back up and the device tucked into my jeans moves, toppling from its safe hold to the deck.

God, no.

How can I be so hopeless at this?

He grabs my shirt, pressing me against the wall as he bends down and plucks up the EPIRB in one hand. The green flashing light oscillates through the small cabin, lighting our faces in a sickening shade. "Oh, now I'm just going to have fun with you," he snarls. He tosses the device to the side.

With both hands, he grips my shoulders and throws me to the deck. I land by the EPIRB and scramble backward, fingers reaching for it. He grabs my legs, dragging me back toward him.

I kick out, snapping one of his fingers back.

"Ah! Fuck you, bitch!" he roars.

A scuffle outside on the deck tells me Timothy is awake.

I make for the EPIRB, scurry to my feet, and rush the door, bursting out onto the deck. I toss the device over the side. It hits the water with a small splash, and I hope the current doesn't steal it too far.

"What the hell is going on?" Timothy screeches, grabbing me when I fail to put enough deck between us.

"Little bitch wants to get roughed up." The big guy fills the cabin doorway.

"No! Get off me." I try to hit Timothy with anything I can. My head, elbows, fists, knees. He blocks everything I send out.

Weak from days of starvation and no water, I sag against his bony frame.

"Coast Guard to Millennia, over."

Emmett.

Emmett!

"You stupid fucking cow!" the big guy roars.

"Coast Guard to Millennia, your EPIRB activated, please respond, over."

"Emmett!" His name is a raw desperate sound. I know he can't hear me, but I have to do something before I fall apart.

"Fuck, just respond." Timothy waves at the cabin.

"Tell them we accidentally knocked it off the boat or something."

"You stupid? We respond, then they know where we are!"

Um, pretty sure the EPIRB has our location pinned . . .

I keep my mouth clamped shut. The two men start arguing. Big guy comes out to the deck, hands flying around, accusations flying further. Timothy releases me, stepping into his space.

I make a run for the cabin. With shaking hands, I snatch up the radio. "Emmett! Help! Emmett! It's Evie! Please help me!"

Static crackles back as the two men fly into the cabin.

"Emmett! Help! Please! It's Eve Holland."

"Ten-four, Miss Evie." Static squeals. "Hold your position. I'll be there in three minutes. Over." His voice is thick. Stoic but tense.

It's perfect relief.

I slide down the cupboard. The intense relief flooding me steals my will to stand.

One breath.

Two breaths.

I replay the short exchange, making sure I didn't dream it.

Rough hands haul me from the cabin. In a sickening tumble of limbs, as the darkness spins around me, I'm tossed overboard. The growl of the engine spurs to life.

The cruiser speeds out of sight. I gasp, spluttering seawater as I tread to keep afloat.

The calm of freedom washes over me with the next rolling mass of water, and I lie back and float. The stars above shimmer. I pull every good memory I've ever had of Callum McCreary to the surface. Closing my eyes, I beg the heavens that Emmett finds me before the EPIRB drifts too far away.

And I'm lost at sea forever.

firefly

Eight

CALLUM

My sister is lying to me. I know she's upset about some missing friend, and now, sitting across from me, she is stone-faced and denying any such thing. I take a sip of the delicious coffee she made and study her as she tries to formulate a reason for getting so wound up at the meeting yesterday.

"I guess I just hate the fact they can toss you out. Fire Island is your home, you've made a life there, and—"

"You said that already, Irry. Tell me what's really going on."

Her phone vibrates on the table, lighting up.

Emmett.

"Shit, I have to take this. Sorry, Cal. Grab some scones before the midmorning rush, will you?"

She slips outside, and I rise from my chair, wandering

to the big bay window, watching my little sister pace. Her hand slaps over her mouth, and she sags with something that looks like relief. When she starts crying on the side-walk, that's the last fucking straw.

I slam the coffee cup on the counter and spill out onto the sidewalk. Without asking, I wrap her in my hold, and she sobs into my chest.

So much for nothing to worry about.

Dammit, Irry.

Her sobs die off, and she pushes away, straightening her hair with one hand, drying her face with the other. "I have to go. Look after Paige for me, will you?"

"Sure, but we are hashing this thing out when you get back."

She winks at me with a scrunched-up face full of love.

Yeah, I ain't getting a thing out of that woman.

I sigh, making my way back inside as Iris dashes out with her bag and phone. I know the doctor told her and Em not to try to fill in the blanks of the three missing years. But being left out of the loop with something like this is hard.

Something feels off.

Like I should be front and center in this unfolding drama.

Instead of charging off after my sister like I want to, I sit my ass back down at one of the smaller tables and pick up the paper. I turn to the community section for the month.

A half page write-up covers the first page of the section.

Talented Fantasy Writer-in-Residence Holds Signing for Bay Shore Library

The photograph is of Sherry from the library staff and a pretty twentysomething with black glasses and a tight smile. She holds a copy of a fancy-looking hard-cover book as she stands at the front of a crowd of people, a line on one side of her table. To the right, a guy hunches by the loans counter, his gaze dead set on the woman holding the book. His scruffy, greasy hair is covered by a cap. Maybe he's her husband?

The way he's looking at her is . . .

Intense.

I shiver, shrugging away the unease washing over me. I fold the paper and check the front-page news. Same old thing, something bad. Nothing good ever sells. The door to the café chimes, and Errol walks in. I glance at the clock. Lunchtime.

He's a creature of habit.

Lucky for Iris, half the town eats here. My sister's

cooking and her personality have won back the town. Mostly.

Errol tosses a scowl my way before plopping onto a stool at the counter. Paige's face lights up as she slides a menu across to him. Without looking at it, he orders and reaches for the counter copy of the paper that's splattered with food spills already.

I rise and roll the paper in my hands, tossing it onto the counter by the old shit. He turns, face not improving any as he says, "Generous of you, McCreary. Just don't get any ideas about buttering me up to get in my grand-daughter's good graces."

The actual hell, old man?

"The fuck you blithering about, Errol?"

"We all know you like them half your age."

I set my shoulders back, setting my feet square as I cross my arms over my chest. My jaw grinds shut. He continues, obviously unaware of the 'no talking about the last three years rule' Em and Iris are abiding by. "Took her over there, early morning, couple weeks back. No clue why she wanted to come back after she got away."

Got away?

She?

Maybe I can get something out of him, after all.

"You did what?" I ask.

"Flew into the watchhouse all hysterical, wanting

Emmett. He was out up north." He studies my face, brows lowering. "She know you ended up half drowned?"

I have no idea what he's talking about, but it's the most recent event anyone's talked about with me since the hospital.

I let my body soften, dropping my arms by my sides. "Wouldn't know."

He grunts. "Figures. Got what you wanted and—"

Paige drops a plate in front of her grandfather. Her frown tells me all I need to know. Iris got to her. She's not going to let Errol or anyone else in this little café slip another word.

Dammit.

So close.

"We're not supposed to talk about anything that happened in the last three years, Grandpa. His memory has to return on its own." Her words are firm.

Gauging by the surprise stretching Errol's face, he didn't know. "Huh. Well, shit. There is a god."

"Grandpa!" Paige scolds the old man.

He chuckles and digs into his food. I retreat behind the counter and head upstairs for the spare room. My belongings are strewn about the space, but this is not my home. I can feel it in my bones. I sink onto the bed and drop my head into my hands. I close my eyes, squeezing them shut, like that will force thirty-six months' worth of life and moments back into my brain.

Nothing gives.

Nothing floods back in.

I'm coddled. Wrapped in fucking cotton wool and set up high on the shelf with the rest of the precious, break-able things.

Fuck this shit six ways to Sunday.

Four hours later, the squeal of wheels on the street outside has me off the bed and standing by the window in a heartbeat. The Jeep pulls up, but nobody gets out. It idles by the curb in its parking spot. Intrigued, I lean on the wall and fold my arms . . .

And wait.

Finally, the engine dies out, and Iris steps out. She rounds the vehicle and opens the passenger door. A woman steps out. With her long dark hair messy around her shoulders, she sways as she holds Irry's hand. Iris folds her into her embrace, and I lean into the glass, fore-head pressing onto the cool pane.

This must be the friend she was upset about.

As they part, Iris palms her face, talking to her.

The woman nods before glancing up.

I jerk back a little from the window when I recognize her face.

The woman from the paper, the twentysomething author. She looks a little worse for wear, but that's her, I'm sure of it. When did my sister become friends with a fantasy author? Must have developed in the last three years. The woman is hugging herself as Iris slides a small bag from the car that looks like it's from the eye place on Main Street, and guides her inside.

I close the door and stand by it, listening, feeling like the world's biggest perv.

But something has me frozen to the spot.

It's . . . curiosity?

She must have been through some kind of ordeal to have Iris this wound up over it.

Footsteps move up the internal stairs. I should move. I should act fucking normal. My blood hammers through me like it understands something I don't. I grab the doorknob.

I won't turn it.

I won't.

It—*she*'s none of my business.

Murmuring fills the hallway, and Iris's bedroom door opens, then shuts. I pull my door open an inch. Heart in my throat, I stare into the empty hallway. Closing the door softly so it makes not a sound, I spin back and lean on it. My head thumps backward onto the hardwood. I try to rein in the thrumming in my body.

What in hell's handbasket's got me riled up over some woman I don't know?

A soft knock lands on the other side of the door, and I jolt away from the sound. With a good distance between me and the door, I shake out my hands, trying to coax feeling back into my body.

"Cal?"

Iris.

I clear my throat. "Yeah?"

"Can I come in?"

"Yep."

I sit on the bed and try not to look as fucked up as I feel. Iris opens the door and comes in before closing it behind her. "How are you feeling?"

She looks much happier than when she left this morning.

"Fine. Bored."

At least I was ten minutes ago. Now, I'm a bundle of whatever the fuck those last few minutes were.

"My, um . . . friend was in an accident, she's going to stay here for a few days. But . . . " She comes to sit by me on the bed. Her green eyes are lit up, but her mouth wobbles to hold a thin line. "She needs some space, okay? I would send you to Em's, but he's on dayshift, and I need someone to be with you as much as pos—"

I hold a hand up. "It's fine. I'll behave. Besides, between Paige, you, and Em, I have enough company. I'm not going looking for more. I'll keep my distance."

"Oh, okay, great."

Iris stares at the door. She swallows before she says, "Have you had any memories come back yet?"

"Nope. Not a damn thing." I shove my head into my hands and groan. "I'm so over this, Irry. It's only been a few weeks and I'm going fucking crazy. What if they never come back?"

I turn my head to find her staring at me. "I don't know, Cal."

"It feels like I lost far more than only three years of memories. Something's missing."

Iris's eyes well with unshed tears as she tilts her head, scrunching up her face. She drops her head to my shoulder and breathes out a wobbly breath. "I know."

She knows what?

"How bad could it be if you told me what I'm missing?" I plead.

She sits up and gives me the most empathetic look that's ever graced her pretty face. "What if that ruins it all?"

"How could it?"

"I'm not telling you how things are. That's for you to find out." She glances to the ceiling, like the next words are hard to say and she needs a little more strength.

"You're lucky, you know. I envy you some. You get to do it all over again. You get to live through that twice."

"Do what? Live through what?"

It sounds like something good, at least? What happened in the last three years that I could get to do over?

She gives me an incredulous look. "Now, if I told you *that*, I would never forgive myself."

"Fine. But if this turns out to be important and you kept it to yourself . . ."

She rises and presses a kiss to my forehead. It's been years since she's done it. The last time was after Ava. After Em found me at the fishing hut with my sanity hanging by a thread.

She reaches the door, then turns back and says, "I'm just happy two of my favorite people are home and safe. The rest will sort itself out soon enough."

She disappears, and I'm left sitting on the bed none the wiser.

Nine

EVIE

"He has no recollection of the last three years." Iris's words repeat on a loop.

I'd sat in that hospital room, so grateful to be safe and off the island and out of Timothy's grip.

"He's alive," Iris had whispered through a sob.

I shook where I sat on the examination bed. And the only words that stuck were the ones where Iris said Cal *doesn't remember me.*

I thought I lost him.

I thought he was dead.

I guess, to me, now he is.

I curl up on Iris's bed, my body starting to shake all over again.

He's only down the hall, and I can't see him. Can't

talk to him. Can't fly into his arms, touch his face, drown in those blue eyes I've kept front of mind for over two weeks. They were my lifeline.

I mean, I could see him, but I'd have to come up with some story about how I'm Iris's friend. I had an accident. I'm recuperating here. Separate from his life.

Just Iris's old friend.

Nothing to him.

Oh god. That hurts.

I wail into the pillow, hands turning to claws around the blanket. They tingle, cramping up as I fail to pull a useful breath in. After all I went through on the island, this small detail shouldn't raze me the way it does. But my heart and soul measure the damage of losing Callum McCreary the same as they do my freedom, my will to live.

The sun has well and truly gone down by the time I have no tears left. My head thumps, and my throat is raw. It's then Iris pads into the room, a tray in hand. She sets it on the bed and closes the door.

I push to sit up, and Iris's face breaks when her gaze finds mine.

"Oh god, sweetheart."

She's wrapped around me a heartbeat later. I want to push and pull and scream and slam my fists into the drywall.

What if . . .

Wha—

Urgh.

"Listen, you have something to eat and drink, and then take a nice long, hot shower. Then we can snuggle up and watch Netflix. What do you say?" Iris looks hopeful.

"Sure, sounds nice." I give her a sad smile.

She rubs my arm before walking to her dresser and fishing out some pajamas. The same ones I wore last time. The boat-neck top and cotton shorts. I gather my few things from the hospital, walk into the hall, and head down to the bathroom. Closing the door, I set my things on the vanity and turn on the water. Stripping down, I step into the warm water. It feels like forever since I had a hot shower.

I wash twice with Iris's lavender soap and wash my hair and condition it before toweling off and dressing in the clothes she gave me. I towel my hair again, trying to remove a little more moisture. I wring it into a long length, twisting it around to pull it over one shoulder. It dampens the one side of the shirt. Hunting in her drawers, I find a new toothbrush and clean my teeth before rolling up my filthy clothes to take back to the room.

The doorknob rattles.

I stand rooted to the spot as the door opens. Hugging the clothes to my body, I step back in the small space as it widens to reveal Callum McCreary.

Alive and well.

Standing, staring at me.

The love and adoration usually filling his eyes is gone. In its place is confusion and something like curiosity.

Nothing registers.

Realizing I'm staring at him, I clear my throat and wave tentatively. "H-hi."

He frowns, leaning on the doorjamb. "Hi." He folds his arms over his chest. His bare chest. "You done?" He nods at the sink.

"I—" I swallow and will the lightning shooting through my nerves to fade. "Yeah. S-sorry."

I move toward the door.

He pushes off the frame. I slip past him, my shoulder grazing his chest. I can't look up at him. My heart will surely shatter if I do. How he doesn't see the heartbreak etched all over my face, I have no idea. His scent fences me in for a heartbeat, and I hover over the threshold, not willing to leave.

"Eve?" he utters.

Hope flares, swelling with a flutter that makes my eyes raise to his.

"Yes?"

"So, you're a writer, hey?" Small talk is painful for him, if the expression on his face is anything to go by.

My hope deflates, devastatingly so.

The awkwardness is palpable. This is him trying to be nice. Stuck in close proximity with a stranger his sister's taken in. Not the boarder who took his home from him for months. That version of Callum was not as nice. I'm torn between laughing hysterically and sobbing where I stand.

"Something like that," I manage.

I slip from the doorway and make a beeline for Iris's room. The instant the door clicks at my back, it hits me like a ton of bricks. The fact that the man I love has no idea who I am . . .

We are strangers.

Strangers.

I collapse to the floor. The carpet burns my knees on impact. The clothes tumble to the floor, expelled from my hold as I sink my hands into my hair. I tug at the roots as a raw, wounded sound spills out.

The door opens, hitting my legs. I don't bother moving. Someone drops to my side as it closes again.

Fine hands brush the hair from my face.

"Hush, sweetheart. Come now, tuck into bed."

I don't have the will to move.

My heart is bleeding through my skin, the remaining shards in my chest liquefied, soaking into the carpet. The inhuman groans leaving my body sound foreign. The agony of losing him, finding him alive and well, only to lose him all over again.

It's too much.

Iris hauls me to my feet, and I stagger to the bed and fall into it.

I rock on my side, gripping at my arms, nails sinking into my skin. My old bedfellow grief slides in beside me.

Iris climbs in on the other side, tugging me into her embrace. She rubs a hand over my head. Her shushing noises tangle with my erratic wails. Her hands smooth my hair repeatedly, her hold on me firm. I let go in her arms. The pain of the past two weeks chokes its way out, burning me alive as it goes.

The days I truly thought Cal was dead.

The pain of thinking I would never see him again.

The air in my lungs evaporates on a cruel, searing blow.

The fear that had me terrified for days, with the threat of unthinkable things hanging between me and Timothy. The dread of realizing I was on the boat with two predators.

The fact that they both got away.

The moments I floated, suspended in time, it seemed, waiting for Emmett to find me. The millions of thoughts that he wouldn't, and it would be too late. That I would sink to the dark depths of the ocean, another soul snuffed out and never found.

That I would never see Cal again . . .

Then him just now, leaning against the doorframe.

Bare chest. Blue eyes curiously studying the woman in his sister's bathroom.

The way simply seeing him leveled me. Like nothing else has before. Not even losing Joshua was as obliterating as loving and losing Callum McCreary.

Nothing compares.

I chug through a string of erratic breaths and choke.

Iris sits me up, rubbing my back. "Breathe, mo nighean."

Mo nighean.

I look up at her, face broken to pieces with one phrase.

"Oh shit, Evie."

As if realizing what she's said to me and who called me that for the last six months.

She swaddles me into her arms, and I bury my face in her shoulder. I grip her arms like the lifelines they are right now.

"Dammit, Cal," Iris mutters.

Every breath burns. My head is pounding. And I finally put space between us.

"What if he never gets the last year back?" I rasp.

Iris holds me at arm's length. "You know, it's been playing on my mind all stinking day. He loved you once. I don't see any reason why he wouldn't again."

I huff a strained sound.

A *second* second chance.

The memories he's lost . . . Could I spend days recreating them?

Would it be deceptive? I couldn't do that to him. It would be like telling him his truth without him getting a say in it.

"You can't make Callum McCreary do anything he doesn't want to." I pick at the hem of my shirt, sniffing back the snot and tears that have swollen and reddened my face.

Iris chuckles. "No, you cannot. But what if I can give you the chance to find what you two had? He needs to go home. He also can't be alone. And I can't think of anyone I trust more with my brother's heart, his head, and his health than his caileag luachmhor."

I tamp down the emotion swelling with the phrase. I wish she would stop saying things like that. Hell, it's like she's testing me. Seeing how deep this thing between Cal and me goes.

Went.

I snap my gaze up to hers. "How?"

She smiles, palming my cheek. "Oh Evie, you two may have been holed up on that little island for months, but we're talking about my big brother. The only other person I know better than myself. He loved you and still he let you go. He broke his own heart to make sure yours was happy and free. Stupid dunderheid should have gone with you, if you ask me. But he's too stubborn for his own good." She sucks in a long breath. "You can travel out in a few days, after Em's cleaned up a little. Look after him for me, will you?"

I don't know what to say.

Em's going out to clean . . . He'll find the devastation I caused. The trashed house. The garden that's probably half dead. The remains of the lamp. The queen who took the fall.

The everlasting evidence of the fact that this maiden saved herself.

At a cost to the man she loves.

firefly

Ten

CALLUM

"Em's here, Irry," I call up from the diner.

"Yep, I know. He's here for you," she yells down the staircase. "We'll be down in a minute."

We.

That's right, her and her author friend.

Pretty little thing.

With her standing in Iris's pajamas last night, I'd have to be dead to not notice her gorgeous frame. The fine angles that make up Eve Holland. Iris gave me the rundown on her and her situation this morning, early. The girl herself slept late. I wrap a hand around the coffee mug on the table in front of me as Eve appears through the door behind the counter.

Like last night, she looks a little lost, and a whole lot of meek.

Not my fucking type.

Good thing she's not staying.

"Morning," she says with a tight smile before sliding onto a stool at the counter and giving me her back.

"Morning, yourself," I mutter.

Emmett swallows a mouthful, leaning back in his chair. "You'll be happy to get home, bud."

"Not a moment too soon, Em."

He huffs a laugh and drains his cup. "I'll be back out to collect you in a week for your scan. But, so you know, Iris has someone lined up to stay out there with you. Doctor's orders." He glances to the counter. "Just in case."

"I don't need a fucking babysitter."

He forces a smile, and when his focus stays on Eve at the counter, the penny drops.

"No, Em. No damn way." I shake my head at him.

A grin stretches his handsome fucking face. "Thought you'd say that. Iris is pretty set on the idea. Plus, Eve needs a place to stay, and you—"

"Why can't she stay here? Where the hell is she supposed to sleep?" I raise an eyebrow at him.

He stares at me for a beat, confusion written all over his face. "Ah, I made up the bunk in the shack. She should be good there for a while. And Iris needs the room." His gaze drops to his hands.

I lean back in my chair, resigned to the fact that she's coming with me, hoping the old shack with no electricity or modern conveniences will scare her right back to the Bay with her tail between her damn legs.

"Besides"—Em imitates my position, giving me a shit-eating grin—"you could do worse, bud."

I mean, he has a point. I could have been stuck with some old hag of a live-in nurse.

I'll count my blessings while I have them, thank you.

Iris rounds the counter carrying a small overnight bag that I assume is Eve's as Eve slides down from the stool. The writer slides her phone in her pocket before shouldering her handbag.

I rise from the chair. "Let's get this over with, then."

Iris slaps my arm, hard. "You will be on your best behavior, lest your actions catch up with you when your memory does." She points a finger at me and walks for the door, sweeping up Eve as she goes.

Force of nature, my little sister. Always has been.

Em files in beside Iris, taking the bag from her hand. She smiles up at him.

Always looking after her. Where would we be without Emmett? He's been my shelter in some of the worst storms of my life.

The walk to the docks is short, and Iris says her goodbyes as we board Firefly. It's strange to be a passenger on my own boat. Em does the prestart checks, and I give the old girl a once-over. Eve settles into the bench seat behind the captain's chair, making herself comfortable.

"You don't get seasick, do you?" I ask, dropping down beside her as Em powers the throttle and we move from the slip.

Eve turns to me. She's tense, like this close, she doesn't know what to do with herself. "Um, no, I don't."

"Good." I turn my focus to the water that opens up in front of Firefly. Em sends her into the blue, engine roaring. Another piece of home slips back into my soul.

Twenty minutes later, the tall structure I've called home for the last two decades comes into view. The tightness that's been winding me up since I moved into Iris's spare room unravels at the sight. Eve moves to my left, and I swear she holds back a smile. Her hands wring in her lap and her leg jumps, the bottom of her elegant flat shoe scuffing the ground as it moves.

"Home sweet home, bud." Em pulls Firefly to a stop by the jetty, and I stand and toss the lines over. They land square around each post I slide the buffers over and brace myself as they make contact with the wooden jetty. The movement of the water beneath the fixed infrastructure makes my head spin. I grip the door to the cabin and wait for it to pass.

A little residual side effect of the concussion, no doubt.

"Are you okay?" a soft voice says from behind.

I turn back to see deep browns studying me where I stand.

"Yep, fine." I cross the deck and haul my ass onto the jetty before Miss Prim-and-Proper can start asking questions. Hell will ice over before I go back to being coddled at my little sister's. She means well, but I don't need looking after. Never have.

Little twentysomething will soon find that out.

"Cal, wait, bud." Em meets me at the edge of the boat. "Let Eve have a look around while I give you some updates."

How will she know where she's going?

But, okay . . .

"I'll meet you up there." Eve steps over, carrying her small bag, and walks up the jetty onto my damn island. Just like that.

She pauses as the grass meets the sandy border to the island, looking up.

"So, I've stocked your fridge and cupboard and cleaned up best I could. But a few things were damaged by the looters while you were gone."

Looters. Assholes who thought it would be a trip to fuck with my stuff while I was held up in the fucking hospital. What the hell is wrong with people these days?

"Whatever it is, I'll fix it." I turn to follow Eve, not wanting her invading my home, regardless of its condition.

Em grabs my arm. "The lamp's gone, Cal. Smashed to pieces. The Coast Guard is trying to get you another one, but it's going to take a while."

"The hell?"

"Someone took a wrench to it, it seems. The glass is shoved into a pile on one side of the lantern room."

Fire laces my veins.

"Fucking hell." I shove my hands through my hair, molars grinding. "That damn thing can't be replaced. We tried. The Restora—"

"Yeah, Irry told me. So we are trying another route. We'll figure this out, Cal."

"Fuck me. What kind of imbecile does something like that? People rely on the light for safety."

"Yep," Em says, wincing as he looks toward the light-house. "They had to have been pretty desperate, I'd say."

"Desperate? More like heinous."

"Anyway, don't stress about it. We'll find another one."

"Shit, geez, thanks. Let me know how it goes."

"Yeah, will do. You better go settle your nanny into her accommodations." He grins at me like a damn idiot.

"Right," I grunt, heading for the house.

Firefly powers up and heads back into the open

water. I glance back, an ache blooming in my chest as she cruises away. I reach the house and walk inside. It's not that different from the night I left it. A few things are out of place, but overall, it's neat and tidy. Em did a great job.

A knock pulls me from my inspection. Eve stands in the doorway, her glasses gone. Her hair is up, and she changed into shorts and a button-down shirt with the sleeves rolled up. Almost like she came to help clean up.

"You needing something?" I ask, fixing the books on the shelves that are not in my alphabetized system.

"I came to see if you needed help?" She looks around the house, almost with a longing expression.

"I'm good."

I turn my back to her and continue sorting the books.

"Sure, okay. Well, holler if you need me?" She sounds so meek, like she's apologizing for fucking existing.

Then it occurs to me, she has no kitchen over there in the hut. She's going to have to eat with me. I'm going to have to feed her while she's here.

My gaze drops to the floor by the coffee table. The ghost of a giggle flits through my mind. My hand tightens around the book I hold. I jerk my head to the side, dislodging the remnant of what feels like a memory.

Something sweet. Something fueled by . . . need.

Fuck.

I swing my attention to the doorway.

But it's empty.

She's gone. And the slip of a memory of whatever or whoever fades before I have the chance to catch it.

With the living room put back the way I like it, I make my way upstairs. The bedroom door is open. The bed is neat and made up, better than when I left it. The dust bunnies under the bed drift around on their own accord. The window by the desk is open. I round the bed and check over the contents of my desk. Opening the drawer, I find EarPods.

Odd.

I don't own any . . .

Maybe the looters dropped them, and Em thought they were mine? The man should know better. He should have tossed them in the trash. Closing the drawer, I pad to the bathroom. The small, clean space looks fine. But dread swells when I think of the next thing I should inspect.

The lantern room.

Bracing myself for the worst, I climb the stairs.

The door has screw holes that weren't there before. Like someone boarded it up or added latches or something. I pull the door open and step inside.

The desecrated carcass of the Fresnel I poured hours

of love, care, sweat, and tears into shines in the morning sun.

Those fuckers oughta damn hang.

Her elegant, majestic body lies in tiny, jagged pieces to my right, brushed into a pile. Just as Em said. And I wonder why he left the mess when the rest was taken care of.

I walk through the room, and glass dust crunches under my boots.

The sound breaks my fucking heart. I run a hand over the few remaining lower panes that sit in the base, broken but still attached.

"Fucking criminal."

"I'm sorry." The words breathe from behind me.

I spin back to find Eve standing in the doorway, hands gripping the doorframe as if it's the only thing holding her up. Her focus is stuck on the pile of glass on the floor. How long has she been there? Her mouth is a thin line, eyes tight and brows drawn, her chest heaving.

I study her where she stands. The glasses are still gone. Maybe she has contacts? Her dark hair frames her beautiful face claiming angles that would be hard to forget. Sweet curves, a narrowed waist that dips in before her hips, and legs for goddamn days.

When I raise my gaze to where it should be, she's staring right at me.

Hell, it may as well be through me. The expression on

her devastated face snuffs out any inkling of need my body was heading toward.

She looks like she's been through hell. Yet here she is, helping me.

I should turn down the asshole a little.

Shouldn't I?

Eleven

EVIE

Impossible is trying to act normal, platonic, around Cal. Pretending nothing lies between him and me. Being back here is the worst kind of torture. Where every memory we made together clashes with the chaos and fear of the last two weeks with Timothy. And I am glad to be near Cal but not in his space right now. Because if I'm honest, I don't think I could be closer without falling apart.

The little shack is fine. It's enough. It's also void of the horrible memories made in the house. I need a little distance from it. I know I want to get back eventually. For Cal and me to go back to what we had before I left. Before the accident. Before the abduction.

That's a lot of *befores* we have to work through.

And I'm grateful to have the time to do it. Less is

more. And the shack is absolutely less. So it's my job to bring the more. More writing, since it helps me process and recover. More time to think over recent events and what I want moving forward. Iris has set me up well, like she did last time.

Where would I be without her?

Em did a great job of the cleanup. Who knows what he found when he came out after he rescued me from the water. I didn't exactly take stock on the way out that day. The day before Timothy and his buddy hightailed it and left me for dead in the ocean.

They got away.

An unfinished story.

A loose end . . .

The police didn't think I have cause to think they would return. Not after being reported present in this area. The officer they sent to the hospital was pretty thorough. I'm guessing he knows what he's doing. Still, the unease in the back of my mind will most likely never leave. The tiny thought that one day they'll come back to finish what they started. After all, six years of effort is a lot to abandon.

"Hello?" The door opens on his heavy knock.

I'm sitting at the small table. My laptop is open, but my attention has drifted out the window. I glance to the door. Cal stands with a bowl in his hands.

"Oh, hi. Come in." I stand and run a hand over my

shorts before tucking a stray strand of hair behind my ear.

He steps inside. "Thought you might like to help me harvest some vegetables and whatever else is still good over there. Hopefully most of it survived."

I realize now the large bowl is, in fact, empty. A smile fights for control of my face. Hope blooms like the hordes of plants I know he has stuffed away in the green-house. "Sure."

Happiness lights up his blue eyes, and he fumbles the door before walking outside.

We wander over the grassy span toward the green-house. The door is closed. He opens it, sliding it on its long tracks, and the humid heat spills out instantly. The scent of growing, thriving plants comes with it. I breathe it in. It may as well be Cal I'm inhaling.

Inside this long, oversized structure is months and years of work. His love and care. Toil and trial and error have all accumulated to produce this. I wander the aisles until I come to my tomato garden. I smile as I find my plants healthy and loaded with shiny red fruit. "Hello, babies, Mama's missed you."

"You always talk to your food?" Cal says with a chuckle.

Shit.

I hope he didn't pick up on that. Dammit, I have to be more careful. Iris told me repeatedly he must remember the last three years on his own. I want him to recover, well and fully. And I will do whatever that takes. Even if it's breaking my own damn heart every day he thinks we're strangers.

"Not usually. These ones are just so pretty, and they smell so great," I say too quickly.

A crooked smile wobbles as he says, "Sure thing, Eve."

Eve.

Not Evie.

No *mo nighean* this time around.

"Put some in the bowl, hey. We can make a salad to go with the chicken Em brought." He handles a plump red tomato, and my mind is stuck on the loop of his mouth stuffed with one, juice running down that square jaw of his, soaking into his short beard. My heart squeezes in my chest.

Holding my composure, I pick a few of the best ones and add them to the bowl in his waiting hands. He wanders to another bed, and I hang back, watching as he trawls the aisles, stopping every now and then to add another find to the bowl. The overwhelming intensity of missing him, even though he's right there, hits me.

"Excuse me," I utter and flee the greenhouse.

I stalk across the grass to the shack. When I'm safe inside, I drop onto the bunk and force each breath in and out of my lungs. The thought that I may never recover what I've lost when it comes to this man burns, and I rub a hand over my breastbone.

Needing something else to focus on, I move to the table and open my laptop. I scan the outline of my romance novel. The one I've waited years to write. Now what was once a grand plan seems like something unrealistic and too hard. I don't want to write it. I'm not in a place to sit and write happily ever afters.

Instead, I tap out notes on a story I know well. One full of grumpy sunshine, forced proximity, an age gap that makes the tension flare from the page, where the hero falls first. One with chemistry, drama and a love to die for. One I hope gets its own happily ever after.

I pray it does, because I don't know how to exist without it.

I tap out a working title:

The Story of Callum & Evie ~ *Mo Ghràdh*

A delicious aroma drifts through the window of the shack. My stomach grumbles. I should go to the house. I should stop procrastinating. I create stories for a living—I can pretend to be something else to this man for an hour. Surely.

I push through the door and pad toward the house, and the gravel crunches under my shoes. The cool night breeze plays with my hair around my shoulders. I'll have to ask if it's okay to shower upstairs, because I may be okay with the bunk and the minimalist way of life, but no running water or hot shower is where I draw the proverbial line.

Sorry, Iris.

I reach the door and it opens.

"Oh, so—I was—"

Cal ducks out with a foil-covered plate. I'm guessing it's for me.

So, I'm not eating in the house?

"Ah . . . Did you want to eat here or there?" he says, eyes darting from the shack to me.

He's adorable when he's flustered. A far cry from the grump I endured when I first came to Fire Island.

"Where do you want me to be?" I ask, truly wanting to know.

"You can eat with me, if you like?"

My smile widens. "I would like that."

He nods and returns through the door.

Inside, the living room is lit up with the lamp and the kitchen light. The table is set. For two.

Like he'd been waiting and decided to come find me.

My stomach is a cluster of butterflies. My heart skips a beat. "Oh, you were waiting?"

"Not too long. Sit. Eat before it gets cold."

I sit at the table, and he hands me the plate before moving to the kitchen. He stands by the sink, washing up.

"You ate already?" I ask.

He turns back. "Yep."

Okay, great. I uncover the plate. A chicken pasta dish with my tomatoes sits on the plate. So similar to the last meal we had here together. Like somehow, subconsciously, this man knows every small part of us, every moment we shared is still in there somewhere. And . . .

I have no idea how to unlock the prison it is held in. No way to pry open the steel bars on the trap his mind has erected around the memories housing everything Evie and Cal. The last nine months.

No idea how to give him back the three years he lost.

I eat as much as I can as he works in the kitchen with his back to me.

Having eaten almost all of it, I set the cutlery down and rise, taking my plate to the sink. I scrape the remnants of the meal into the bucket by the sink he uses for compost and slide the plate, knife, and fork into the soapy water as he cleans a glass. My hand brushes his, and the plate falls from my fingers.

He stills. His hand closes around mine, lifting it to the running water automatically. Just like the times I burned myself trying to cook.

I stare at him, praying just one memory gets through.

When he drops my hand and shakes his head, I know nothing made it through.

Blue eyes find me. "Sorry, I—"

"Callum, it's okay."

He turns to look at me. His face is a tangle of pain and confusion. "No, I—"

"Really, it's fine. It's . . ."

He pulls away, and his composure changes instantly, his jaw setting as his face hardens to stone. "Turn the lights out when you leave."

Just like that, Grumpy McCreary is back.

I huff a small laugh as he ascends the stairs. He disappears, and I can't help the hysterics that have me doubling over. Tears leak out of my eyes with every new bout of laughter. This version of Cal I love.

Oh god, and I do.

If I had my way, I would walk up those damn stairs and wrecking-ball my way into that head of his. Take back what we were and drag him kicking and screaming —most likely growling—with me.

I finish the washing up, tidy a little, and turn out the lights before I leave. Just like McGrump asked me to. I smile as I pull the door to the house shut behind me. The moon is up and huge in all her glory tonight, and I take my time wandering home, diverting out onto the grassy spans between the lighthouse and the forest.

I haul in long, deep, calming breaths. They stretch my lungs like happiness.

I tilt my face to the beaming queen overhead. Her light soaks into my skin and I sigh. The light in the bedroom is on upstairs, and I imagine Cal is getting ready for bed. Showering . . .

Without me.

Good lord, I have it bad.

Slipping into that cozy bed of his. Like he did during the cold snap when we were both freezing. The fright I got waking up next to a very naked, very perfect Cal. I still feel the thrill in my bones even now as the memory takes.

Writing in his journal. The one I tossed at his feet the day he kissed me.

That was our catalyst. That very moment.

A small cluster of seconds that changed my life.

Completely.

Entirely.

Relaxed and getting sleepier by the minute, I walk back to the shack and change. When my head hits the pillow, I smile, thinking of all the moments Cal is going to find when his memory returns. The joy I will witness as he discovers the depth, the intensity of what we had.

I only hope he hasn't changed his mind about me.

Hopefully he'll conveniently never remember the

ridiculous promise he made me swear to. That's one part of us he would do well to forget permanently.

The hope that's been poking its head up since the moment I found out he was alive and well rears up for another look. It's a shy little thing. But in its defense, it has every reason to be afraid. Despite that, I stay positive. I can do this.

After everything we have been through, falling in love again should be the least of our worries.

We can do this.

I can do this.

firefly

Twelve

CALLUM

I can't do this.

I lie in my own bed. In my own damn house. The shower is running. The door is open. What the hell? Has the twentysomething never heard of boundaries? She hums away like she hasn't a care in the world. And my traitorous mind is flooded with images of her naked, wet, and soaping her elegant fucking limbs one by one.

Now I'm goddamn hard.

Impossibly so.

With a groan, I roll over and bury my head into the pillow on the other side of the bed. Something floral hits me, and I jerk back up. It smells suspiciously like the woman now occupying my shower.

The hell?

Did the little pervert sneak in here in the middle of the night and sleep in the big bed?

Who does that?

My engorged cock presses into the mattress, not helping where my head is at right now. The water shuts off, and I do my best to feign sleep. The door is half open, steam curling out as I force my eyes closed. The curtain rustles, gliding along the metal rod. I imagine she steps over the side of the tub with one long, elegant leg.

Fuck's sake, pull yourself together.

Christ, must have been a solid three years since I've been laid, too, if the rock-hard cock in my boxers is anything to go by. Just my luck, holed up on a floating rock with the only woman that's ever had this effect on me. The only woman who is entirely out of bounds.

She's far too young. She ain't staying. And she's Iris's friend.

No-go zone.

A *hard* no.

Urgh, that makes it fucking worse. I tried being nice, thinking it would help. But the moment I saw her in Iris's tiny bathroom back on the mainland, biting her bottom lip like she was keeping back a million thoughts that were desperate to transform into words, I felt it.

The duality of déjà vu slips over my mind. The closest thing to a memory I've had since I woke up. Her bottom lip through her teeth.

Fuck.

"Oh, morning," a happy voice chirps.

I open my eyes to find a dressed woman toweling her long hair, a sweet smile plastered over her face. Like she isn't in my bedroom while I'm in bed. Like she didn't just get naked mere feet away from me. Making herself at home.

Christ.

"You shower in strangers' homes often?" I grunt out.

She opens her mouth to respond but closes it a beat later.

I slide my hands under my head, letting the blanket slip down my bare torso. Two can play this game. Her gaze snags on my body before she schools it away. "I'll just . . ." She points to the door and pads for it.

I suppress the chuckle that wants out and throw the covers off. My boner tents my boxers. Gonna have to take care of that before it drives me crazy.

Before *she* drives me crazy.

So I head for the shower.

When I close the door, I see two towels on the rack instead of one. She didn't take hers with her. Two toothbrushes stand in the cup on the vanity.

A live-in caregiver would stash her own shit in her room. Not leave it around my goddamn house like she fucking lives here.

I fling the shower curtain back further, and sure

enough, body wash and conditioner sit on the shelf by my stuff.

Who the fuck is this little woman? Why are her things in my house?

Does she live here? If so, what is she to me?

Iris has some explaining to do.

I don't give two shits what Jamieson said, I'm getting answers. As soon as Em comes back and I can get to the mainland. For now, the cheery little twentysomething is going to give me something to work with if she wants to keep living here.

I slam the bathroom door.

Finding my reflection in the mirror, it looks like I've aged a decade. Not just the three years everyone keeps telling me I'm missing.

Which begs the question, how did a woman so young wind up here with me?

"Who are you?" I corner her in the greenhouse.

She sets her shoulders back, but no fear shows on her face. Like it damn well should. A strange man who she's only just met, as far as I know, has cornered her against the back of the greenhouse by the flower bed. Instead, she glances at the green shrub littered with white flowers and hordes of small yellow butterflies.

"What do you mean?" she says softly.

"I may have lost my memories, but not my damn marbles, woman. Who are you?"

"I'm Eve." She pushes her chest out, tilting her head up in the slightest. "Eve Holland."

"Cut the shit, you know what I mean." This mind-fuck has run its course. I'm done feeling helpless in my own mind and body, in my own fucking home.

"I—I'm Iris's friend, from New York."

"Oh yeah, how'd you meet?"

"Livvy, she's my editor." Her face shows no sign of a lie.

I cross my arms. "Livvy's your editor?"

"Yes, for over six years now."

"So, since you were twelve?" I ask, raising a brow.

Her mouth gapes, and an incredulous expression contorts her pretty face.

"Sorry," I say, tamping down the chuckle bubbling in my throat. "Inside joke, I guess."

Inside my own damn head.

"I will have you know she was my editor for my debut novel at twenty-two. And every book after. I'm twenty-eight, not eighteen."

"Sure."

Her brows drop as she glimpses the butterflies once more.

"Should I leave you with your friends, then?" I nod to the bush bustling with the small yellow insects.

She shakes her head, rolling her lips together.

"Alright, Eve. Tell me about this accident you were in."

It's the Spanish Inquisition, I'm aware. I'm also aware I'm an asshole right now. But every single person in my life is walking on eggshells around me, holding a wealth of information about *my life* from me. It's as good as lying, if you ask me. Which nobody has . . .

"My accident?" she asks, the trill in her voice making it evident she wasn't expecting to have to talk about it. By the way her voice skipped an octave, maybe she should.

"The reason you ended up banged up and at Iris's house, now here. To do what? Recover? Help out? How did you end up on this island, Eve?"

She hugs her arms around her body as her gaze hits the ground.

Fuck. Too far.

I should stop.

I should let her process her own things on her own time. It's most likely nothing to do with me. By the way she glared at the shattered glass in the lantern room, I'm guessing car accident?

But then, her things are in my house. Was she in the boat I found?

I'm clutching at straws here.

And it's winding me up like a spinning top, ever-revolving, never-ending, but set to topple over at any second its foundation isn't perfect.

"It was a car accident. And I'd prefer to leave it in the past where it belongs, if you don't mind."

She stalks past me, her shoulder brushing mine. I don't miss the silver lining her eyes as she gets the hell away from me as fast as she can. The greenhouse door slides shut, and I hang my head.

"Fuck me."

Was I really willing to destroy someone else's peace just to find mine? I need to apologize. Christ, that was uncalled for.

I trudge my way to the shack. Looking through the door, I find it empty. I head for the house. Inside, I find my living room empty. I take the stairs two at a time, only to find my room and bathroom also empty.

Would she go to the top?

Surely not.

I climb the twisting stairs and step into the lantern room. She leans on the wall of the round room, wiping furiously at the tears streaking down her face. The louvers shine in the morning sun. The brilliant chamber is a stark contrast to the storm clouds lining her beautiful brown eyes.

"I don't want to talk about it, Callum." She doesn't look at me.

I lean on the doorframe.

"Sorry, that was too much. You don't owe me anything. If you want to put your things in my house, go ahead. I got my wires crossed. Thinking we . . ."

Now she turns and stares at me. "You thought what?"

I study the tight look on her face and decide better of it. "Nothing, I thought nothing."

I roll off the frame and pad back down the stairs.

So the woman put her things in my house. She doesn't have a bathroom. She's comfortable here, that is all this is.

Of course it is. She's far too pretty, young, and smart to end up stuck on an island with a grump of a lighthouse keeper.

God, I feel like an idiot.

I *am* an idiot.

Best I keep my distance. As soon as the three-month checkup rolls around, she can go home and I can go back to my life of solitude. Just the way I like it.

Deciding to distract myself with my chores, I check over the weather station and report the daily update to the watchhouse on the radio. Next, I head for the locked-up shed. I've been meaning to ask Em to help me clear this old crap out for months. Twisting the combination, I tug the lock open and slide the chain from the handles.

The old weathered doors swing open of their own accord, like they've been waiting, holding their breath, and only now has it been released. Dust and piles of old things that used to hold meaning greet me. Boxes of books, old records, random items I haven't used in the house for years take up far too much space. But I'm only focused on one thing in the back.

I pad to the bulky shape covered by a sheet. The material has yellowed and started to rip in places. I tug it off in one fell swoop, and dust explodes around me. I cough, waving it away. It finally settles, and my beloved Indian Chief motorcycle stands stoic, right where I left her just shy of twenty years ago.

Even covered in filth, she tugs on my heart strings.

I walk around her, taking in the damage that years of sitting hidden away have done as memories of speed and wind in my hair flood in. Ava holding my waist, giggling before she buries her face in my neck as we roar along the highway. Going nowhere in particular, just happy to be together.

Happiness is a man and his motorbike, the girl he loves wrapped around him.

My last breath chokes out . . .

Fishing hut. Bunk . . .

My arms wrapped around a soft body flickers and fades.

That one was definitely a missing memory. Or the film negative of one. The inverse, static, and untouchable facade of someone, sometime in the last three years.

In the fishing hut.

Who would I take there? To my sacred place that not even Em goes to? She must have been—

I shove my hands into my hair and sit on the bike. The old leather creaks and splits with my weight.

"Dammit," I say on a groan.

A knock rattles the hanging door of the shed. I look up to find Eve, her hands sunk into her back pockets as she looks around the dim interior of the shed, her eyes finally landing on me. "There you are."

Her gaze drops to the bike I'm sitting on. A soft smile blooms before she clears her throat. "Did you want some lunch? I made sandwiches."

I rise from the bike and brush the dust out of my hair, then from my clothes. "Sure."

I walk from the shed and close the doors. I don't bother with the lock. Who would want anything in that old shed, anyway?

"An Indian, hey?" Eve says, glancing up at me.

"Yeah, years ago. Know much about bikes?"

"Not really, this guy I once knew had one." She shifts her focus toward the house, and we walk in silence. I hang back a little as she reaches the door to the house. The sway of her hips has me mesmerized, the way she sweeps a hand over her hair and pulls it around her shoulders, letting it drape over her chest as she turns back. "Hope you like chicken on rye. It's all we have left."

Blood harrying through my veins, I swallow past the rock in my damn throat and simply nod.

She steps inside, and I force my feet to move forward.

"Ain't happening, McCreary," I mutter before crossing the threshold, etching that particular hard line in my mind.

Shutting the effect she has on me down.

Thirteen

EVIE

The sounds of tinkering echo from the now-open shed near the tree line. Cal's been in there for days. With no lamp to polish to a shine every other day and his lighthouse first responder duties on hold for the next few months, I'm pretty sure he's bored to death.

The chance to restore his Indian is a very welcome blessing.

Selfishly, I can't wait to see him on it.

Maybe he'll let me ride with him sometime . . . But I understand the connection the bike has to Ava. So I won't get my hopes up about it.

I wander the greenhouse every day under his strict instruction, harvesting what I can. It takes everything I have to pretend I'm learning all this grow-your-own-food knowledge for the first time. I listen as he talks about the lighthouse duties and how, as a first responder, he has daily maintenance and checks. That on top of his chores, he's usually kept busy.

Now, not so much.

He's counting down the days until Emmett comes back.

I'm not. I'm perfectly content in my delusional bubble.

The rest of the world can stay the hell away.

Gravel moves behind me, and I turn back from watering the long row of summer crop salad varieties.

"Can you give me a hand?" Cal says.

I place the water can on the edge of the bed and turn back. He's covered in grease, a cloth tucked into the waistband at the hip of his jeans. The faded, old blue T-shirt he's wearing highlights his toned chest and bulky arms. His hair is messed up, and a streak of grease covers his cheek. He takes my breath away.

I compose myself before closing the distance between us.

"May I?" I ask, searching those gorgeous blues for any sign of recognition.

He swipes at his face with a hand, smudging the grease. "Shit."

"Here, let me," I offer, pulling the rag from his hip.

His lips part like he's about to object. I rub the cloth

over the grease, getting most of it off. "Better, but still not clean."

He stands stunned, hands hanging by his sides.

I pray the frozen moment means memories have started piling up in his head. And this is him viewing each, one after the other, realizing who is standing right in front of him.

He shakes his head and diverts his eyes. "Sorry. Could you help me with the bike? Need smaller hands."

My hope dies in my throat, my gut plummeting like it did the moment Iris told me Cal had lost three years.

"O-of course, um, just let me . . ." I walk outside and suck back the emotion burning the bridge of my nose. Heavy footsteps catch up with me, and I lose a breath.

I can do this.

I can.

Hell, I lived through days of thinking the man behind me was dead.

Nothing will ever compare to the devastation that brought.

"Over at the shed. I need small hands to tighten a bolt," he says to my back.

Small hands.

Huge stupid damn heart.

I spin on my heels and smile up at him. "Sure. How's it coming along?"

"Slow." He pads across the grass at my side.

The wind plays with my hair, the sunshine warms my skin, and my lungs fill with life-affirming fresh air as my hand brushes his.

I try not to let the way the small touch spreads like lightning through my entire body affect me. The way my breath hitches at the tiniest contact.

He doesn't seem to notice. As we reach the bike now standing on the grass with tools littering the ground around her, he squats. I kneel close to his side and follow his hand as he points out the task I'm assigned. "This bolt here. If I hold the nut with the wrench on the other side, can you tighten it all the way?"

He passes me a tool I'm sure is a socket driver or something.

"Yep, I'll do my best."

He rounds the bike and secures the head of the wrench to the nut. "Okay, tighten her up."

I slide the socket over the head and turn it to the right.

Righty tighty, lefty loosey.

I learned it from my dad, I think?

Not that I spent a lot of time fixing stuff with him. I was always inside with my head in a book. This one I remember, most likely because it rhymes. The bolt turns, revolving its way into the hole it was built for. Cal's grip on the wrench hardens when I reach the last bit. Each turn is tougher than the last, and the tool slips in my hand. The small spot I had to slide my hand into doesn't allow for much visibility.

I reaffirm the head of the socket on the bolt and drop to my seat, squaring up with the task like it's my opponent. I send the socket around once more. With it as tight as I can get it, I stretch up to look over the seat of the bike. Cal's messy hair is all I see. "That's as tight as I can get it."

"Good. Thanks." He looks up, removing the tool from the bike, and for a moment we stare at each other over the worn and cracked leather of the bike seat.

Neither of us speaks, so I return the tool to its grassy bed and push to my feet. "Let me know if you need any more help," I offer with a smile.

"Thanks, Eve."

"Sure thing." I shove my hands in my back pockets, wishing this awkwardness between us would simply disappear.

Knowing it won't until his memories return, I wander back to the greenhouse to finish up my chores. Watering, weeding, and then collecting anything ready for harvest for tonight's dinner. It's just like before. But at the same time, it's not like before at all.

With a basket full of wonderfully fragrant produce, I pad to the house and into the kitchen. I start the process of washing and sorting the food in the refrigerator.

Bending over, I replace the container with tomatoes and shift the root vegetable container to one side.

"You're finding your way around well enough, then?"

I startle, rising and hitting my head on the inside of the refrigerator. "Shit."

I rub my head and turn back to find a shirtless Cal leaning on the counter, sipping from an enamel cup. He wasn't there when I came in.

"Damn, you scared me." I push my glasses up my nose and pull my T-shirt down as his gaze travels my body.

His jaw feathers, but he doesn't say a word.

"Dinner plans?" I ask.

He raises an eyebrow.

"I mean, what did you want to cook for dinner? I'll leave the veggies out." I wave to the basket behind me, still half full of produce.

"Anything's fine. You cooking?"

I stare at him. "I—"

"Don't cook?"

"Not very well."

He chuckles. "Some live-in caregiver, hey."

I would take offense, but he has a point. "I'm usually writing, not doing . . . this." I look around the house as if something more sensible to say will present itself. Nothing does.

"Well, I'll cook, you clean. Deal?"

I can't help the smile that blooms. "Deal."

"Anything you can't eat I should know about?" He places the mug on the island counter.

"Nope, all good."

"Good, we don't do fussy here."

"I know," I say, thinking back to the first days I arrived on Fire Island.

I know.

Like I've been here before.

Crap.

"I mean, I guessed that would be the case."

"Okay . . ." he drawls, giving me a strange, confused look.

Shit. Iris is going to kill me. I can survive this McCreary. Not sure about the other one, though.

"I have words to write." I scurry from the house and bust through the shack door in a flurry of self-deprecation. "Dammit. I will not screw this up."

There is far too much at stake.

Too much.

I've never been so happy to see Firefly as I am this morning. Em waves from the cabin as the trawler closes in on the jetty. I stand beside Cal, waiting for the boat to slow enough that we can board. Cal has a scan scheduled today, and I have time to kill with Iris. Hopefully she won't murder me for the many slipups I feel I've had in a mere seven days of being on the island with her brother.

"Hey, Miss Evie." Em wraps me in a hug, and I can't help but return the gesture.

Callum clears his throat behind us, and Emmett releases me, saying, "You want a hug too, bud?"

"Fuck off, Bradford."

Em chuckles and we board the boat. I sit on the bench seat the way I did on the way out here. Em starts Firefly up as Cal moves to stand by the console. "Handing over control today?" he asks.

"Sure, she's all yours."

Emmett turns back and sits with me as Cal powers the old girl up and sends her out over the blue water. Hands on the wheel, the rumble of the engine under our feet, he looks good in his element. The rock of the boat as she charges over the chop sinks into my soul. It's so good to have the dynamic somewhat recovered.

But it's not back to normal by any means.

"How's things?" Em asks, not taking his focus off his friend.

"So far, so good. No developments yet." I hope he gets my meaning, because I can't say it outright.

"He'll come back, Evie. I know he will."

I smile, but it's sad. Wistful, like the type of smile you give when someone is sorry for your loss. It doesn't feel very dissimilar, despite the man in front of us being alive and mostly well.

Em slides an arm around my shoulders and hugs me into his side. "He'll come back, I promise," he whispers.

I lean my head on his shoulder at the moment Cal glances back.

He takes in his best friend cozy with his live-in care-giver. God knows what's going through his mind at the sight. I move out of Em's hold, and he gives my shoulder a squeeze before removing his arm. We don't want to create any new narratives in Cal's head, and this one would be so far off the mark.

"Running to your standards, Cal?" Em says, rising and heading to the console.

"Fine," he grunts, shifting on his feet.

"You know, you could say thanks for all the hard work and hours we poured into your old tub." Em winks at him.

Cal's face is stone as his jaw feathers. "Thanks."

He returns his face to the water. If I didn't know better, I'd say Callum McCreary is jealous of his best friend. Em shoots me a cheeky grin over his shoulder. He totally set us up.

Who'd have thought . . .

firefly

Fourteen

CALLUM

Iris meets us on the sidewalk by the café. Em drags the cap from his head, giving her his best smile. I see some things never change. She wraps me in a hug before taking Eve inside. Probably wants to quiz her on my every move. She won't get much out of the woman. We've ate together most meals, but apart from that, we stay out of each other's way.

"I have to head back to the watchhouse, Cal. But I'll be back to take you to the appointment in an hour."

"I can take my damn self, Em."

"Sure, but humor us, will you? If anything happens to you, I don't think those two wou—" He snaps his gazes away, cursing under his breath. "Iris would have my balls, bud. Just play nice, okay?"

"Whatever." I wave goodbye and walk through the

front door of the café. Iris and Eve sit at a table, heads together as I assumed they would be. "My ears are burning, Irry."

She flips me off, not breaking her stride as she quizzes Eve on the last week.

I lift the lid to the muffin display case and snatch one up. Blueberry, my favorite.

I round the counter and mess with the coffee machine. Only because I know it gets under her skin. I have no idea how to work this fandangled thing. I'd probably break it before I get a cup of coffee out of the contraption. "Irry, your machine's acting up."

"Hold on," she says to Eve, rising from her chair with a sigh. "You break that and I'll have your hide, Callum. Step away." She waves me off. Her fingers fly over the levers, gadgets, and buttons, and a moment later, the thing steams before dark, rich liquid pours from a tiny spout over the mug she placed under it.

"When it stops, add your cream. Then get out of my kitchen."

"Yes, ma'am."

She narrows her eyes. "I know what you're up to, and it won't work."

"No idea what you're blithering about."

She slaps my arm and returns to the table. Eve looks up from her phone as Iris settles in to talk some more. They chatter away, laughing as hand gestures fly with the escalating storytelling. I wander outside and leave them to it. Outside, I sit on the step. Sipping my hard-won coffee, I take in the marina. The small, quaint town I've lived, loved, and bled in my entire life.

With the hour up, Em arrives in his truck, and we head to the hospital for the scan. I'm in and out in under fifteen minutes, and the doctor is happy with the results. I'm free to go until the twelve-week checkup, as long as someone is with me.

Great. No escaping the pretty little twentysomething.

Sarcasm drips from my own syllables, like maple syrup seeping into my grey matter.

Huh.

Not getting attached, are we, McCreary?

My life is good. Full, almost. But it's like the last three years included one thing I can't put my finger on. The one thing that would fill the void that's been growing since I got home with Eve at arm's length. I'm grateful for her company. She's no trouble, having slipped into the way of life and routine easy enough.

And it will be too quiet when she leaves.

Em pulls the truck over at the café, and I climb out, sending him off with a wave. I cross the sidewalk and push through the front door. Iris meets me at the door. "You should stay the night. Em's going to be hours and then he'll be exhausted. Stay, please?" Her hands are pressed together in a prayer-like position.

Good lord, Irry.

"You don't have a sofa, Iris. Where are we supposed to sleep?"

"Eve can snuggle up with me again."

She tilts her head, smiling up at me like that will make me agree.

"Fine."

"Yay! Dinner's on me. We'll get takeout, save cooking. I'll see if Em wants to come over."

She whizzes back into the kitchen, bubbling something to Eve. She talks fast when she's excited, always has.

Em arrives hours later as the sun is setting, and we are sent to collect the takeaway. *Nicely played, little sister.* We stand outside Bay Shore's only Chinese restaurant in a comfortable silence. So, I decide to obliterate it.

"You and the author, hey?" I ask.

Em looks up from his phone. Something like shock fills his face before he schools it back to aloofness. "Nah, just being a good friend, is all."

"I mean, she's a little young for you, bud." I hold his gaze.

"You could say that."

"How's Iris feel about it?"

Now his face falls, the slight amusement that it held over the past minute fading.

I raise an eyebrow. "She's her friend, isn't she?"

Let the inquisition commence.

"No." He shakes his head now. Seriousness claims his face.

"No, they're not friends or no, you and Eve aren't a thing?"

"We—"

"Order up!" the little lady in the takeout window calls. Em frowns as he turns back to collect the food, thanking the woman.

"Drop it, Cal." Em's mood has swung like the weather on the open seas.

So, they are a thing?

Well, fuck.

I can't help the slither of jealousy as it heats its way down my spine. Dammit.

Not getting attached.

Back at Iris's, we sit at the table as she dishes out takeout onto our plates like the mother hen she is. Em sits by her side opposite Eve and me.

"The wine," I blurt out.

Iris stills, looking over to me with the spoon suspended over the plastic container. "Wine?"

"There was wine . . ." I breathe.

Holy shit.

Fucking hell.

Eve is staring at me.

Em is staring at me.

Iris sits and drops the spoon onto the plate. By the look on their faces, this was a memory. Trying desperately to reclaim the sliver that drifted through my mind a second ago, I close my eyes.

But as hard as I try to envision what could have possibly unfolded around this table involving wine and these people, I can't find the thread again.

"It's okay." Iris lays a hand over mine as she leans over the table. "It'll come back, I know it."

Tears line my little sister's eyes.

"Excuse me," Eve utters, pushing up from the chair and leaving the dining space. She treads upstairs, and Iris rises, following after her.

"Em, just tell me. Please?" I beg.

His face twists a little like he's holding back emotion, but he simply says, "I can't, Cal."

We eat our food and leave some out for the girls. When Em leaves for home and I head upstairs, they still haven't come out of Irry's room.

I knock on her door. "You want me to pack the food away?"

Murmurs slip under the door. It opens a second later, and my sister's face fills the gap. "No, I'll be down in a minute to fix it up. Go to bed, Cal."

Yes, ma'am.

I nod and wander to my room. How can one fragment of a memory trigger such a dramatic effect? What the hell was going on here before I went on that damn rescue call?

I shower and slip under the covers in my boxers. When the heaviness of sleep calls for me, I let it take me down.

"Cal!"

I jerk awake.

"No! Please, stop . . . No, no." Someone is screaming, and it doesn't sound like my sister. "Callum!"

I'm off the bed and out the door before the next heartbeat. Iris meets me in the hallway. Her worried gaze alternates between me and the woman tangled in the blankets.

A heartbreaking wail leaves Eve's restless body.

Iris steps into the doorway, shaking her head. "No."

"Callum, plea—No!" Eve screams.

FUCK.

"Move, Irry." Every inch of my being is strung tight with the need to get to Eve. I have no idea where this protectiveness is coming from, but it's burning me the fuck alive.

"Help, ple—Cal, I'm sorry . . ." she sobs, tossing violently.

I shove my sister aside and crawl up the mattress until I'm level with Eve. Her tank top is askew, her hair messed all over her face and over the pillow. Her belly is bare, the small sleep shorts barely covering her hips. Her body trembles, her hands curled like claws as she grips the sheet beneath her. A strangled cry tumbles from her lips.

I lift her shoulders, brushing the hair from her face. "Evie, baby. I'm right here."

Evie, baby.

Where the hell did that come from?

She struggles in my hold. Her hands fly up, swatting at me.

"Wake up, Eve."

Her palm connects with my cheek.

"Enough. Open your eyes," I growl.

I'm someone else.

I'm me.

I—we are . . .

Her eyes fly open. She cowers back instantly.

Did I hurt her? Is that why everybody's holding out on me?

God, fuck, *no.*

My hold on her slips. I can't breathe.

No wonder my sister didn't want to tell me what happened. I would never . . .

I don't understand.

"Cal?" Eve gasps.

"Right here," I manage past the stone filling my airway.

She sits up, crawling into my lap.

She's not scared of me. So, my last theory's out the window. Something shuffles on the carpet to my right. I glance over to find Iris leaning on the doorframe, tears running down her cheeks.

. . . And it hits me.

Em isn't with Eve.

I was.

That's the part I was missing. The part I can't remember one moment of. So, she's not some friend of Iris's. She's my . . . I have no idea what she is to me. How far this thing between us went.

Fine hands press against my chest. I haul in a breath.

To know but not remember.

"You good?" I ask Eve.

She moves off my lap, and the realization of what just happened sends her face falling. "Cal, I'm . . ."

"It's fine. Go back to sleep." I step off the bed. Iris moves, letting me leave.

I stalk back to my room.

I shut the door, locking it behind me. How the fuck

can a man forget someone like her? What the hell is wrong with me?

I sink onto the edge of the bed and shove my head in my hands, tugging at my messy locks. It makes sense now, the way she knows her way around the island and took up the routine so easily. Why her things are in my bathroom. Because I'm not just a man on his island anymore, I'm a 'we.' We must have had a life there together before the accident.

Her accident . . .

What's that all about? Did she go out looking for me after the rescue? Was she coming home and got into a car wreck?

God, I wish someone would fucking tell me what the hell is going on.

Fifteen

EVIE

The nightmare I had three nights ago was so intense I was sure I was dying. The only thing —person—I wanted in the final moments of my dream was Cal.

And he heard me.

He came.

To find me a *mess*. I can't get the thought that I've ruined everything out of my head. Iris was quiet when we left, but I know she's upset about what happened. I'm kicking myself now. How could I be so stupid? Of course the man would come if I was screaming out his name.

I drop my head onto the small table in the shack. The laptop in front of me is open on a blank page. Chapter four of this new project, and I'm stuck. Stuck in my own damn head. Never to return to reality.

It's hard to work in an imaginary world when your real life is imploding all around you.

Urgh, I need a break.

From nothing.

From everything.

I wander from the hut and head for the tree line. Some forest time should help.

I cross the invisible line from island grasslands to forest and keep walking into its cooling embrace. I feel better already. After five minutes of wandering through the trees and inhaling as much fresh air as my lungs can tolerate, I stop and lean on a rough tree trunk. Eyes drifting shut, I let my mind meander.

"Don't go too far," a gruff voice calls from the tree line.

I barely hear his low tone over the breeze.

"Alright!" I call back.

I slide to the ground and listen to the beautiful sounds of nature around me. Those sounds are soon drowned out by heavy treads over the debris-covered forest floor. Steps halt in front of me, and I crack one eye, looking up at Cal.

"You okay?" I ask.

He looks conflicted. He has since we left Iris's, if I'm honest. The awkwardness that's been swinging between us since the nightmare is driving home the reason why nobody's supposed to talk about his past.

Our past.

I've set him back, and I hate myself for it.

"Don't get lost, is all." He glances around the forest.

"I won't."

"You know your way around the forest?" His brows fall.

"Mostly."

I decide honesty is my only path forward at this point.

"Course you do." He sighs, searching the forest around us.

I push to my feet. "I can go back to the mainland, if it would be easier."

He turns on me, stepping into my space. "Why would that be easier?"

"For you, I mean," I breathe.

"You think being away from you would be good for me?"

"You did," I whisper. "Better for me, that was the idea."

This complicates things further, and I need to shut the hell up. Maybe if he has a reason to send me away . . .

But the doctor said he had to have someone with him. Surely, Iris could find a real live-in caregiver?

"Eve." He lifts my chin with a finger. I'm looking into those blues with nowhere to go. No refuge when he says,

"I don't want you to leave. Now, or when my memories return."

That takes my breath away.

"That might change."

He searches my gaze before he leans in, and his breath caresses the shell of my ear. "Come home."

Emotion floods my senses. Him this close, I can barely manage a solid inhale.

He puts a little space between us.

I hate it.

I want the distance to disappear again.

"Lunchtime," Cal says, walking back the way he came.

He leaves me gasping for air, back pressed against the rough bark of the tree, my body alive from one small interaction. If it was possible to fall in love all over again with this man, consider me tumbling down to earth at speed. Only this time, the chance of splattering all over the ground on impact is a solid possibility.

Because to lose this man twice would render me unrecoverable.

Cal pulls out the chair at the table. All I can do is stare at it. The image of being tied to it as he pushes my thighs apart burns, sending the hottest crimson all over my neck and face. A quizzical look captures his face as he takes in my flushed face.

"It's just a chair, Eve."

"That's what she said." I drop into it and pull myself closer to the table for lunch. The table is loaded with fresh salad, chicken, ham, something that looks like a casserole or stew. Warm bread rolls sit in a basket by it. A bottle of wine is the centerpiece. A red. It sticks up out of the plates of food like the lighthouse it's in.

If food was a love language, this would be a proposal. Or a really big apology.

"Eat before it goes cold." Cal passes me the heavy casserole dish, and I spoon some onto my plate.

"What's all this for?"

He continues to load up his plate, taking a little of each. When he's done, he looks up. Uncorking the wine, he pours us each half a glass. "Trying something different."

"Oh?"

"I can't ask you to tell me about"—he waves a hand between us—"but maybe if we spend more time together, things might come back."

"They might."

"You don't think it'll work?"

I shake my head. "I don't know if forcing it is a good idea."

"Does this feel forced?" He frowns.

"No, but—"

"We're going swimming after this. Eat up."

"You're not supposed to swim on a full stomach, Cal."

He grunts. "Wives' tale. You'll be fine. Besides, it'll take us a half hour to get there."

Does he mean the waterhole?

I narrow my eyes playfully. "Fine, but if I need rescuing, I'm absolutely calling Emmett."

His cutlery hits the table. "Fucking brat." He tosses a carrot at me.

"Hey! Stop wasting our hard-earned food!"

"Our food?" He raises an eyebrow.

I can't help myself. I rise and pad to where he sits. He looks up at me, all blue eyes and handsome angles. I pluck up a tomato. If this doesn't jog his memory, nothing will. I shove it into his mouth, and his eyes widen as he chews. I lean down. "I like you with your mouth full."

I swear he growls.

I pluck up my plate and hightail it out of the house.

I took it too far, but I am not missing that swim. Not for anything.

An hour later, a knock rattles my door. I look up from the huge word count of eighty-nine to find the man filling the doorway as he does, leaning on the jamb.

"Got time for a swim?" he asks.

"You have Em's number on speed dial?"

He rubs his chin with a hand, as if contemplating leaving me behind.

"It's fine, you'll do. Let's go." I grab a towel and slide on my flip-flops.

We walk in a comfortable silence on the way through the forest. As the trees give way to the large spans of water and the small waterfall trickling down the ledge at one side, I toe off my footwear. Tossing my towel into the tree, I pull my shirt over my head. I changed into my swimsuit after lunch, still hopeful he would bring me here.

Cal tugs his shirt over his back, running for the waterhole like a kid. He jumps and cannonballs, his legs tucked up, arms tight around them. The splash explodes around, wetting me where I stand. I pad to the edge. Its grassy mud-rimmed border is squishy underfoot, mud squelching through my toes. I wade into the water as Cal comes up for air and bobs, arms wading out beside him.

Just how deep is this little oasis pond?

It's incredible. In up to my belly, I suck in a breath. For a warm day, the water is cool. I brace myself, walking until it's up to my shoulders, then I swim out to where Cal is.

"Guessing they don't have anything like this in New York?" he says with a wide smile.

"Nope, not at all," I say softly, leaning back until I'm floating on my back. The surrounding canopy frames the blue sky overhead. It's amazing.

Not unlike the night I floated and waited for Em.

But unlike that time, now I am content. Happy.

Safe.

The water sloshes, and I glance over to find Cal gone. I fix my focus back to the sky, not bothered he's decided to do something else. Inhaling, I relax, letting the ripples lap at my side, arms, legs, ribs, and neck. My hair floats out around me.

This is as close to heaven as a girl can manage by herself.

A head rises to my left, water running from his hair, over his face and his cheeky-as-shit grin.

"Ah! Shit." I roll and sink, spluttering on the liquid that finds its way into my lungs when I forget to hold my breath. Warm hands haul me to the surface, and I gasp. Mouth open and hair curtaining my face like some swamp monster, I slap his shoulder. "You ass!"

He chuckles, not letting me go.

I swipe the hair from my face and the water from my eyes. Cal's laughter fades as he realizes we are barely inches apart.

I could so easily lean in, crash my mouth to his.

Devour this gorgeous man, palm his face with my hands. Hold him until one of us breaks away, breathless.

Instead, I simply float in the water.

The absence of our love is an anchor weighing between us, tied off at both our hearts. Neither of us dares to move, lest we both sink to the dark depths below.

"Can I touch you?" he whispers. "To see if anything happens."

"I—you're already touching me."

His hands adjust on my waist, and to my surprise, he pulls me closer. With only an inch between us, he says, "Your face, your lips. To see for myself."

I nod, and my breath stalls out when his hand rises and his knuckles brush over my jaw. I want to roll my head into his embrace. To close my eyes and let my instincts take over, like they've done so many times with this man.

"Eve." My name is gravel.

My lips part as my chest caves under my choppy breaths. I can't take my gaze from his as it falls to my mouth. His thumb sweeps over my bottom lip, and I swear his eyes dull to something close to navy. My legs wrap around his waist automatically. I still, waiting for him to object.

He doesn't, and I plant my hands on his shoulders.

He cups my face in his hands, eyes searching my own as he brushes his lips over mine. "What were we?"

My throat closes over.

I want so badly to fill in every blank he's suffering through. To give him the relief he so desperately needs. But if I do, I will tarnish or twist the memories his mind has stored and protected so well.

I don't answer, and his hands fall from my face.

"They are worth the wait," I whisper, catching his hands before they can dip below the water. "I can promise you that."

He forces a smile, but I can almost taste his disappointment. I know that feeling all too well. I'm dying here, too, for the moment we get back what we lost.

But I refuse to ruin our chance at something incredible for a moment of curious relief.

Cal wades toward the waterfall, and I follow. He stands now where the water must be shallower and runs his hands through his hair as the fall pours over him.

I hang back, watching this god of a man in action. Something so simple, yet so damn overwhelming.

He walks from the water toward the edge, not coming back. I swim to the waterfall and let it pound its heavenly way over my shoulders. A girl could absolutely get used to this.

An hour later, we break through the tree line, almost home.

Cal tried to make small talk on the way back, but I was quiet. I don't trust myself to not screw this up. The last thing he needs is more drama to deal with. With the lamp and losing three years and all. Enough is enough for one man. Besides, it's nice being in his company. It's what I longed for in those darkest moments. The bargains I made, every one included him.

And they came good, so there is no way in hell I'm ruining this. For Cal.

For me.

For us.

As we reach the house, the screech of the radio splits the air.

"Watchhouse to Fire Island. Over."

Cal rushes to the radio and plucks up the handheld receiver. "Watchhouse, this is Fire Island. Over."

Emmett sounds tense.

Static channels through the room, and he glances at me.

"Hey, bud. Ah, your sister needs you back here. ASAP. Over."

"Em, really, tell Irry to text me."

"You know that's patchy at best. I'll pick you up first thing tomorrow morning."

"Can't it wait?" Cal says, focusing on me.

"No. This time it can't. Over and out."

firefly

Sixteen

CALLUM

The bell to the diner door jingles overhead, but inside is oddly vacant. I look up to find my sister standing shy of the door. Her face is a war between upset and anger. Evie files in behind me. I couldn't leave her on the island by herself. Besides, she said there's no way she was staying out there alone.

I search the room and find Em sitting at one of the tables toward the back. His face looks as vacant as this room, as if he's in shock, his focus fixed on one spot across the room.

"Hell, if you tell me Errol died, Irry, I'll shout for the after-party."

The grin that splits my face with that particular thought fades when her expression doesn't change. Em clears his throat, fighting with his cap in his hands, and I track his gaze to where it hasn't moved from since I stepped inside.

What I find has to be some kind of sick dream.

One I'm sure I will wake up from any second now.

Maybe I never survived the rescue after all, and this is simply a screwed-up version of the afterlife.

Because the woman sitting at Iris's counter should be dead.

She stands, straightening her shirt as she offers up a tight smile. She's older, but I would recognize that face, that blonde hair, and those blue eyes anywhere. Only now, she has the same aloof air about her that her mother did. Her hair is cut shorter, just above her shoulders, and it's straight, not wavy like it used to be. A single string of pearls sits around her neck above a beige top over dark jeans, a prim-looking handbag hanging from one slim shoulder.

With . . . rings on her finger. And not the one I gave her.

"Ava," I choke out.

Iris spins back to glare at the woman we all thought was dead and gone. "If you don't want her here, say the word and I'll shove her sorry ass onto the curb faster tha—"

"Callum," Ava says, moving closer. A chair scrapes to my right. I glance back to see Eve sitting at a table with her hand over her mouth, shock etched into her face.

I open my mouth to say god knows what, but every last thought I have isn't fit for human consumption. The realization she's standing here, alive, means she lied. The entire fucking town lied to me, then treated me like a goddamn criminal. Blamed me for her death. For the tragic death of our . . .

I stumble back and hit the closed door.

The ridiculous bells jingle.

I mourned for her. I grieved for years.

Fucking years.

I turn and rip the door open. It slams into the wall as I stumble onto the sidewalk and stalk toward the marina. The wood clacks under my boots. Everything blurs as I make Firefly's slip.

Then I'm in her cabin, firing up the engines.

I'm out on the water before I can bother to remember I've left Eve behind. I contemplate going back, but the sight of Ava has me push the throttle forward.

Fire Island comes up in what feels like a moment later, and I slip her up by the jetty, kill the engines, and tie her off. The tower I call home blurs as I stagger toward it. Grass meets my knees as the burning in my lungs and the squeeze in my chest take me down. I crash into the grass, sobs keening from my throat.

I haul myself to my feet and wander in a circle, hands tugging through my hair.

"Fuck!"

Did Em know? Iris?

This entire fucking time?

The roar of the Coast Guard boat drifts in, and I turn back to see it dock on the other side of the jetty. Eve flies from the boat, sprinting for me. Her face is as devastated as my own.

I collapse under the weight of the sight of her. She's on the ground with me a heartbeat later, holding me as I chug through each horrendous breath.

"Oh, Cal," she sobs, hands running over my hair.

"Bud, I'm so sorry." Emmett comes to my side.

I pull out of Eve's hold, scrambling to my feet. I'm on him a second later. "You knew!"

He's shaking his head furiously, emotion twisting his face. "No. Cal. I had no idea. Nor did Iris. We are just as shocked as you are."

I scoff a harsh laugh. "Yeah, right. I'm just the idiot the entire town pulled a fast one over. Then treated me like the fucking animal who killed her for their own entertainment. And what about the ba—"

Fuck. I can't even say it.

Em stares at me as he rubs a hand behind his neck. "Ava should be—"

"No! You tell me. Tell me something, Emmett. Just *one* thing!"

I'm in his face.

It's not his fault. I know that. But he's here, and I'm so damn fucking angry.

"I would if I could," he breathes.

I roar at him.

His jaw feathers, but he stands his ground.

I falter backward.

Ava . . . Un-fucking-believable.

Now, I want to be anywhere but this godforsaken island. I want to rail Ava until she gives me every fucking answer I want. I want her to understand the suffering she put me through. The toll she took on a man by faking her goddamn death and that of our baby.

Did they survive?

It suddenly registers, heavy and unrelenting . . . I may have a child.

I fall to the ground, legs tangled underneath me. Finally looking up, I find Eve waiting, tears coursing down her cheeks, sobbing breaths chugging from her like this cuts her the same as it does me.

I bleed, she bleeds.

In this one moment, I understand what she is to me.

Everything.

It only took the worst blow of my life to figure it out.

I reach for her, and she drops into my lap. I fold her in my arms, and she palms my face before dropping her head to my chest. I let the tears fall over my cheeks. They soak into my beard and then into her hair. Neither of us moves from the spot when the Coast Guard boat rumbles to life.

I should apologize to Em.

It's not his fault.

God, I'll get around to it as soon as I take care of my girl. I hold her tighter, breathing her in.

Ava can go die in a hole for all I care.

But hell, I want to know what became of the baby.

So much it twists my heart on its axis.

How many years did I wish to the heavens I'd just met this kid? Had the chance to hold my baby. To be a father.

I toss and turn through the twisted sheet. My mind is racing at light speed, and I have no hope of slowing it down. Every interaction, every moment I thought I remembered right is under scrutiny. How the hell did an entire town lie to me, and not one person slip up?

It seems impossible.

I'm alone. Eve insisted she still sleep in the hut until my memories return. But all I want is to be close to her. The memories would be nice, but now I understand who she is to me. At least, I think I do.

I guess I won't truly fathom that until my mind rights itself. That's what eats me, gnawing its way down to the bone. After all I've lost, it feels right that what lies between Eve and I was something . . . deep.

"Urgh! Fuck me." I sit up, rubbing my hands down my face. "Christ above."

I wander downstairs to grab a mug of water. The small lantern hanging in the hut is still on. I glance at the time on the wall clock by the bookshelf.

Midnight, or near enough to it.

Eve's up late.

I head for the door before I realize I'm only wearing boxers and it's the middle of the damn night. Hesitating, I turn back and head for the stairs. The last thing I want to do is force something that may or may not be between us.

The second my head hits the pillow, memories of Ava file in, contrasting with the woman I saw this morning. The shock rattles me for the hundredth time around. And I wonder how much of a choice she had when we were young. She was barely seventeen when we got pregnant. Still a kid in most people's eyes.

How much of her disappearance was her parents?

Knowing the way things went down, she probably had as much say in it as I did. But why wait twenty fucking years to come back? Why come back at all?

I fully intend to have my questions answered the

moment I calm down enough to have a civilized conversation. The moon shines her silvery beams over the wooden floor, and I finally relax, weary from the day's drama.

Heaviness creeps in, and I stretch, willing myself to surrender to it.

My eyes shutter closed. I turn my head to the side, and oblivion finds me.

I'm floating. No—lying on Firefly's deck. Something touches my hand. I turn to find her. The sun is setting to the west, lighting the sky up with its pastel pinks and oranges before it changes to gold.

The boat slips away, and I stand with my hands by my sides, my breathing labored from the axe that is in my grip. Bare-chested, a journal at my feet, I am frozen in the moment, entranced by the woman calling me out. By the fire I see in her eyes for the first time since she came to my island.

Something between my ribs snaps.

Fireworks float overhead as the realization she's defending me against the town swells.

The ground spins, and I'm lying on Iris's tiny fucking spare bed. Eve's warm body is pressed into mine, her ass against my hard cock. A heartbeat passes. I can taste her. Thighs spread wide, my hands the ones holding them back.

My surroundings flip, and I'm on my feet. Brown eyes,

lined with silver, look up at me. Her mouth—my cock sunk deep between her perfect pouty lips.

Heady and raw, I groan, out of breath—trees flying past me—so desperate to get to her. My name, a scream, carries on the wind through the forest.

The fishing hut closes in around us, and I can't fight what aches inside for her any longer.

Then we're spinning. Happiness exploding from the epicenter we've made.

A beat and I'm naked.

Wet.

She stands in my shower, brown eyes pleading. Unable to rein in my control for what I know is the umpteenth time, I take her, slamming her heaving shoulders into the tiled wall, mouth crashing over hers.

Whimpers pour through her lips.

My heart splinters in my chest.

Mo nighean.

I'm choking. Hands reach for me, closing around my jaw. Her lips brush over mine. Dark hair falls around me. I look up to her strung-out face, her need for me etched all over her face.

Tomato juice trickles from my lips. The beautiful dark-haired woman sitting on my lap laughs, her head tipping back. The scene wobbles and . . .

She's leaving the dock with Em, who carries her bag. My fucking broken, tattered heart trailing along behind her, leaving its bloody stain in her wake. I can't move from Firefly's cabin. I can't even say goodbye. Air in my tight lungs turning to ash . . .

I'm suffocating.

Burning swallows me whole. I jolt awake with a painful groan. Sitting on the bed, I stare at some inane point across the room as the last nine months or so flood back into my reality. I—

Eve, she . . .

Evie.

Fuck.

"Fuck, fuck, fuck," I cry.

I jump off the bed like it's on fire, stalking a short distance before turning back. Repeating the route, I run my hands through my hair.

I told her to leave.

I love her.

And I made her promise to leave me.

But . . . she's still here.

Tears burn my eyes as the room blurs. I groan.

What have I done, baby girl?

My—

Mo ghràdh.

Irry told me she'd been in an accident. What fucking accident? Where was she for two whole damn weeks while I was held up in the hospital, clueless?

She—

I fly from the bedroom and stumble my way down the stairs. The front door slams against the wall behind me as I send gravel flying, crossing the small path from the house to the shack.

Halting abruptly at the door, I find her light off.

I rest a palm on the door.

My heart flings against my ribs. I can't spend another second without her.

Seventeen

EVIE

The door rattles. Heavy breathing—more like consecutive rasps—comes from the other side of it. Now, I'm glad for the chair I stuck under the doorknob. I feel safe here with Cal, I really do. But the knowledge that Timothy is still somewhere in the world will always have my nerve up.

"Evie," Cal groans.

Evie.

Not Eve.

I sit up.

"God, baby girl. *Please* . . . Please, let me in." His voice breaks on the last syllable.

"Cal?" I scramble from the bunk and fly to the door. Knocking the chair out of the way, I tug it open. His choppy rasps that barely hold back sobs disintegrate as I find him distraught.

Tears shine on his cheeks. His face is wrecked, and he shakes as he heaves through every lungful. Standing rooted to the spot, his hands hang, his eyes burning into mine.

"Cal," I whimper.

He sets his face and takes one step closer before strong arms sweep underneath me and I'm in his hold, hugged to his chest before the next heartbeat has a chance to fall. I wrap my arms around his neck and study his face through my own stream of tears.

"How will you ever forgive me, mo ghràdh?"

I huff a strangled laugh that comes out more like a whimper as my head shakes. "Nothing to forgive, sweet man."

His raw exhale turns into a moan as his face sinks into my hair. Wordlessly, he lifts his head and turns on his heel, walking into the house. He kicks the door closed behind us and takes the steps one by one, his gaze never leaving me.

He stops and lowers me onto my side of the bed, and I can't help but scrunch up my face to stem the ridiculous flow of tears that refuses to stop. He crawls into the bed and hauls me into his arms.

"Never again, Evie."

I sob in his embrace, fingers curling around his neck,

fingertips sweeping through his hair. I wail in his hold until my face feels too swollen to take a proper breath. "I thought I lost you." My voice cracks, and I haul in a ragged parcel of air. "Twice."

He chugs through a sob and tightens his hold.

"You broke your promise," he rasps.

"I know," I wail.

"I'm so fucking thankful you did."

"Don't you *ever* send me away again."

His head is shaking.

No.

"I couldn't even if I wanted to."

I steady my racing heart with long, calming inhales as I put a little space between us, taking him in. This stoic, grumpy man that's tried so hard to do the right thing for so long. Nothing burns quite like the love I have for him. It's soul-deep. An ethereal existence.

Running a finger over his jaw, I lift it to his lips, then trace over his eyebrow. He cocks it under my touch, and I smile.

"I *missed* you," I whisper.

He pushes up onto an elbow and looks down at me. With a quick kiss to my lips, he says, "I was missing you."

"You can stop now. I'm right here." I brush a finger over his temple.

He chuckles and wipes the moisture from my cheeks

with his knuckles. I lean into his hand like I've wanted to for the past few weeks. His palm catches my chin, tilting my face up toward him a little further. "Yes, you are, baby girl."

His lips find mine.

I melt where I lie.

Opening, I sink my hands into his hair as he claims my mouth, devouring me like a man starved. My body responds to his, needing him everywhere. Needing his soul wrapped around my own. Only then will this nightmare come to a close.

He breaks away. "It's been too long since I tasted you. Every fucking day you've been here with me since I came home, I've dreamed about what you feel like. Taste like. And having the memory back isn't going to cut it."

"Making new memories could help?"

"Mouth or hands?"

I huff a stunned sound. He remembers that?

"Everything."

"Greedy, greedy girl." He dusts kisses over my neck, working his way down to my T-shirt. He loses a low growl when he finds my hard peaks. "Fuck, Evie, how did these ever slip my damn mind . . ."

"I—" He clamps his teeth around one. "Do—n't know."

I arch off the bed. Rough hands grip my rib cage. He moves, knees digging into the mattress on either side as he straddles me, never losing contact with my aching nipple.

Heavens above, I missed this.

I missed *him*.

To think I could have never had this man ever again . . .

"Cal," I whimper.

"Mhmmm?"

"God, please . . ."

"Slow down, Evie. I'm taking my time. Whether you like it or not."

I can't respond.

Of course he is.

"These clothes need to come off, or I'm ripping them to pieces," he growls, lifting the T-shirt as he rocks back, staring down at me.

These are the only pajamas I have here. I lift from the mattress and tug the shirt off. Locks of my messy hair tumble over my shoulders and down my chest when I lean forward to toss the shirt to the end of the bed. Cal traces a hand over my cheek before he tucks my hair behind my ear. He studies my face, as if committing it to memory in some place that can never fail him again.

He brushes his knuckles over my shoulder, sweeping my hair away, one side then the other. It's all I can do to stay still as his gaze travels my body inch by inch, letting him remember me.

Who I am to him.

Who we are.

For the promise I made, the promise I will regret till the last day of my life, to be dead and buried in his mind. Like it should have been the only thing to *not* survive his memory loss.

"Irry was right," he breathes.

Iris?

We're talking about Iris right now?

"She was?" I chuckle.

"Yeah, she was. I'm one lucky bastard. Getting to fall in love with you twice." His voice is raw.

That steals the amusement from me, along with my breath. I sit up and drag his mouth down to mine. Hungry doesn't even begin to cover the response I get from Cal. He devours me, covering my body with his delicious weight. Growling into my mouth before he nips at my throat.

His lips. Teeth. Travel lower. Until they close around my nipple.

I whimper, arching to offer him everything I have.

His tongue swirls, and I open for him automatically. Hips widening, legs pressing against the mattress, chest open, shoulders digging into the blanket.

"Fuck me, Evie baby," he rasps as he dots kisses over my belly.

A searing open-mouthed kiss brushes over my hip. Then the other.

Methodical.

Taking his time.

Patient.

Mine. Again.

Thank God.

The bland days I spent between losing him and the moment he knocked on the hut door not even an hour ago are forgotten. I never want to live through another one of those ever again.

His beard tickles my thigh, and I glance down to see blues looking up at me.

"Picking up where we left off?" His face twists with desperation.

He's asking permission.

Like, somehow, the time I spent without him—the promise I made—could have changed my mind.

"We never should have stopped, sweet man. That's the last time I promise you a thing."

A cheeky, sweet smile blooms on his face before fading to need.

Rough hands spread my thighs. My last breath burns out as he kisses his way up my right thigh to my aching center.

"Fuck, Evie. A man could die of starvation just—"

He closes his eyes briefly before he growls, "You're fucking soaked for me, baby."

firefly

Eighteen

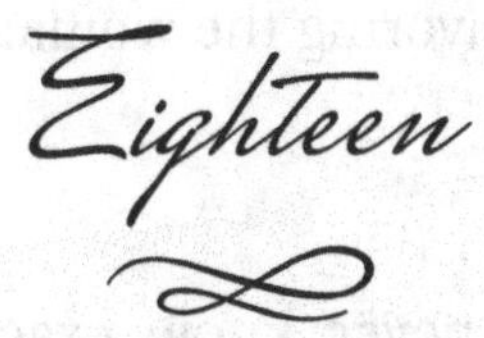

CALLUM

Evie spreads wide for me. *This* is my favorite new fucking memory. Hell, I'd lose them all over again just to recreate each moment between me and her. I knew she wa—

Brown eyes look down at me, the fire in them burning all the way to my soul. Her need for me, grounding. The way I can barely control myself around this woman, incredible.

I sweep my tongue through her center, and her hips buck from the bed. The smile wanting out, I hone into another slow, delicious stroke of my tongue.

Cruelly slow.

I'm rewarded with the prettiest little whimper. Her breaths snap in and out so quickly I doubt any air graces her lungs at all.

Watching her writhe under my hold . . . I could do this all damn night. All damn day. We're never resurfacing from this bed, not if I can help it.

My rock-hard cock aches as it presses into the mattress. But I'm savoring the woman who lived through hell and still stayed.

For me.

I guess I will never know exactly what she went through, waiting for me to find my way back.

I nip her sweet little bud, and she cries out. Her teeth settle over her bottom lip, and I suck her clit into my mouth and sink two fingers inside her.

So wet. Her need covers my hand as I pump her higher and higher.

Shaking, she grips the blanket, chest arching. As she tightens, claiming my fingers, her hands hunt and find their way into my hair. Elegant digits pull with a harsh grip as she mutters something incomprehensible. I tug at her clit with my teeth, flicking my tongue, soothing it after each vicious pull.

"Come for me, baby girl. It seems like I've been waiting a lifetime to see that beautiful face wrecked."

With a lingering stroke of my tongue, I suckle her clit. Curling my fingers forward, I coax her to where I want her. And, like I knew she would, she arches off the bed, coming hard.

She is stunning.

All angles.

Sweet-as-fuck little noises.

Driving me absolutely feral.

My cock pulses as her release spills over my hand. I suckle her through her release, drawing out every last incredible wave she rolls through. My balls tighten as I taste her release. And my own follows. I couldn't stop it if I tried. I groan, the raw sound vibrating against her clit. She flies up, sinking her hands further into my hair.

"Cal," she cries.

One syllable.

One fucking goddamn sound, and my heart all but snuffs out.

When her doe eyes find mine, I crawl up to kneel between her legs. Cradling her, I press a kiss to the top of her head. How did I forget a love that hurts this much? This good . . .

"You—" A fine finger slips behind the waistband of my boxers.

"You have that effect on me."

"I know that." She gives me a cheeky grin as she slides the boxers down. "My turn to taste."

Christ above.

She frees my cock, her eyes darkening as she studies the mess I've made. "What a waste . . ."

Gripping the base, she licks the cum from my shaft, rolling her tongue around the tip.

Fuck.

Fuck.

Now my hands find her hair. My restraint is threadbare at this point. Still impossibly hard, I could flip this little woman over and claim every inch of her as my own. She cleans me before looking back up, her thumb brushing a stray drop of my cum into her mouth. Like she won't waste a single drop.

I brush her hair from her face, slipping my palm along her jaw. "Fucking perfect, Evie baby."

She rises, and my hand drops from her face. "Yes, we are."

I fold her into my arms. There is no way in hell I'm ever letting this woman go. As long as it's her choice to be with me, that's where she'll be.

Not willing to let each other go, we lie on the bed in a tangle of arms and legs. I drop my chin to the top of her head as she snuggles closer. "Goodnight, mo nighean."

"Night, Cal."

A kiss presses over my heart.

Mostly content, I could let the night take us where it wants. But the vague thought that one piece of the puzzle is still missing . . .

Where my Evie was for two weeks that made Iris such a mess.

That thought sees my eyes snap open.

Each version of what could have happened to her while I was out of action is worse than the last.

So much for sleep.

Yellow wings fly past my vision, flapping through the air as a butterfly circles back round, landing on the bush at the rear of the greenhouse to rejoin its flutter. Evie stills at my side, the watering can in one hand, a basket half full of harvested produce in the other.

The memory of her fear of the small insects sinks to the front of my mind.

"You never did tell me about the butterfly thing."

She looks at me, hesitating before she sets down the watering can and basket to take my hand. "I need to show you something."

Confusion takes hold as she leads me to the house, up the stairs. Higher still, to the lantern room where we come to a stop by the pile of glass I still haven't had the heart to clear out.

She hugs her arms around her body, nodding to the glass shrapnel at our feet. "I did this."

"No, you—"

"I smashed the Fresnel. With a wrench. I had no choice."

Maybe they were desperate. Em's words fling back around at me, the meaning no longer obscure.

"How?" I manage.

I mean to say what happened, but my brain is reeling right now. What could have had Evie so desperate *this* was her only option?

"I left, like you made me promise. I did. I went home, but—" She looks out the glass wall circling around us. "I received a text from Iris, which was odd. We don't text often as a rule. Something felt wrong, I just knew it. So I came back, but Iris had no idea what I was talking about when I showed up asking her why she'd text me saying you were in trouble."

"Hang on, Iris knew I was in trouble? When was this?"

"The day before Em found you in that upside-down boat."

"That doesn't line up. Why would Iris text you the day before it happened?"

"I know," she whispers, like she understands something I don't.

"Did Irry tell Em something was up?"

"No, Emmett was out on shift by the time I got here the next morning. I got Errol to bring me back to the island."

I raise a brow at that.

"He said he wouldn't stay, but I didn't care. All I could think of was finding you."

She didn't. Find me, that is . . . by the feeling of dread that's started to swell in my gut.

"The next part is hard to tell, because I've kept it a secret from every single person. For . . . six years."

I need to sit down.

I pad to the wall and sink to my seat, leaning against the curved wall. I pat the floor by my side. "Come here."

She tilts her head, her face twisting like she's not sure I'll want her there when I hear what's about to come out of her mouth.

I don't care what it is.

Nothing will stop me from loving this brave little woman.

Finally, she closes the space and sits beside me. Her head falls back onto the wall and her eyes close. She continues, "I have been receiving letters from a guy for six years. First off, they started out friendly, you know. And I was kind of excited to have such a great fan." She huffs a sigh. "Around six months later, the letters started being inappropriate. Possessive in nature, I guess you'd call it. Joshua and I were married six months later, and that's when . . ."

The accident.

"My husband died." Her words from the first time

she shared this with me are like glass under my skin. I knew what she went through. I'd lived it myself.

I scoff a sadistic laugh at the thought.

Fucking Ava.

"Well, the letters kept coming. And just before Livvy sent me here, I'd received another one. So, I was happy to leave the city, thinking it would put an end to it. But he found me."

"The mail Iris gave you the night of the festival . . ."

She nods.

"Fuck, baby. You should have told me."

"I couldn't." Her gaze intensifies as she shakes her head. "He killed Joshua. That's what was in the letter. A confession that read like a warning. And he knew you and I wer—"

Her chin wobbles as the first tear spills over from the silver lining those beautiful eyes.

"He set that boat up to—" She rocks forward.

"That was *him*?"

She nods.

"Christ."

I rub my hands down my face. "How does this fit with the Fresnel?"

Now, a sob chugs from her lips. I pull her onto my lap.

"You don't have to tell me, not if it's too hard. Let time pa—"

"No. I want you to know. Because I don't think it's over."

I can only search her face, hanging on tenterhooks as she composes herself.

"He stole Firefly, beached her on the eastern side, and I was stuck here. He had me chained to the generator for the first week. That part was okay . . ."

Okay? Heat rises in my core.

The fuck?

"Evie, no . . ." I grind out.

"I tried to sabotage the generator but failed. I thought maybe that could help somehow. He wanted me. Upstairs. I fought him on everything. He locked me up here. There were two locks on the door. The lantern room was boarded up so I couldn't try to climb out or signal for help in any way. He was thorough, I guess."

That explains the screw holes on the door.

"I thought maybe Em would have come out to check on things. Only, the one time he came out, I was still in the basement, and Timothy must have hidden. I don't know."

Timothy. A name to the pasty little fucker who tried to off me. Tried to hurt Evie . . .

My hands curl to fists.

Evie moves from my lap and sits in front of me. Now her gaze drops, her hands fidgeting with the hem of her shirt.

Fucking hell, I have a fair idea of what comes next.

"He wanted me to . . . I was instructed to scrub myself clean in the shower, and then he cuffed me to the —our—bed. Every time he touched me, I flinched. I couldn't help it. I was so scared. So he sat at the end of the bed and made me spread wide for him while he—"

She bunches up her face.

"Stop."

"No. You need to have all the information before we go any further, Cal. I wanted control back. I wanted to escape. I thought that would be the way. So, I did what he asked. I bared myself, opened up, literally. He saw everything."

"Did he . . ." My voice cracks, and I can't rein back the fury welling up.

"No, that's as far as he got before I decided to kill the queen."

"The queen?"

"He brought me back up here, must have been satisfied with—" She glances up and worries her bottom lip through her teeth. "I was running out of time, I thought surely next time he drugged me and carted me downstairs, he would—"

"He drugged you?" Horror pinches my face.

"So, I smashed her. I found the wrench, and I couldn't stop." Her voice breaks. Her mouth flattens to a thin line as tears course down her cheeks. "I had no choice. It was the only way to get someone, anyone, over to the island. And . . . it worked. Em came. But then he had a gun, and I couldn't scream for help. We went to the fishing hut, then his friend came. They'd been in on the whole thing, together. It was the middle of the night when I finally got a chance to grab the EPIRB. I was screaming over the radio for Em. Eventually, he found me tossed over the side in the water where they left me."

The last words fade as she hauls in a much-needed breath.

My body vibrates with rage where I sit.

Christ. *Fucking.* Almighty.

I push to my feet, pacing a short length. If the Fresnel wasn't a pile of glass already, I'd obliterate it to shards myself.

They would have abducted her.

Done god knows what, and then . . .

Six fucking years she's been living with this. I rake my hands through my hair, letting choppy bits of air grace my lungs and burn.

If I ever find those motherfuckers, I will take immense pleasure in snuffing out their last goddamn breath. And their torment will be long, drawn out, and painful as sin.

Nineteen

EVIE

I sit across the table from the woman who destroyed Cal's life. And she has the audacity to smile some fake-as-hell smile at me while we wait for Iris to bring the coffee. Em and Cal are out the back seeing to Iris's hot water system, which she says has been playing up.

In truth, I think he's procrastinating. Ava didn't come back from the dead for no reason. To think she has the balls to waltz right into Iris's café, thinking whatever she wants from the McCrearys wouldn't do damage.

"You don't look like Cal's type," Ava says with a sniff as she tilts her head up, looking down her nose at me.

I purse my lips together, grinding my molars down tight as a beat passes. "With all due respect, I don't think you can comment on that."

A huffy breath escapes her lips as she moves her attention to outside the window somewhere.

Her rigid posture barely moves as Iris sets coffees down in front of us before returning to gather the rest. Em appears by her side a moment later. He leans down close, whispering into her ear.

Is Cal okay? Are we leaving, like we should have the second we stepped into this ambush?

As Cal walks through the door to the diner from Iris's living quarters, I see he's resolute. He wants answers. That's entirely understandable.

Hell, he deserves more than that if you ask me.

I give him my best smile, and he winks at me, running a grease rag through his hands before tossing it into the trash and moving to the sink to wash up.

My heart rattles in my chest.

He's braver than me.

My nerves are set to detonate at any second. The long list of things Ava could say or want flips over in my mind like one of those cartoon flip-books from the nineties my dad collected.

I realize, for the first time since Ava appeared, Cal may still have feelings for this woman. They have history. They spent some of their best days together.

Wild and free.

Completely opposite to anything I've ever been.

I swallow past the emotion closing my throat. Hands

firm around my mug, I take a tentative sip. It tastes bitter. I can't help the surge of crimson flushing my neck as Ava studies me from across the table.

I've never felt so small at such an inappropriate time in all my life.

She should be the one with her tail between her legs after the stunt she's pulled. But apparently, she's fine with the way things are playing out.

"Have you known Iris and Callum long?" She sips her coffee, wincing like it's warm vinegar before she sets it back on the table.

"About a year," I hear myself reply. The words are meek. Like an apology I'm too chickenshit to say out loud.

I've never felt like such a flake as I do now.

I clear my throat, rummaging for something more solid to say, but Iris drops into her seat with a tray of three coffees. Em sits on her right, leaving the last chair for Cal. Between Ava and me.

Awesome.

Em shoots me an encouraging smile, but I can't reciprocate. I'm lost in the woe-is-me vicious hamster wheel of my own head. It's all I can do to glance at Cal when he drops onto his seat. His hand squeezes my leg under the table before his gaze moves to Ava. His hand slips away, and he picks up his coffee and takes a long sip.

Oh god.

"Well," he finally says, "what the actual hell?" His voice is rough, clipped.

Ava forces a smile, dropping her gaze to her mug, and Iris leans forward, her face hardening. Em leans back, his arm draped over the back of Iris's chair as his stare sets on Ava.

It seems like we all wait for an age before she sighs and clears her throat. "I heard about the accident. And I —" She glances up to Cal. "I couldn't stop thinking about you. My husband, Craig, suggested I come and see if you were okay. He doesn't know I was supposed to be . . ."

"So that's it, you just heard I almost drowned and thought that would be a good reason to flip my fucking world upside down?" Cal's jaw grinds shut as he waits for her response.

She opens her mouth to say something but snaps it shut.

Iris frowns. "Bullshit, Ava, you had twenty years to undo what you did. And you didn't. You let Cal think you died. Your baby died."

Cal's breathing kicks up as his grip around the mug whitens.

"I guess that's true." She swallows and glances at me, like the next words will do me the most damage. Not Cal. "And I should have come back, Cal."

"Callum," Cal snaps.

Her gaze falls along with her face. *Nice try, Ava, but you and your wrecking ball are not welcome.*

"I should have come back. I realize that now. But we were so young. My parents moved us clear across the country. I had no money, no means to get us back. That's what they were counting on."

"Us? As in your parents and you, or . . ."

Ava sits up a little straighter now. "You have a son. Reese."

All expression disappears from Cal's face.

I watch as he moves from shock to anger to pure devastation.

"Where is he?" he growls.

"He's at home. With his father." Ava sets her shoulders back.

Cal rises from the chair so quickly it topples over. He's out the front door before any of us can get a word out.

How could Ava do this?

How could she say that?

"You mean to tell me my brother has a son, and all this time some other man has raised him. Taken care of him . . . *Loved him?*" Iris hisses.

"He was the better man, Iris. Yes, it is unfortunate Callum hasn't met his son and he's missed those formative years. But this is what was best for me and for Reese."

I glance at Emmett, whose face is utter shock. His hand supports his forehead as he glares at the woman across the table.

Iris stands. "Have you any idea what you've done?"

Ava goes to say something, but Iris cuts her off. "You didn't just break him once, you had to come back for a second go. Get the hell out of my café."

I stand as if in agreement. And when Ava doesn't budge, Em pushes his chair back and closes in on her. It's the first time I've ever seen Emmett angry. He hauls her to her feet by an arm, and she slaps him away before stepping back and smoothing over her pristine clothing. With a flick of her long hair, she raises her chin. "I should have known better than to try and do something nice for ignorant riffraff."

My jaw drops.

Iris flies at her, Emmett catching her in time before she tears the bitch to pieces. As they seethe and stare at each other like two feral cats around the last dead pigeon by the furthest dumpster, I excuse myself, heading outside to find Cal.

The door closes behind me, and I wander toward the marina. The man is a creature of habit, so I'm betting he's sitting on Firefly. Reeling.

The thought sends panic through me, and I pick up the pace. By the time I reach our slip, I'm at a sprint. Sure enough, I find him sitting on the bench in the cabin, his head hanging, his elbows on his knees. I round the bench and lift his head with my hands on either side of his jaw.

A storm brews in the brilliant blue eyes I adore so much.

"Hey," I whisper.

He pulls me into his arms and drops his head to my belly. I run my hands through his hair, not knowing what to say.

What could I possibly say?

He groans into my stomach. His grip falls to my hips and tightens. I drop into his lap and tilt his face up, forcing his gaze to meet mine. "Listen to me, Callum McCreary. You have done nothing wrong. None of this is your fault. Other people made decisions for you, and they took away your choices and they took away your son. You did not deserve any of this. Promise me you know this."

His jaw feathers on a groan.

His face twists as silver lines his eyes. Then, on a ragged sob, it breaks, and I fold him into my chest. The only place I have to keep him safe. To try to soothe the hurt and pain tearing at him right now. I know how much he blamed himself for Ava's death and how badly he wanted to be a father to the child he thought he lost.

This has to be destroying him.

And she stole it all.

Just to, what? Come back and rub it in his face? Good lord, I want to—

"Evie?" Em says from the dock. "You guys in there?"

Cal sucks in a breath as he wipes his face dry.

"Yeah, Em. Be out in a minute," I call back.

"Iris needs you back at the café, only for a minute."

Urgh.

What more can this sweet man take?

"Be there in a bit," Cal calls out, standing as he slides his hands behind my neck. I look up into his sorrowful blues. "Come with me?"

"Of course."

He presses a kiss to my forehead. We take our time wandering back to the café. When we push through the front door, Ava stands with her bag by the counter. The same place she was when Cal first saw her days ago.

She adjusts her bag on her shoulder as she clears her throat. "I wanted to apologize and say goodbye."

Cal folds his arms. The deadpan stare he gives her is beyond cold. "Go on, then."

"I—you should know . . . I never meant to cause you any inconvenience."

"Inconvenience?" He steps toward her, releasing his arms to his sides. "I thought you were *dead*, Ava. For twenty fucking years. I mourned you. I mourned our son. This entire town turned on me. You destroyed my damn life."

"Yes, well, I—"

"You should probably wrap it up." Emmett gives her a pointed look.

"I'm sorry I lied to you. I regret a lot of things that happened between us."

Cal shakes his head. "Does he know?"

"Pardon?" Ava frowns.

"Does Reese know anything about me?"

She holds Cal's fiery stare. "He does."

"Does he know where to find Cal?" I hear myself ask.

"I told him his biological father lives in Fire Island."

Biological father.

The balls on this bitch.

"Yeah, I think that's about all we can take for now." Em moves closer to Iris, who looks set to rip Ava's head from her shoulders.

I would pay good money to see that.

"Here is my card, if you have any questions. All I ask is that you let Reese come to you, if and when he decides to."

Without waiting for a response, she glides out the door. The bells jingle as the door closes behind her.

The four of us stand, stunned, our stares penetrating the white wooden door, shock sinking her filthy talons deep in each one of us.

firefly

Twenty

CALLUM

He would be around twenty.

Twenty fucking years I missed out on. For what? So Ava could marry money?

I see the apple doesn't fall far from the tree.

I raise the axe above my head. Sweat trickles down my spine in the heat. We don't need firewood, but if I don't smash something, I'm going to lose my goddamn mind.

The axe falls. The wood splinters. The groan that leaves me with the swing takes a tiny piece of hurt with it. I know Evie's worried about me. The fact that she's been sitting in the sun pretending to read the same page for an hour gave her away.

But hell, I love her for it.

She's selfless in all the ways I need her to be right now. And I fully intend to be there for her when she needs me, while praying she never goes through anything like this.

Night and day, Ava and Evie.

My memories of Ava don't match the woman she is today. I can only assume that is the makings of her parents. Of being a seventeen-year-old girl with a baby. Having her life and plans upended.

But to stay away this long . . .

"Cal?" a soft voice coaxes to my left.

The axe hangs in my hand, my stare fixated on the chopping block. No wonder she's worried. I'm not exactly handling things well.

Fuck.

"Come inside for a bit?" she says softly.

When I turn to face her, her face is red, flushed from sitting so long in the sun. Her top is sticking to her skin, sweat beading at her brow and her neck glistening with it. A bead breaks and runs down between her breasts. She slips a hand over mine, holding the axe. I release it to her hold, and she leans it against the block. "Time to cool off."

She laces her fingers between my own, and I follow as she leads me into the house.

Inside, two glasses with ice sit on the counter. A light

snack of chopped crudités and cottage cheese in a small bowl waits.

"Sit." She drops my hand and reaches for the snacks.

"You don't have to coddle me, baby. I'm fine."

Studying my face, she leans on the side of the table after placing the tray between us.

"I—" She angles her head with a wobbly smile. "I just can't get over this, for you. I can't process that this is happening to you. I hate it."

I reach for her, and she steps closer. I push the chair back and tug her between my legs, looking up at her brown eyes, tight with emotion for the man in front of her.

"I don't know how I'm supposed to feel," I say.

Confused and angry would be two emotions I can identify. But at the same time, I mourned Ava. I said my goodbyes. The lingering hurt for me all revolves around Reese. Or, more accurately, the absence of him. The absence of me in *his* life.

Replaced by some stranger Ava's parents no doubt thought was a better alternative.

"Do you want to see him?" Evie asks, palming my face.

"More than anything," I mutter.

She smiles at me, scrunching her nose. A gesture I know means she is trying to hold back tears.

"Hey, you don't worry about this old man, baby girl. One day at a time."

I've had my pity party, my meltdown moment, finding out Ava is alive. And the way the sight of me broken wrecked this gorgeous little woman will forever be etched into my memory. My heart.

I will do everything I can to make sure she never endures a drop of that pain ever again.

She nods, but she's shaking now.

"Hey, come here." I pull her down onto my lap. Brushing her hair behind her ear, I trace the incredible angles of her face. Sliding the glasses from her nose, I place them on the table. Her eyes dart, studying my expression. I can only imagine what's going through that brilliant mind of hers.

"What if having Reese in your life means I can't be?" she finally asks.

I tilt my head, frowning.

I'm lost.

She presses her palms to my chest. "Cal, I'm barely seven years older than your child." Her chin wobbles.

Right.

She is.

"What if it's too weird, and you have to choose?" Her hand covers her mouth, and she struggles to hold it together.

I cup her face with my hands, hers falling away. "That is *not* going to happen. You and me are nonnegotiable. You got it?"

"But—"

I shake my head, jaw feathering. "No buts. This right here, you and me, this is it."

She groans but nods.

"*Now* I feel like an old man." I chuckle to lighten the mood and her wobbly smile splits as she slaps my shoulder. But she slows, her hand tracing the muscles of my chest.

"You don't feel like an old man to me . . ." she breathes.

I drag her mouth down to mine. She opens for me instantly, and I devour her, growing harder by the second. I grip her ass and lift her onto the old table.

This I remember, we have been *here* before.

"The food," she protests. I lift the tray and lean over, sliding it onto the counter. Ice water sloshes over the rims of the glasses.

She's all worked up over nothing.

These clothes have to come off. The sweat-soaked T-shirt comes away easily enough, and I tug at her tiny shorts as she lifts her hips. She lies on the kitchen table in nothing but her pale-blue lacy underwear, and I pause a moment, taking her in.

Fucking perfection.

As pretty as they are, the lacy things are coming off, too.

Spreading her legs, I step between them and lean over, plucking up a sweet, hard nipple in my teeth. Arching, her hands fly to the sides of the table, fingers closing over the edges. I slide a hand around her, releasing the clasp.

She huffs a laugh as the lacy bra leaves her skin, hitting the floor.

The most incredible fucking tits fill my gaze. Christ, she's magnificent.

She's mine.

All fucking mine.

"Caileag luachmhor, I couldn't live without you even if I wanted to."

"Precious girl," she whispers.

She knows the phrase. Of course she does. Some of my most sacred memories of her and me are lined with Gaelic phrases my father reserved for my mother. From Henry to Merri. The depth of understanding of what they had hits hard, knowing that's what Evie and I have.

Now, I truly understand it.

Evie reaches for me, and I come down, hands tracing up her ribs, mouth dusting kisses up from her belly, between her fleshy, addictive mounds, to the space where her neck meets her jaw. She writhes underneath me already. My rock-hard cock digs into her soaked center. Even through my jeans, I feel it.

So fucking wet.

Panting, she shoves on my shoulders. "Please, Cal. It's been so long."

It has. It was before she left since our souls have been tangled together. Since I've been buried so deep in this woman it's impossible to tell where one of us ends and the other starts.

And, fuck me.

Overwhelming need spirals, crashing out my breaths.

Sliding a finger behind the band of her panties, I hold her gaze as I trail them over one hip and then the other. With her pussy bare, I spread those pretty thighs wide.

A growl puffs from between my parted lips.

Evie pants where she lies, as wound up as I am.

She's dripping wet. My cock aches painfully. The only cure for my madness is the woman spread upon the table before me. Evie sits up, pulling her legs up so her feet rest on the edge of the table. She grabs my T-shirt, pulling me into her space.

My girl, taking what she wants.

A man has never been so fucking proud.

Or so fucking desperate.

I want to touch her. Taste her. Sink balls-deep into this pretty pussy that's mine. I want to take her rough.

Take her, period.

But after all I've put her through, I'm letting her call the shots.

"Lose the clothes, Cal," Evie pants.

I don't move, simply letting my gaze burn into hers. A strangled sound escapes when she rips the shirt from my body. Next, her hand pops the button of my jeans, and they are shoved down my legs.

"We're doing this at your pace." The words are ash on my tongue, my restraint barely holding.

"I don't want my pace. I want yours." Her mouth opens, and she spreads her thighs wider, reaching for me.

Fucking hell.

I sweep her up off the table and onto my hips, my mouth crashing into hers. Her hands are in my hair. I knead her ass as I ascend the stairs to our room.

Our fucking room.

My goddamn woman.

Mine.

Kicking the door shut—for god knows what reason— I slam her into the wall. She moans into my mouth. I break away, nipping her neck as she squirms against the wall, her soaked pussy grinding against my hard stomach.

My throbbing cock is desperate for her sweet, wet heat wrapped around it. I haul in a lungful.

"Cal," she utters, a whimper stealing the rest of that particular breath.

"Yeah, baby girl."

"I need—I want to see you."

I raise my head. "You want to watch us?"

She nods. Her face is flushed, the brown of her eyes so dark you could drown in their depths.

I peel her from the wall and pad to the desk by the window. Depositing her on the cool wooden surface, I give her a little space. She pulls me right back in, opening wide for me. I run a finger down her stomach, stopping shy of her clit.

Capturing my mouth with hers, she whimpers.

I'm an asshole, I know.

Making her wait. Teasing her . . . Taking my damn time.

Breaking away from her kiss, I drop to my knees. Worshipping this woman the way I fucking should. Her head falls back to the round windowpane as I claim her glistening pussy with my tongue.

Fine fingers find their way into my messy hair.

I sink my tongue through her again, and she bucks on the edge of the desk.

"Cal-lum . . . oh—my god."

I chuckle, my beard moving against her slick opening. Her breaths peter out.

"Come on baby, that can't be all it takes," I say as she trembles.

She's shaking her head.

No? Yes?

"Words, mo nighean. I know you've got them."

With a strained, raw little sound, she nods. "Mouth, fingers . . . Please."

"Good girl."

I suckle her clit and sink two digits deep inside her, curling them forward. She shoots off the wall, looking down at me with desperate eyes as a mewl pulls from her chest.

Good girl, my love.

Sending my tongue around her clit, I graze it with my teeth before plucking it between them. I wait for a response. And I get one.

"Oh. Hell—fuck." She tightens around me.

"Come on, baby, ride my fucking face," I growl out.

Her hips roll as I pump in and out in time to her movements. I suckle down on her clit. She grinds against my mouth as the sweetest little whimpers string out of her. She milks my damn fingers, coming hard.

Arching, she leans her head back. The creamy column of her neck presents itself, and I can't wait to take a bite.

Fuck. That was incredible.

She's grabbing for me a moment later, and I slide

between her legs, lining my throbbing cock up with her soaked entrance.

Palms cup my face, a thumb brushing my bottom lip. "Slow, sweet man. I want to see every inch of you sink into me."

Christ.

I grab her hips, hauling her toward me, and do my best to only notch the tip in her swollen lips.

And it almost takes me out at the knees.

Twenty-One

EVIE

Heaven is Callum inside me.

He grips my hips in a rough hold and pushes his tip into my swollen entrance. The delicious stretch chokes out my last breath. Inch by exquisite inch, he slides inside me, eyes set on my face as I watch us come together. My mouth waters with the pure bliss only Cal will ever be able to give me.

"Fuck, nighean leanabh," he growls. "I don't know how much longer I can give you what you want."

His control when it comes to this has always been touch and go.

It's one of the things I love the most about this man. The way even the slightest touch elicits a response. The way he falls apart for me.

Like he was built for me.

And I him.

He pulls out, slow. Teasing. Exactly what I asked for. I tighten around him too soon.

"Move, we need to move," I rasp.

One sweep of his arms, and we're off the desk. Cal presses my back into the bed, letting his weight settle for a moment before pushing up on corded arms. He thrusts in slower, the reckless, desperate streak he has for me straining to break free.

I slap a hand to his chest. "Too sweet." I'm shaking my head. His hand tugs my leg up under the knee, and he leans back, flipping me over.

"I distinctly remember telling you once before, baby girl. I am not sweet."

He remembers *that* . . .

I can't help but smile as he fists my hair, pressing my cheek into the mattress as a rough hand tugs my hips up to his cock.

He slams into me. The fit so tight, so overwhelming, I cry out, wrapping my fingers around any bit of blanket I can.

Long, hard vicious strokes thunder into me. His grip on my hair shifts, tugging my face back so I'm forced to look at him. "Still think I'm sweet, Evie baby?"

I open my mouth to respond, but my brain is nowhere ready to form words. Instead, I whimper as another orgasm crests. He slams harder, faster.

"That's it. Come on my cock. Milk the ever-fucking life out of me. I'm going to watch this perfect damn ass bounce while you do. This is your reminder you are mine, mo ghràdh."

"I know," I rasp. "I understand now."

With a low growl, he thunders into me, leaning over to plant kisses up my spine. Warmth spirals from my core, sending lightning through my body. Every inch of me vibrates around him. Ecstasy consumes me in the most beautiful waves as I look back to see his jaw feathering. His eyes are a dark shade of deep ocean blue.

Cal's domineering thrusts wane as they turn erratic. He roars, sending ropes of release into me. And I want every last drop he has.

Finally, I am home.

The early morning ocean breeze is in a playful mood, sending my locks about my face as I sit on the sand. I sweep my hair away, refocusing my attention to the page in front of me. I'm on book three of the latest popular fantasy series. It's safe to say I'm addicted at this point. The world is magnificent. The plot is plotting. The banter and spice between the two main characters . . . life-altering.

Cal runs past, jogging his way up and down the stretch of beach on the eastern side of the island. He runs when he needs to process. At least, that's what I've figured out. And he has more on his plate than any man should.

I turn the page.

The heroine pulls her fighting knives from their sheaths as she is cornered in the fight. Five to one . . . .

Eyes flying across the page, I don't notice the man beside me until he drops onto the beach next to me. A kiss smashes against my cheek. "Good book, baby girl?" he pants.

"So good."

"Mhmmm, I can think of a better way to spend your time . . ." He carefully removes the book from my hands, marking my page and closing it before setting it down.

In only shorts after an almost hour-long run, he's all glistening corded muscle as he sweeps me up off the sand and runs for the waves.

"No! Callum McCreary, you put me down."

We splash over the waterline, slowing as we move deeper and deeper.

"Still want me to put you down?" Cal's face is lit up with mirth, the cheekiest grin wrapped around his gorgeous face.

"Don't you dare!"

He jerks, pretending to drop me.

I squeal, sending the heartiest laugh rolling through his throat. For a tiny beat, I'm back at the south end of the island, hunting for food. Me Jane, Cal Tarzan. I'm being spun around, and the happiness that consumed me then does again right now.

"Cal," I whisper, and he drops his gaze, the rambunctious laughter fading.

"Yes, my love?"

"*Now* you can put me down."

He releases me, and I sink into the dense, wet sand, the water soaking my shorts to the waist as we move further into the water. I slide my arms around his neck, and his forehead drops to mine.

"Sunshine looks good on you, Evie."

He's right. I feel positively alive. Alive, and overwhelmed in the best way possible, and so completely loved.

"I need to tell you something," I say softly.

He raises a brow, but his eyes stay locked on mine. And to his credit, after the last bomb I dropped on him, he doesn't flinch.

I press a palm over his heart and reach up on my tip toes. "I—"

"You . . ."

I expel a nervous laugh.

The one thing I regretted most when I thought I would never see this incredible man again was that I never told him how I feel. So now, in the sunshine and the swell, utterly enraptured, I brush my lips past his as I pull his head down a fraction and say, "I love you, Cal. I have for months. When I thought I would never have the chance to tell you. That I left without telling you . . . It broke me."

"Sweet gir—"

"No, I need you to know how I feel, especially now."

Now his hands are cupping my face, his eyes intensifying with earnest as he shakes his head. "Evie, you've been part of me since the day you tossed my journal at my feet. I was gone before I even stood a chance. I told you—you and me, we're nonnegotiable. No delusional stalker guy or ridiculous dead woman are going to tear us apart. Not happening."

"Nonnegotiable . . ." I echo softly.

"You got it."

"So, does that mean I can stay? I can turn the little shack into my library-slash-writing room?" I ask, biting my bottom lip, giving the best pleading face I can summon up.

"You can do whatever you like to it. But Evie, if they decommission the lighthouse, we won't have a reason to stay here."

I drag his mouth down until it brushes against my

lips. "I can think of a good reason to stay tucked away on this little island with the man I love."

He chuckles and claims my mouth, hungrier than I expected.

Breathless, I break away. "Where would you go? I mean, where would *we* go?"

"Now you're getting the nonnegotiable part."

I caress his jaw, studying his expression. "We could go anywhere."

"And what if we can't?" His face turns serious. "What if this island and lighthouse are all we ever have?"

"Then you will polish your lamp, and I will write my books, and when we are not busy doing that, we'll make beautiful, beautiful babies."

His mouth gapes.

I have no idea where that came from. I mean, Joshua and I talked about the idea of it before we got married. I've always wanted kids, but the words slipped out like they were the next natural thing for Cal and me. And I realize that was a mistake when he closes his mouth without a word.

"Sorry, I—"

"Please don't be sorry, you just took me by surprise. I neve—"

"We don't have to talk about it, especially now," I add quickly. I need to get the hell out of the water. I can't believe I said that. After finding out about Ava and

Reese, that's possibly the worst thing I could have said. God, I hate myself right now.

"Evie," Cal calls after me.

I can't stop. I break free of the oscillating water and swipe my book up as I march for the house. I am the world's biggest idiot. To think—

A rough hand grips my arm, and I spin back to face a flustered Cal. His chest cycles through quick breaths. "Mo nighean . . . I want all those things for you. I do. And we can talk and plan, when we've made it through the current crisis."

"I'm sorry I said it. I just . . ."

"Besides, we never really had a proper start. I want to do things right."

"What do you mean?"

"Dinner, movies. Kissing the girl I love on the sidewalk in the rain . . ."

I roll my eyes at him and huff a laugh. "You want to date me? I think we're past that, Cal."

"I want to do *everything* with you. But we're doing this thing right."

"I guess you're going to need my number?" I ask, the coy sound of my voice taking me by surprise.

"Yeah, I should probably ask Irry for that." He gives me his best shit-eating grin.

I narrow my eyes at him and cross my arms. "If we're going on a date, we're doing it in style."

"We are?" he says with a chuckle.

"Yep. I want to ride on the back of an Indian, arms wrapped around a gorgeous man."

"Well, shit. Now I have to fix the bike and find some guy . . ."

I chuckle at him, and he sweeps me into his arms, his mouth dropping to mine in a searing kiss.

A girl could get used to this.

We make it inside, and the radio squeals before settling into a familiar voice. "Watchhouse to Fire Island Lighthouse. Do you read? Over."

I wander to the radio and pluck up the hand piece. "Watchhouse, this is Fire Island Lighthouse. Over."

"Hey, Miss Evie. Fancy hearing you on this old channel."

Em's amusement makes me smile. Like I haven't done enough of that today. I drop my book onto the small table the radio sits on and sit on the seat.

"What's up, Em? Over?"

It feels weird having to add *over* to every single comment.

"Ah, you know, the usual. Iris wants you two here for the weekend. Over."

I chuckle. "You use this channel to set up your social engagements often, Emmett Bradford?"

He laughs over the radio before adding, "Only for you and Cal."

"We'll be there. What's the occasion?"

"Ah, nothing special. Some shopping and then a movie night, I think."

I gasp. God . . . Yes, please! I could absolutely use a girls' day out with Iris. "We'll be there Friday, that soon enough?"

Cal smiles over the glass of ice water he's holding.

"Perfect. See you then. Over."

"See you then, Em. Over and out."

Leaving the glass on the kitchen counter, Cal wanders toward me. "Movie night with Iris and Em?"

"Yep, if you want, we can call it a double date. Or our first date . . ."

"Em and Iris would have to be dating for that to work, Evie."

"Yes, they would." I peck a kiss to the cheek of his currently confused face.

Honestly. How he hasn't picked up on that little detail already, I will never know.

With writing to get done, I down the last of his ice water and head for the shack, leaving Cal to shower after his run. Or should I say, my new writing-room-slash-library. Oh, the plans I have for this tiny rustic space . . .

I open my laptop and continue the scene I'm working on. The heroine is settling into her new routine at the isolated cottage on the east coastline. A slight variation to our story, but effective nonetheless. Fingers flying over the keyboard, I tap out a good chunk of words before the sun starts to sink over the horizon.

After the first unwanted letter arrives at its new location, I save and shut the laptop, ready to head inside and help fix dinner. Pushing out of the chair, I stretch. It's been a good day. I'm content.

I find Cal inside, stirring something that smells like chicken in the frying pan.

"Hmmm. Smells good," I offer, sitting down at the kitchen counter stool.

"Chicken pasta, with your gourmet tomatoes." He winks at me.

"Can I help?"

He chuckles. "I got it. You want to set the table or find some drinks?"

I slip from the stool and pluck out two glasses from the upper cabinet before spinning back to find the red in the base of the island counter cupboard. Padding to the table, I set the wine down. Cutlery goes down next, and then two plates. My stomach grumbles. This is my favorite dish.

Our dish. Cal's cooking, my tomatoes.

Perfection.

firefly

Twenty-Two

CALLUM

Well, this is fucking cozy . . .

Iris is squished between Em and me on the new sofa. Evie is at my right, legs crossed as she leans into my side. The opening credits roll, and the girls settle in. Em throws me a helpless look as *Titanic* starts up.

You have to be kidding me.

Nobody moves.

Evie is shaking beside me. Em slides a hand over his mouth, his shoulders shaking.

"Very fucking funny," I grunt out.

Iris cracks up. "Too soon?"

She points the remote at the television and the screen flips back to the Netflix menu.

"Pick something good, Irry, or I'm pulling out the board games."

"Good lord, Cal, not that slow, mundane torture, please."

My little sister has always done everything at a hundred miles an hour. No wonder what most people think of as fun or relaxing only serves to drive her insane.

"Well, choose wisely." I raise my eyebrows at her.

"Fine."

She scrolls through the options until we find something we all like. And like the old man I am, I groan as I lie on the sofa and hug Evie closer.

"Oh, the popcorn!" Iris jumps up, jostling Em and I. "Be right back."

"Whose idea was the sofa?" I ask Em when she's out of earshot.

He chuckles. "All Iris. She's wanting to spend more time enjoying life instead of slaving away at the café every waking hour. Something positive to come out of your accident, Cal."

I'm impressed.

By my little sister. By the way Em has her back. I'm guessing he's the muscle she called to install the sofa. I suppose I shouldn't be surprised—he's always been there for us.

"Is the television bigger, or is that just my eyes?" Evie notes.

"Now that one was my idea." Emmett smiles.

"Nice one, bud," I say, and Evie snuggles in closer again, tucking her legs underneath her. Iris returns with two bowls of popcorn, handing one to me. She drops back into her spot beside me and places the bowl on her left leg so Em can reach.

I mean, we're in pretty close quarters, so that's a nonissue.

The movie plays, and Evie softens into my side. I glance down to see her sound asleep. We had a big day. Chores out in the sunshine, and she spent even longer writing. No wonder she's wiped out. I turn back to the movie, only to catch a glimpse of Em's arm sliding around Irry's shoulders.

She leans her head on his arm briefly, as if letting him know she knows he's there, then rights herself and shovels more popcorn into her face.

As the end credits roll, I move slowly to my feet and scoop Evie into my arms.

"Night, Cal," Em says softly.

"Night." I turn to move but hesitate when I see Iris asleep against his side. "You want me to come back for Irry, too?"

"Nah, I got her."

We stay locked in the quiet moment, brother and

friend hovering. Finally, I simply nod and carry Evie upstairs.

What's the deal with Iris and Emmett? Evie asked me once before.

Em wouldn't, would he?

We've been friends for decades. He's known Iris as long as he's known me. If he was going to make a move, wouldn't he have done it by now? And I would have had to rectify that stupid train of thought.

Iris isn't someone to be taken lightly.

She's a strong woman. All storm, no rainbows some days.

I doubt our friendship dynamic will ever change.

Padding into the spare room, I walk to the bed, leaning to one side to pull back the covers as I hold Evie in my arms. I place her on the bed, and she rolls over, curling up.

"You want those jeans off, baby?" I say.

"Hmmm."

I release the button and remove the jeans, one elegant leg after the other. She mumbles something and curls back, hugging the pillow as I cover her up with the blanket. Brushing her hair from her face, I sit on the bed and tug my shirt from my back. Stripping down to my boxers, I cross the room to put our clothes on the chair by the door.

On my way back, I glance out the window. Something on the street below glints in the dim light of the crescent moon. Chrome.

Curved.

A motorbike. One of those cheap knockoffs of a Harley-Davidson idles outside Iris's. I lean on the wall by the window and wait to see what the guy does next. No helmet, a battered old cap covering his shaggy dark hair. After a few minutes pass, he pulls his cap down and shoots away from the curb, opening her up on the quiet, small-town cobbled street.

As he rounds the block and rides out of sight, my gut flips.

Who the hell was that?

I wake up to an ass pressed against my groin.

Déjà vu.

Or . . . typical Evie, hunting my warmth the way she always does in her sleep. With a growing boner from her simplest touch, I tug her closer. Sweeping the hair from the back of her neck, I dust kisses up her neck to the tender spot below her ear.

She moans, wriggling in her sleep.

And fuck, if that doesn't turn my cock to concrete . . .

"Wake up, baby girl."

"Mhmmm. I'm awake."

She wriggles her ass into my groin to prove her point. That's all it takes to snap my control. I toss the blanket off and flatten her to her stomach. Straddling her, I rake her hair into a rough fistful, turning her head round. I want to see those stunning browns as I spread her and sink into this pussy.

I tug her panties to one side and run my finger over her glistening entrance. She cants her ass up to me, begging.

"You want more, mo ghràdh?"

"So much. Please, Cal."

"Keep begging and you'll get it."

She smiles up at me. But it's not a pleasant smile. More like a woman who knows where she has her man, safe in the knowledge she put him there.

Fuck me.

I slap her ass hard, punishment for her cheek. A soft whimper tumbles through parted lips.

Christ.

I rip her panties at the seam and toss them behind me. Losing my boxers, I fist my cock. The throb all but drives me over the edge.

Evie spreads her legs wide, her knees digging into the bed. She pants, chest pressed into the blankets. Her perfect damn pussy waits for me. Reaffirming my hold on her hair, I nudge the tip into her soaked center.

"Oh, fuck." Her face breaks.

I know, baby girl. I know.

The mirth that lined her expression is long gone, replaced by desperation, a need burning too hot as her body starts to tremble and I sink in slowly. Inch by heavenly inch. Watching her come undone in one goddamn stroke.

"Good girl," I offer as I seat myself fully into her tight center.

"Cal, don't move. Please."

She tightens around me as she groans into the pillow. The muffled sound does something to me. All I can think of is her wrapped around me, her delicious nipples in my mouth as she rides me, us, to oblivion. With a harsh slap to her ass, I pull out.

Her whimper is tainted by incredulous disbelief. "No."

I settle over my heels and wait for her to come to me. She looks back to find me watching her and rises, turning about on all fours. She crawls across the bed to me.

Those perfect tits bouncing with every movement.

My mouth waters.

I close my eyes, shaking my head.

Hell.

Fine hands find my jaw, pushing through my short beard as she straddles me. "You want me here, sweet man?"

"Fuck, baby girl, I want you every-damn-where."

"Good to know."

I open my eyes as she clamps my lip through her teeth before releasing it. "Mine." The word is no more than a whisper. Her hips roll. My cock throbs with an ache only she can cure.

"Rough or slow, Evie baby."

"Slow, really slow."

She rolls her hips again, and I groan into her neck before nipping my way down. As if she needs my mouth on her as much as I do, she leans back a little, arching up. My tongue swirls around one hard nipple, and she pants out little breaths that squeeze my heart tight.

"God, I love that," she whispers.

I bite down, and she jolts on my lap, her pussy rubbing along my cock in one firm, delicious movement.

"Ah fuck, baby," I mumble against her breast.

"Do it again, please . . ."

The fucking beg on this woman.

Christ.

"Say it again," I rasp.

"Please, Cal. *Please* do it again."

With a harsh suck to the nipple in my mouth, I let it pop from my lips and move to the next one. Swirling my tongue around her dusky peak, I cup the other with a hand, my thumb drifting over the point. I bite down a little harder than last time, and she rocks on my lap with a cry.

I suck the sting away and she takes up a grinding motion, her hands hunting through my hair.

"Fuck, you keep doing that . . . this is as far as we'll get."

"God, I can't stop."

Raising my head, I crash my mouth to hers. She's starving. Lifting her a little, I line the tip of my cock with her entrance. So much for slow. Neither of us are capable of that right now.

"More, please."

I slam her hips down, filling her completely in one thrust.

She tightens around me before I have a chance to move. I take her face in my hands, guiding her gaze to mine. "Slow, baby, slow."

"Watch," she pants.

I nod.

Rising so goddamn slow that I feel every glorious inch of her, she hovers at my tip, lips parted, waiting.

"Tell me," I rasp.

"Mouth, hands."

I sink my mouth over her nipple, a finger tracing down her belly before sweeping over her clit. The sound leaving her lips when she sinks down is something I will never forget. The wrecked form of her beautiful face will never leave my mind. Ever again.

This is who I am.

I'm hers. I was a man alone on his island. A lighthouse keeper with a solitary existence. Now, I'm whatever the fuck she wants me to be.

And . . .

She's mine.

Like I said, *nonnegotiable*.

Iris hands me a blue top she spent ten painstaking minutes to hunt down. "I knew it was here. I saw it last time and thought it looked like you."

I take it from her outstretched hand as she turns back to the secondhand shop rack, searching for who knows what. The small shop has so much stuff, I have no idea how they find anything. Not one thing here is the same as the other, and it's almost like a treasure hunt.

I love it.

I trawl through the jeans and shorts, trying to find something else to add to my collection. I love wearing shorts in summer, tank tops and pretty blouses I find online. Now, nothing will beat this new thrill I have discovered of rummaging through racks to find a gem.

I've never really been a shoes-and-bag girl. More

money for books that way. Even without the big book-stores and one-day shipping from the big one-click merchants, I have managed to start a small collection of fantasy and romance books in the shack.

My mail has been redirected to Iris's café for the fore-seeable future. Something I felt bad asking to do, but she was overjoyed I'm staying. And so am I. I've written a good chunk of my new project and spent more time outside touching grass and getting sunlight than I have in the last six years.

I feel . . . Alive.

Before Fire Island, life was a mirage of various tones of grey.

Now, I see in Technicolor.

Urgh, that is so corny, Evie.

I chuckle at myself, flipping items along the rack.

"Something funny?" Iris stops beside me, one sweet brow raised.

"Just my corny mind."

"I doubt it. I think your beautiful mind is what makes you a great writer."

I scoff at that. No, it doesn't. It makes me eccentric at best, antisocial at worst.

"And your big heart," she adds, handing me another top. "This one, it'll bring out your eyes."

Such deep conversation for a shopping trip. I realize every piece Iris piles into my arms is for me, apparently.

She doesn't have anything for herself besides an emerald scarf she found on the way in.

"You're not getting something?" I ask.

"Oh, I raided this place last month for myself. I thought I would take you to all the best spots, you know. Make a girls' day of it. Show you what this little town has to offer. This is the last stop, I'm afraid."

We've covered the little bookstore, the pharmacy that doubles as a gift shop and has amazing stuff, and had morning tea at a teahouse at the other end of town. Is Iris trying to convince me to stay?

Like I have any choice at this point. In fact, I doubt I'll renew my apartment lease in the city when it comes due in a few months. At least, I hope I won't have to.

I know we've talked about it, but I guess that's another conversation I should have with Cal. Because giving up my apartment would mean I have no other place to go, if . . .

Apart from going home to my parents, I guess.

Good lord, no way.

"I think we've covered every rack," Iris says as she walks toward me. Her arms carry a few more clothing items.

"Find something good?"

"Of course! I can't wait to get home and see you try all these on."

She beams that stunning smile of hers at me, and I

can't help but be consumed by her infectious happiness. It's like Iris inherited all the happy genes and Cal got all the grump. It makes me wonder what their parents were like.

We make for the checkout counter, and the girl rings up my huge spend of twenty-three dollars for five items. Some, after a quick sort, I decided to leave behind.

Iris simply winks at me and heads toward the door. The girl hands me my bag of treasures, and I follow after Iris. Outside, she waits a little way down the sidewalk. I push through the glass door, checking my phone is still in my back pocket. My glasses slide down my nose. I really should wear contacts instead.

A rough shoulder bumps into mine.

Snapping my head up, I mumble an apology as a tall, dark blur hovers too close. Something flutters to the ground.

"Forget it," he utters. Dressed in black jeans and a black T-shirt, black motorcycle boots with a ratty old cap pulled down over . . .

I shake my head.

Messy brown hair.

No, it can't be.

I press a hand over my heart, trying to stifle the fear that's clawing its way up from the pit of despair that materialized with the black masculine form.

Images of Timothy flood my mind, turning my stomach on its head.

I slide my glasses up my nose and focus on the guy whose gaze has dropped but travels back up with a frown. His eyes level with my own, and I don't recognize him.

At least, I don't think I do. I frown, studying the planes of his face.

"You okay?" Iris says, coming to my side as her glare swings upward. "Watch it, buddy."

Her stance softens as she hooks her arm through mine, and she pins him with a curious look. "You passing through?"

"Maybe." He walks away, not bothering to look back.

Rude.

Grumpy ass.

He'd be around twentysomething. Now I sound like Cal. I drop my focus to the small slip of paper on the sidewalk. Something is handwritten on it, but it's folded in half.

"Hey!" I call out after him, now seeing him much clearer.

He spins back, a frown creasing his face, blue eyes narrowing. "What?"

I bend and swipe the paper up. "You dropped this."

He looks away, as if contemplating whether retrieving said paper is worth the four steps back. A beat passes before he strides to where I stand, slipping the paper from my fingers. Without a word, he walks back the way he was heading.

"You could say thank you!" Iris calls out after him.

He throws a hand over his shoulder and, without looking back, says, "You could look where you're walking."

"Urgh! Ass!" Iris seethes.

I chuckle. There's something so familiar about this short exchange.

The café is buzzing when we return. Paige is swamped. Errol sits at the counter, his usual lunch order in front of him.

"How's things?" Iris asks Paige as she shucks her bags behind the counter and dons her apron.

"Okay." She gives her a little awkward smile.

"Oh, I know that face. What happened?" Iris says.

"Ah, some guy came in asking odd questions." Paige glances at me.

"Told him to take a hike," Errol says.

That's the first time I've ever seen Errol defend a McCreary.

Wow, news sure travels fast in small towns. I'm guessing the fact that Ava is alive has shocked a lot of folks.

Maybe even Errol's softened.

"Don't need any more riffraff from your lot coming around here. He can go back to where he came from." Errol bites his sandwich like it killed his firstborn.

Well, there goes that theory.

"How do you figure he's 'one of our lot'?" Iris asks, using air quotes.

"Why would anyone else bother with a McCreary? Has to be family. Maybe that brother of yours owes the guy money . . ." Errol's contemplating his theories when it hits me.

"What did he say his name was?" I ask.

Errol's gaze is still sour when it swings round to me. "Didn't. And I wasn't bothered to ask."

Helpful. Really helpful.

"Well," Iris says to Paige, "if he comes back, ring me if I'm not here, okay?"

"Will do," she says with a smile, then wanders out to the tables to pick up and check on patrons.

I slide onto the stool by Errol, and he glances sideways at me, chewing.

I see some things never change.

I text Cal, letting him know Iris and I are done. We can go home anytime now. The sooner I'm back on Fire

Island with Cal, the better. Coming to town is nice, but I miss our solitude. The one place where we are just us. No peopling to be done. No rude pedestrians. No hateful old men.

Just us.

Firefly slips in by the jetty, and I haul my bags from the deck and drop them over the side onto the wood. Cal kills the engine as I step over, grabbing my bags. He follows, his overnighter in one hand as he catches up with me, taking my bag.

"In a hurry, baby girl?"

"Done with other people, is all. And so glad to be home."

He chuckles, but it catches in his throat. When I feel him hang behind, I stop and turn back. "What are you doing?"

He simply stares at me.

I drop the bags to the grassy ground. His falls from his hand as he closes the distance between us. His hands cup my face before he's even in my space. Sliding my arms around his neck, I arch up as his mouth crashes down to my lips. He pulls away breathlessly, and I search his face. "What's this about?"

He swallows, hard. "I didn't think I would ever get this."

The chance of having love?

I shift on my feet, running a hand down his chest. "So, about that . . ."

His expression blanks, hands falling from my face. He sets his jaw, like this is the moment he's been waiting for. That deadly blow he's certain is coming.

"Evie . . ." His throat works.

I'm scaring him. Shit, I'm no good at this. So I blurt out, "I'm not going back to the city."

He frowns, confusion working his face over.

"I mean, my lease comes up soon, in a couple of months . . . and I don't know if I renew it or . . ." Now, I search his expression for any hint of how he feels about me staying.

"You're letting your apartment go?"

"Am I?"

His face shifts like the wind changing in a wild storm, cheekiness lining it now. "Are you?"

I growl at him, tugging him closer by the front of his shirt. "If you're waiting on me to decide what I want and demand it, then . . . I'm letting my apartment go."

The most gorgeous smile splits his face. A beat later,

I'm hauled onto his waist and his warm hands run up my back. "You and me, tell me what we are."

I huff a soft, emotional laugh and whisper, "Nonnegotiable."

"You got it."

I slide my hands over his jaw and into his hair, claiming his mouth.

Claiming this stoic, steady, and incredible man as mine.

Meeting my hunger with his own, Cal devours me. I can't breathe. I can't get enough.

I never want to be anywhere else but right here in his arms. Right here on our little island. In our huge old wrought iron bed. In our little world, growing food, writing books, watching the weather, and being in each other's orbit.

And it hits me . . . Cal isn't the only one who never thought he'd never have something like this.

I didn't either.

Not after Joshua.

Not after Timothy . . .

I'd resigned myself to hiding away, staying as antisocial as possible to avoid involving anyone else in my disaster of a life. Even now, with those two men still out there somewhere, I will never relax. Every time Cal's late or I'm by myself, I will worry Timothy kept his word and be looking over my shoulder.

Cal knows everything, and he's not fazed—in the slightest.

This doesn't remove my fear that something will happen to him again. But at least with him knowing, the odds are stacked in our favor now.

We haul our bags into the house, and Cal totes them upstairs while I rummage through the refrigerator for a snack. Finding cheese, some sweet cherry tomatoes, and crackers, I put together a plate. I toss some ice cubes from the freezer into two glasses and fill the glasses with tap water.

Cal winds his way down the stairs slowly as I carry the glasses to the coffee table. Sinking onto the sofa without a word, he's caught in his head. I sit beside him and pluck up some food. Handing him a glass, I tilt my head. "Spill it, McCreary."

He chuckles but clears his throat. "Evie?"

I close my lips around a tomato and suck it into my mouth. "Mhmmm?"

I bite down, the red sphere exploding with delicious juices.

"Mo ghràdh, will you go on a date with me?"

I swallow the tomato and smile, shifting to his lap. "Absolutely."

He presses his forehead to mine, closing his eyes. "This kind of feels backward. We've already . . . But I want you to have every good experience I can give you."

"I would go anywhere with you, sweet man."

"You may regret those words," he says with a chuckle.

"Why?"

"That old Indian is going to need a good long road trip to iron out the kinks, get her running smoothly again."

"I stand by my earlier statement."

His gorgeous smile is contagious. "How the hell did I get so damn lucky . . ."

I lean back to grab a tomato. One of my favorite things to pop between his lips. "Oh, I almost forgot. Iris and I ran into this guy today in town . . ."

firefly

Twenty-Four

CALLUM

When Iris called this morning over the radio, I thought I was ready.

I also thought this day would be one I'd never have.

The water is choppy as Firefly powers over it, bow proud. The sea is a direct reflection of my gut. I've spent the last two hours trying to find the right words to say to someone I've never met.

An impossible task.

Will he be anything like me? Or has Ava nurtured the McCreary right out of him?

Contemplating a thousand scenarios of what his childhood was like—what his relationship is like with his parents—I grip the wheel too hard.

The bitterness of missing my son's life churns sour in

my gut. I remind myself it wasn't his doing. It was Ava's. Her parents.

Oh, of all the ways our parents can screw us up, this one's a clusterfuck.

Bay Shore comes into view, and I slow Firefly. I'm not entirely certain what's going to happen, and it's doing my head in.

"It's only a first meeting," Iris had said. "Ava thought it was fair that Reese comes to you, that way he can see a little of your life. And maybe next time, meet Evie."

Evie will be pacing the living room floor with bated breath, no doubt. She's up in her head about this, too. But what took me aback about her reaction was the fear I would choose my son over her. I highly doubt it would ever come to having to choose. Like I said, after all we have been through and the soul-deep need we have, nonnegotiable.

Em's waiting as I slip into the dock and kill the engine. He moors the lines and shoves his hands into his pockets. "Easy trip?"

"Choppy."

"The water or that mind of yours?" He raises a brow.

"Both."

"You'll do fine, Cal. I mean, come on, who wouldn't want you for an old man, hey?"

I punch his arm, and he sways with the impact, chuckling.

"Is he here?"

"*They* are here."

Shit, I'm late. Great first impression.

"Ava's here, too?"

"Yup. Apparently once she comes back from the dead, she's hard to get rid of."

I shake my head at Em's ridiculous sense of humor. "Let's do this, then."

I sound far more confident than I am. My own hands have worked up a shake, and I wring them as we make our way to the café. It's busy. Too busy for an intimate meeting of father and son for the first time. The doorbell jingles, and everyone but Errol, who's sitting at his usual spot at the counter, stops and stares.

Fucking Christ, the last thing I need is an audience.

I'm about to do a swift about-turn when Em nods toward the counter. Iris is waiting, and she smiles at me, gesturing for us to come out back. Thank god.

Em goes first as I run through my rapid thoughts for the least idiotic thing to say. I don't trust my words at this point, and I wish Evie was here. Since they're her thing. And she's literally my happy place. I have no doubt one glance of those beautiful browns would calm me down.

"Callum." Ava stands from where she's sitting at Iris's dining table.

Em and Iris huddle before making themselves scarce.

"Hey," I say, but the word is strangled as it wedges past the stone in my throat.

The young guy sitting on the seat beside Ava has his head down. The same shaggy brown hair as mine covers his face. He's staring at his phone, like nothing interesting is going on. Wearing a black T-shirt and a black jacket, his moody vibe is emanating around the room.

"Reese," Ava starts, glancing at her—our—son, "will you get off that thing?"

He ignores her.

"Hey, bud."

He scoffs. "I'm not your bud."

Now he looks up. It's like someone spun a goddamn mirror around and I'm catching my own reflection. A few decades ago, but still. He's the spitting image.

Exactly the way Evie described the guy she ran into in the street the other day.

I take a seat and lean back, crossing my arms.

Since my carbon copy sits across the table from me, I have a fairly good idea of what's going on in his head. As soon as the thought formulates, I scoff at myself internally.

"What year is she?" I ask.

His head pops up, the phone forgotten. "Who?" His face doesn't improve—in fact, the frown turns into a scowl.

"Your bike."

"What bike?"

"The one you've been scouring the streets of Bay Shore in."

Ava's face turns to surprise laced with annoyance. "I told you to stay off that thing. It's a damn death trap."

Reese rolls his eyes at his mother. I suppress the laugh wanting out at his defiance. I shouldn't laugh. She's raised him, housed him, and fed him. Kept him alive and thriving for two decades. But that bitter little streak in me centered around her keeping him away lets the chuckle escape as a barely contained smile.

"Just a piece of junk I picked up secondhand. Nothing like what I plan on getting."

He looks at his mother as he says this, as if this is her punishment for keeping the bike from him.

This boy isn't a chip off the old block. He's the exact replica of it.

The attitude. The defiance.

The contempt at anyone trying to tell him what to do . . .

That was me from the month my parents died to the moment I met the woman in front of me right now. Five years of running riot without a care in the world for the damage I caused.

And it cost me.

Everything.

"You working on modifying it or going to upgrade?" I ask.

"This is what you came here for? To chat about bikes? You don't want to hear what my first word was, or when I lost my first tooth, or how my shitty grades were?" He leans back, imitating my position.

I smile at him. What else can I do? I imagine this is what the town saw back then. A boy with an attitude bigger than the chip resting on his shoulder.

"Nah, past is in the past. Besides, I don't reminisce."

He scoffs, looking away.

Ava shifts on her seat. "I'm going to grab some coffee." She leaves the table and disappears from the room.

"So you're like some loner locked up on an island in some lighthouse, then?"

"Absolutely, and you're some misunderstood guy with shitty parents, right?"

"I don't want your sympathy. Or anything else from you. I came here because my mother wanted me to."

"So, you do have a conscience . . ."

"Barely."

"Right, because that doesn't sit well with the broody guy act." I lean forward and study his face.

"Fuck off," he mutters.

I sigh. "I understand this is a lot. You're not the only one whose world got flipped like a goddamn trash can."

He doesn't reply, simply stretches, his hands clasping the back of his neck as he stares out the window. So we sit in a companionable silence for a moment. The first part of this encounter we both agree on. I can just hear what Iris would be saying: *Pot, kettle. Pigeon pair, you two.*

Reese lowers his arms. "What's your island like?"

"An island. Quiet. No place for young blood, that's for sure."

"Yeah, right . . ."

Two men of few words, we sit in silence once again. As if she's been watching, Ava reenters the room. "Well, how's it all going?"

"We're eloping next Saturday," Reese drawls with an eye roll.

"Reese," she scolds. Looking at me, she tilts her head. "Sorry, I don't know where—" Her face tightens with a flat smile.

Oh, he absolutely gets that from me. I resist the urge to chuckle at the two of them.

"Are you staying on the mainland for the rest of the day?" Ava asks, sitting down.

"Nah, gotta head back."

"Oh, sure." She forces a different kind of smile.

"You're welcome to come over to Fire Island any time," I say to Reese. "If that's something you want."

Ava studies her son, but his expression doesn't change. "I'm sure that would be fine, when he's ready."

"Yeah, whatever." Reese stands and swipes up his phone.

He's tall. Built like me, and I even recognize the gait as he walks away, disappearing through the door to the café.

"I would appreciate it if you would run any offers past me first." Ava's shoulders are set back, her chin tilted up.

I raise an eyebrow at her. "You want me to ask permission to see my own son?"

Her mouth opens to say something.

I don't give her the chance. "So we're clear. You faked your death, turned an entire town against me, and ran off with my flesh and blood. And now you're trying to set the rules?"

"I—"

"You don't get a say, Ava. He's twenty-one. He doesn't need your permission to do a damn thing. And neither do I."

I stand and stalk from the room.

She can sit in her propriety and stew, for all I care. If she's doing such a wonderful job, why is the boy not in college? Why is he being chauffeured around by his mother? And why the hell is this town so okay with what she's done?

It's almost as if . . .

Small-town business is everybody's business. But this is surprisingly not getting the reaction I thought it would. They either truly do hate me that much, or something else is going on here. I find Iris behind the counter with Paige. They are tallying the bill for a disgruntled customer, and I give them a wave as I head for the door.

Iris mutters something to Paige and slips out from behind the counter, following me out. The door jingles to a close behind me, and she grabs my arm. "So? What's he like? How did it go?"

Her green eyes are lit by hope and curiosity.

"As I'd expected. Awkward and short."

"Urgh, come on, you have to give me more than that."

"He's a chip off the old block, that oughta tell you all you need to know."

Her eyes narrow and she folds her arms over her apron-clad chest. "He looks so much like you. Is he coming back?"

"I have no idea. I invited him out to the house, but something tells me Ava isn't on board with that."

"Well, he is old enough to do what he wants. So maybe he will?"

"Maybe." I move to leave, but she stops me, a hand on my arm.

"Cal, I'm—" She tamps back emotion. "This feels like a good thing."

"We'll see, Irry."

She shakes her head, stepping out of my space. I press my lips to her forehead. For all she's done for me. For the way she constantly fights for me. With a brief squeeze of a hug, I leave her on the sidewalk and head for Firefly. The only person I want to see right now—to talk to—is Evie.

Twenty-Five

EVIE

Laying on the grass by the shed, I let the sun's warmth soak into my skin. The ocean breeze is my friend today, caressing my skin as it warms me, lulling me into a restful doze. The days have started cooling off, and I will catch every ray of warmth I can before they disappear.

"Pass the wrench, will you?" Cal's grunt snaps me back to reality.

I sit up and scan the tools laid out at my side until I find the one he needs. He sits on the other side of the old Indian bike, hands filthy with grease, some smudged over his cheek, and his beard darkened with it where he's been rubbing his hand as he thinks.

"How long until she's ready?" I ask.

"Another few weeks, give or take."

"Real helpful. How's a girl supposed to plan her first bike trip without a solid deadline?"

He leans to one side, catching my gaze through the gap in the bike's frame. "Who you road-tripping with, baby girl?"

"Hmmm, haven't decided yet."

I give him my cheekiest grin, and he drops the wrench and pushes to his feet. Rounding the bike, he stands, looking down at me.

I lean back, my hands pressing into the soft grass. "You could convince me to take you, I guess."

He takes one step forward, and he's between my legs. His body is alive from the labor of fixing the bike in the sun, grease and dirt stain his clothes, his tight T-shirt sits over his toned chest and bulging biceps. My heartbeat, which was slow and content moments ago, triples its pace. Now, it thunders through my core and lights up my body inch by inch with its needy heat.

"You want me to beg, mo ghràdh?"

"I think it's only fair . . ."

He bends over and hauls me from the grass to his hips. My arms slide around his neck, where they belong, as he studies my face. "You want to see the world with me, *please*, baby girl?"

"Hmmm. I think your plea needs a little work."

"Which part?" He raises an eyebrow. The angles of his face are addictive.

"All of it," I breathe. "How much do you want to leave this island for me, Cal?"

His eyes tighten and I'm sure he's going to put me down and tell me that's never going to happen.

I wait, suspended in time just as I am in his hold as he considers my request.

It was a fleeting idea, anyhow . . . I open my mouth to take back the stupid words.

"How far?" he rasps.

The smile stretching my face takes me by surprise, just as those two words do. "Anywhere . . . Everywhere."

"Just on the bike?"

"What are my options?" I ask breathlessly.

He looks up like he's thinking over a long list of possibilities. "Well, there's the bike. We could fly. Train. But my favorite would be to sail."

"Sail?"

"Yup, wind in your sails and hair. Sunshine that melts you to your bones and all that." The grin on his face steals my breath.

"You can sail?" I clarify.

"Uh huh."

"You have a sailboat? Like a decent one?"

"Semi-decent?"

"Are you like the master of old things in need of restoration?"

"More like old enough to have things that need

restoring. The boat is dry-docked in Em's bay in the boat-yard. We'd always dreamt of getting her seaworthy."

"You totally should. You and Em could sail around the world . . ."

He swoops in, nipping my neck, and I squirm in his arms as a giggle bursts from my lips. Teasing this gorgeous man is the highlight of my day.

Well, almost.

The laughter dies out, and I palm his face as it rises, his gaze meeting mine. "Don't you dare see the world without me, Callum McCreary," I whisper.

"Never."

His hold on me turns desperate. His hands spread over my back. I'm crashing my mouth to his a second later. Hungry for every last piece of him, I sink my hands into his hair. My butt meets the warm seat of the bike, and he releases his hold as I steady myself on the Indian.

"Cal, no, I'm going to fall off." I try to find purchase, leaning back a little. My hands wander over the fuel tank and the back of the seat as I hunt for something to grab onto.

Rough hands slide under my thighs, turning me until I'm lying back on the fuel tank, my head resting on the handlebars. The metal of the back of the bike is hot on my calves. I pull my knees up.

Cal raises one leg and slides onto the seat.

"Still need me to beg, Evie baby?"

My last breath stalls. The thought of this man begging me . . .

"Absolutely," I manage to say, and the cheekiest smile tugs up one side of his face.

He hooks his fingers around my cotton shorts and tugs them down over my hips. The bike moves as he removes them, leaving behind my pastel yellow lacy panties. On the black motorbike, my lemon-lace-clad body is something out of a boudoir shoot. The sun has tanned my limbs, put color in my face. My T-shirt slides from my head, and I settle back. I can't help feeling like this is one memory we are making that's going to make me smile—and my children cringe—thirty, forty years from now.

I live for it.

I live for this man.

The endless possibilities that are Cal and Evie.

All the life we have to live through yet . . .

Lost in my head, clouds drift in the blue above as the breeze tangles through my hair, now draped over the bike's small console.

Open-mouthed kisses dust up my stomach toward my bra, and I tilt my head to one side to watch him. Every time his lips press to my skin, I float higher. Every embrace is confirmation of our love.

His love.

And the way I am going to return it, tenfold. Because not doing so would break my heart.

"Cal, I don't hear any begging . . ." I pant, but the last syllable fades like my will to resist his touch.

Hands gripping my hips, he looks up from under those lashes framing the blues I adore. "I'm getting to that part."

His finger slides beneath the lacy panties and sweeps over my aching center. "Is this where I come to pay my penance and beg for you by my side for—"

His jaw feathers before it grinds.

My chest rises and plummets as I take in the emotion toying with his handsome face.

I rise a little, brows lowering. "You don—"

He shakes his head. "Yes, I do."

I want to say something to ease the burn that's taking us both down. Having no idea what words could hold such power, I press my lips together and slide my hands over his, still at my hips. They slide away and he tugs my panties down.

With a soft nudge to the inside of my thighs, his hands lace with mine at my hips again.

"Close your eyes, baby girl."

My eyes flutter shut of their own accord. My body, his plaything. His will, my command . . .

His tongue runs through my center, and I cry out, a quick arch pulling me off the bike. It moves under my weight and I still, torn between moving with the pleasure he brings and the need to not tumble off this damn thing.

"Evie . . ." he rasps. His tongue swirls around my clit.

I open my mouth to respond, and his hands squeeze my fingers.

No talking back, got it.

"Please, baby."

He nips at my aching center.

I resist the urge to tilt my hips upward to his tantalizing touch. And fail . . .

"Let me come with you, *please*?"

His tongue dives into me, hot and fast.

The whimper that leaves with my exhale crumbles to a shattered cry.

One hand leaves. The pad of his finger—no, his thumb—brushes over my clit.

"Baby, take me with you. Wherever you go."

Two fingers sink into my swollen core. He traces my soaked entrance with his tongue before lapping at my clit.

"Say yes, Evie. Let me come."

"I—" I pant. Stars fade into my peripherals. "You—"

I tighten around his fingers, now pumping in and out in a slow, torturous rhythm.

"Is that a yes?" he growls before sucking hard on my aching nub.

I come hard around his fingers. Each blissful wave heavier, more delicious than the last. The bike, almost forgotten, moves with my writhing weight. I settle with ladened breaths, hands hunting for Cal. For the man I will never leave behind.

Who am I kidding? He didn't need to beg.

He'll never need to ask for the things he needs with me.

Because the feeling goes both ways.

I need this man more than oxygen. At this point, suffocating would be easier, less painful than spending another day without him in my life.

An hour later, I'm standing beside Em on the Coast Guard boat, heading for the mainland for lunch with Iris and some solid library time. God, I have missed the internet, the smell of hundreds of books, the soft chatter of book talk as I tap away on my laptop, brain whirring, the story building.

Tensions rising . . .

Plot, plotti—

"Iris is excited to have a girls-only date," Em says, interrupting my reverie.

I chuckle, pushing my glasses up my nose. I really should wear my contacts. "I'm starving. Did she say where she's taking me?"

"Some place over in Huntington, I think."

"Have you been there before?" I study his expression, trying to discern from his answer whether he and Iris eat together and how often—besides at the café, that is.

"Nope. You must be special."

Well, that gives me nothing to work with, Em. Disappointing. Feeling a little nosy and a lot bolder than I should be, I ask, "So, you and Iris? How long are you going to make her wait, Em?"

He glances at me, too quickly, as his face surrenders to a blush I'm sure can be seen from space. Clearing his throat, he tightens his hands around the wheel. "Wait for what?"

I give him my best *you have to be shitting* me look and roll my eyes at him like some teenage girl.

"What?" he says with a chuckle.

"Nothing. Keep your secrets, Officer Bradford. But you should get onto that, if you ask me."

"Well, don't take this the wrong way, Miss Evie, but I didn't."

It's all I can do to beam up at him. A smile wobbles over his lips, and he keeps his focus straight ahead.

"You want me to change the subject?" I ask, nudging his arm with mine.

"Please," he mutters.

"Okay, sure, what's with you and Cal and having old relics lying around needing to be fixed up? Old before your time?"

"Relics?"

"The Indian and the boat in your dry dock?"

"Oh yeah, I kind of forgot about those. Cal's rolled the old dust bucket outta the shed, has he?"

"He has. We're fixing it up."

His stare holds for a beat. "That's great. I never thought I'd ever see him ride that bike again."

"So, about the boat? How much would it take to make her seaworthy?" I sound ridiculously like I know what I'm talking about, which is stupid.

He rubs a hand behind his neck. "The Pearl—and don't laugh, Cal let Iris name her when we got the boat not long after their parents' accident—would take a fair bit of fixing. But the bones are there. The problem is, nobody has the time. Not me, and least of all Cal. Especially now, he has something else consuming his every spare moment."

"Ha, ha. Could we find someone to do it for us? What would it cost?"

"Geez, Miss Evie. That would take a significant cash injection."

"What kind of numbers are we talking?"

"Well, she would need re-rigging, a new comms and nav system, paintwork. and probably some upgrades on the inside living area."

"Can you put a price on it, even roughly?"

"Maybe somewhere between fifty and seventy-five, depending on who does the labor?"

"Okay, thanks."

I turn my gaze to the water ahead, leaving Em hanging.

Serves him right for holding out on Iris, if you ask me.

Not that anyone did. But life's too short to be indecisive about the things you want. The past six years have taught me that.

firefly

Twenty-Six

CALLUM

The lid to the lantern room is open and hanging on her hinges in the ocean breeze that's decided this is the very minute to become the problem child. I wait, holding my breath, as the crane lowers the new lamp through the small, round opening.

The freighter with the crane and new lamp arrived an hour after Evie left with Em, and it's my surprise for her. She's heartbroken about the way the lamp met her timely end.

I mean, it needed replacing, anyhow. So I guess you could say this backed the Restoration Society into a corner. With the help of the Coast Guard, we were able to afford a new Fresnel.

We are officially back in business.

If the lamp makes it onto her platform without smashing into a million tiny little pieces, that is. As soon as I can reach, I take her sling-bound body in my hands to steady her as she lowers down. Everything is ready for her. I only need to make the connections, then secure her to the base. The test run will happen very soon.

And I have a plan for that.

The crane operator squawks out something over the radio. I snatch mine from my hip and count him down until the lamp is in position. Unhooking his apparatus from her, I squeeze the radio buttons again. "Up and out, bud."

The oversized crane hook and straps float up and out of the lantern room. I hold my breath until they clear the glass-walled room. Checking the new lamp is in fact stationary and stable, I use a long stick with a hooked end to bring the lantern room's dome back down and latch her shut. With a tug to double-check she's down tight, I turn back and fix the lamp.

The connectors don't take too long to put together, but smaller hands would have made things easier. I realize I've gotten used to having Evie around. So much so, she factors into every part of my life now, consciously and subconsciously.

Every thought and decision runs through the Evie lens. How does this affect her, what would Evie want . . . It shouldn't surprise me like it does. I've known for weeks how far gone I am for that little woman. Longer, if you count the nine months we spent before . . .

With the lamp in place, I double-check every point is installed correctly and head downstairs. Wiping my hands on a grease rag, I pad to the sink for a mug of water. I gulp down the cool liquid, staring out the window. On the distant offshore waters, a small boat sails along at a steady pace.

Or is it?

I squint, leaning closer to the window.

No, it's anchored?

I cross the living room and grab the binoculars. Back at the window, I hold them up, taking a while to refocus and find the boat.

Odd.

Why would you anchor all the way out there? It's too exposed. Too choppy, even on a good day.

They're far too close to a shipping lane to be standing still. I can't make out the name on the side of the boat. It's either too weathered or too far out for the binoculars to focus on. With a grunt, I push from the sink.

I should radio out and see if they need help.

I should.

But I don't.

Not after last time. It may be my duty to render assistance to all vessels who ask for it, but they ain't asking. As far as I'm concerned, they're right where they want to be.

Hell, so am I. I'm not risking that for anything.

Not anymore.

The drone of Em's muscle boat carries in with the late afternoon easterly. I finish repotting the gnarly old citrus plants for what may be their last season. With the cooler weather around the corner, my chores have shifted like clockwork, as they do every season.

The footsteps crunching over gravel outside are unfamiliar.

I turn back in time to see the greenhouse door slide open.

"Hello?"

I don't recognize the voice straight away. But the figure standing in the doorway is as familiar as looking in the mirror.

Reese.

Dropping the pot to the ground, I toss some mulch around the soil and water it as quick as the watering can will drain. Dusting my hands on my jeans, I walk toward my son.

"I didn't know you were coming," I say in lieu of hello.

"Wasn't really the plan. But, you know . . ."

His hair is a mess, his clothes crumpled like he slept in them. It's then I notice the small backpack hanging by a strap on his shoulder.

"Running away from home?" I raise my eyebrows.

"Bit old for that," he says, his gaze not breaking from mine.

"Em bring you over?"

"If you mean the big guy in the blue uniform with the gnarly boat? Then yes."

"That'd be him."

"Is he like your brother or something?"

"Close enough."

He gives me a meek smile and nods.

"Let's go to the house. It's coming up on dinner."

"Oh, Iris gave me this to give to you." He hands me an envelope. Inside is a piece of the café's stationary.

I unfold it. Right away, I recognize the handwriting. Evie's.

Cal,

We had the best day. When we made it back to the cafe, you had a visitor. So, I'm going to stay with Iris for the night and let you boys talk. Hash out the things you missed.

"You gonna be long?" Reese interrupts.

"You got some other place to be?" I give him a leveling stare.

His gaze hits the graveled path, and I drop mine back to the page.

I will miss you. And when I get home, it will be my turn to beg—

I flip the page over, sliding it back into the envelope. I'm not reading this with Reese hovering. The last thing I need to do is have to explain away a random boner while he's here.

Christ.

"You can help me with dinner. I assume you eat." I walk past him, heading for the house.

When no footsteps follow, I turn back.

He stands staring at me, an unreadable expression scrawled over his face.

"Come on, boy, you can tell me all the ways you hate your mother. I might even listen."

The smallest of smirks moves the corner of his mouth, and he trudges after me.

I may have missed twenty years of his life, but we ain't going to be able to fix that standing around staring at each other.

Inside, I toe off my boots and shove my cap on the hook next to Evie's sun hat. Reese hangs back before the threshold. I glance back but decide to let him take his time. Everyone reacts differently to their first time here.

The fact that his father lives here, has lived here for his entire life, may have a distinct impact on him.

I pull the refrigerator open and slide out a pack of steaks. Seasoning them in a tray, I set them aside. Gathering ingredients for a salad, I toss them together with a smidge of Evie's dressing. Deciding to add tortilla chips and guacamole for a side dish, I load it all up onto a tray and head to the small grill on the eastern side by the fire pit.

As the steaks drop onto the grill, they hiss and smoke. Flames lick the meat, caramelizing it with every brush of heat. Reese drops into a chair at the firepit, a beer—my beer—in his hand.

Okay then.

"You eat it how it's cooked. Serve the sides yourself," I say, handing him a plate with the steak, nodding toward the sides on the chair between our seats. A six pack of beers sits at his feet.

I grab one and tear it out. Resting it beside my chair, I decide on eating, putting food into my mouth before something harsh runs out of it and I can't take it back.

Reese eats like he hasn't eaten a solid meal in days.

I know better than to feel sorry for him.

"Spill it, what's got you out here?"

He lifts the beer to his mouth, hesitating before he takes a sip. With a swallow that moves his throat like he's holding back something, he sighs before uttering, "She kicked me out."

Not having anything constructive to say, I finish my food. Scraping the plate clean, I set it on the gravel and lean back and take a sip of the cool beer.

"She never used to be like that," I offer up softly.

He scoffs. "I wouldn't know. My whole life, she's tried to control who I hang out with. Who I talk to. Where I go. And Da—" He clears his throat. "Craig says its genetic, I don't get the rebel streak from him."

"You got along with him growing up, though?"

He stares at me. "As much as any boy gets along with his dad." He chugs a few mouthfuls of beer. "At least, I thought that's what he was."

"He's still your dad, Reese. He raised you."

"You're very accepting of all this. Why didn't you try to be part of my life? After Mom left?"

My mouth hangs slack. She didn't tell him.

"I didn't know you existed. Ava—your mother—" I clear my throat. "You want the truth or the sugar-coated version?"

I don't know if I should be saying this to him. Hell, I'm no parent. I'm winging this, at best.

"I want the truth. I'm done being in the fucking dark."

I force a smile. Sometimes the dark is less painful.

"She faked her death. Her parents moved away. I

mourned you both. She was six months pregnant when I got the call she'd died of some pregnancy complication. I was at sea, in the Navy."

His face goes through every registrable emotion. Finally, it settles on disgust. "Why?"

I take a sip of my beer. "I wasn't exactly the town's favorite kid. I was trouble. Off the rails. I'd done a lot of bad shit before I met your mom. She was adored. It was never going to end well."

"That—" He tilts his head, his face bunching for a brief moment before he schools it back. "You sound like me . . ."

I huff a laugh, but it's not the amused type. It's strained, weighed down by two decades of baggage and grief. "I was way worse, bud. I was a mess. I ruined everything I touched. I guess the town thought they knew better."

"You don't know a thing about me." Reese stares at the ocean, finishing one beer and starting another.

"I know enough."

"What's the town got to do with it?"

"They—well, many folks—took pleasure in my downfall. I'd finally got my shit together when your mom got pregnant with you. It was the first time since my parents died that I'd had hope."

"And she took it all away." He stares off into the distance.

"More like your grandparents did. But she never came back. Never sent word. Nothing. Until a month ago."

"Jesus. That's fucked up."

"Yeah, it's fucked up."

We sip our beers, sitting in the quiet.

Father and son.

My hope races ahead of reality once again. I couldn't rein it in if I wanted to. As I glance at Reese, I can't help but think maybe I can pull off this second chance.

Twenty-Seven

EVIE

Cal waits for me on the jetty as Em slips his big-ass boat in beside it. I can't sit still. One day—twenty-four hours—away from him and I'm climbing out of my skin. And I fully intend to climb him like a tree the nanosecond Reese leaves with Em.

Em moors the boat, and I'm down the steps and flying up the jetty with no care for my bag left on the cruiser. Cal's big, wide grin splits his face. I jump up as I reach him, wrapping myself around his waist. His hands palm my face. His mouth crashes to mine.

I open, luring him in as deep as I can. So deep we can never fully recover would be just about far enough. He follows, devouring me. His hands explore my face as my own crawl through his hair. I wonder how long it will take him to notice what's missing.

God above, I missed this man.

A voice clears behind me, and I ignore Em. This is my reward for going without my heart for one night. And no gorgeous Coast Guard big-brother type is going to steal our moment.

Cal doesn't break either. We're both as desperate as each other.

"Get a room," a voice says from behind Cal, lined with the disgust that can only come from a kid witnessing their parent kissing.

I pull away, breathless.

Briefly closing my eyes for courage, I lean to one side to find Reese standing with his hands in his pockets, trying to look anywhere but at Cal and me.

And this feels weird.

I knew it would.

My stomach twists, sending my nerves aflame. A blush creeps up my neck, dousing my face in its heat.

"Sorry," I mutter, letting my legs unravel and my feet touch the wooden surface of the jetty.

Cal turns back. "Hey, not your home, bud. You don't insult a woman in her own home."

Reese stares him down.

"Okay, well, here's your bag, Miss Evie. Reese, I'm your ride, if you're ready?"

It's then we all notice the absence of his backpack.

"I'm good." He simply rocks on his heels and folds his arms over his chest.

Chip. Off. The. Old. Block.

"Well, radio back when you change your mind. Otherwise, I'll see you two in a few days." Em waves as he climbs aboard.

Cal pulls me into his arms, sinking his head into my neck, face smothered in my hair.

"No glasses, baby?"

I smile up at him. Took him long enough.

"Contacts are easier than those bulky things. Mostly."

"Good. I like seeing your face. So fucking beautiful, mo ghràdh."

"I missed you. Lying in that bed without you was *hell*."

He chuckles, and we head for the house, my bag in his hand, his other laced with mine. The house looks the same. I don't know why I thought it wouldn't. The door to the shack is open, and Reese moves about inside. Avoiding the cringy adults, no doubt.

"He's staying?" I ask.

"Ava kicked him out. I can't turn him away."

He doesn't have the heart for that. And I am one hundred percent certain when he looks at his son, he sees himself.

I do.

It's like a window into the years of Cal's I missed.

"Why did she kick him out?"

"Hasn't said. Guess it'll come up soon enough."

"Guess so. You want to go upstairs, or do you need a hand with your chores?"

"Later I will. You got writing to get to?"

"I do, actually. But is my stuff still in the shack?"

"Ah, fuck. Yeah, it is. Told him not to touch your things."

"It's fine, I doubt he's an avid romance reader." I make my way to the shack and knock politely on the door. Is this how Cal felt when some random twentysomething woman turned up that one time?

I smile at the memory of our beginning.

The door opens, and Reese stands with a frown. "Yeah?"

"I need to grab my work stuff?"

Why am I asking? All those months of learning to say what I want are nowhere to be found.

He waves a hand and steps to the side. I try my best to shoot him a smile, but I doubt it reaches my eyes. Neither of us seem comfortable with this situation.

He moves across the small space and drops onto the bunk. He picks up his phone, tapping the screen, but tosses it back to the table.

"No service. At least, it's rare here," I offer.

"Figured."

Man of few words. I know one of those. In my experience, they just take some warming up. I'll give him his space. If he's anything like his father, there's an amazing man in there somewhere. Under all that angst, attitude, and gruff exterior. The roughness he wants the world to see.

Luckily, a few of us can see past that particular shield.

Iris, Em, and I being the most notable.

I gather up my belongings and select a couple of reads, not really knowing how long he'll be here. Just in case he's here longer than a few weeks . . .

"You done?" he snaps.

I toss the last book onto the growing pile in my arms and turn to him. "Ah, yup."

He waves to the door.

Wow, okay.

I hold my stare on him for a beat before heading back to the house.

Well, that was pleasant.

The fire crackles in the fire pit, and I pull the light blanket around my shoulders, my gaze stuck on my book, the book light hanging precariously from the side as I flip the page with more enthusiasm than I can hold back. Cal walks behind me, dropping a kiss to the crown of my head. "Good book?"

I nod quickly and wave him away.

He chuckles, dropping into the Adirondack seat beside me. His son, who has been sitting out here with me for the last twenty minutes, scoffs. And it's the shortest sound he's made since I sat out here. I swear to god, if Reese talks to me again while I'm reading, I'm going to sail—drive?—him back to the mainland in the dark myself.

And like clockwork . . .

"So, this is your Friday night, hey?" His words have a slight slur, the kind tipsy brings.

Glancing at him, I don't respond before tracking back to the paragraph I was on.

"Bud, unless you want your balls served up for your breakfast, don't interrupt the woman while she's reading."

"Yeah, unlike her husband, I'm not pussy-whipped."

I snap my head up.

Husband.

I swallow past the emotion swelling with the idea.

Reese's stare finds my face, and he frowns before sipping his beer. "What is it all about? Money? You into old guys or something?"

The warm fuzzies I had a second ago are sucked right out of existence. Confused, I can only try to form words that won't eventuate.

"Watch your mouth, Reese." Cal's voice is low, and when I turn back to look at his face, it's pure stone.

"Whatever, I need to piss."

He pushes out of the chair and wanders inside. Cal rises and moves to go after him. I rest a hand on his forearm. "It's okay, he's probably out of sorts with everything that's happened."

"No, Evie. This is your home. He'll learn the boundaries and maybe some goddamn manners." My hand slips from his arm, and he stalks inside.

A moment later, Reese reappears. Instead of an apology, which I had assumed Cal went inside to tell him to give, he sinks into the chair and takes another beer from the pack and twists the top off, tossing it into the fire.

"What are you, like five years older than me? What's your angle here?" He points his beer toward me. "I would go for gold digger, but there's nothing worth digging for on this island. So what is it? What's your angle, Eve Holland?"

I set my book down, fumbling to turn off the light as I formulate my response. Cal simply leans against the doorway to the house. His large figure catches both of our attention. "Her angle is kindness and selflessness. But I doubt you have matured enough to possess those traits yet. Another syllable of disrespect from you, and you can find your own way back to the Bay first thing in the morning."

Reese slumps back in his Adirondack chair, chugging another sip. He runs a hand through his shaggy hair and closes his eyes. I study his face for a moment, waiting for another insult to slip. But he seems to be put in his place.

I pick up my book and continue where I left off. The hurt sinks in as the silence takes up every inch between the three of us. I know he's rough around the edges. I know he's hurting from having his life upheaved in the most complicated way possible. I knew this would happen, and it's more uncomfortable than I imagined.

Cal sits by me, his face tense, his gaze alternating between me and his son.

After I reread the same sentence four times, the page blurs. I swallow past the stone wedged in my throat and gather my things. "I'm going to bed." I rise, kissing Cal's cheek.

He grabs my wrist. His eyes are tight as he shakes his head.

"It's okay, I'm tired."

I slip from his hold and mutter a goodnight to Reese as I pass him in his chair. His eyes are still closed, like he can't look at me. Not able to witness the hurt he caused. Inside, I pop my blanket and book on the sofa and pad upstairs. The stairwell outside our bedroom is cold. I close the door behind me and pad toward the shower.

A nice, long, hot shower will right my ragged feelings.

I shuck my clothes and step into the steaming stream of water. The weight crushing my logic and reason falls away.

Reese is just a kid.

He may only be seven years younger than me, but his parents were too young. I'm older, even more so if you gauge age by life experience. He needs a stable adult and a place to crash. I'm not saying I'm part of that, but I won't make his life harder than it already is. If not for the broken young man downstairs, I'll do it for the man I love. For his chance to be a father.

I find myself rubbing my hands over my belly. The thought of it swollen with Cal's child.

The moment I would tell him he's a father. Watching him with his child from day one.

Tears course down my cheeks, washing out with the water running over my face.

All the life we have to live yet . . .

All the life we can create.

Anywhere we want.

firefly

Twenty-Eight

CALLUM

Reese is in the shack. Check.

Evie is finishing up her words—five minutes, she said. Check.

The sun is setting slowly. Check.

The small navy velvet box sits on the east ledge of the lantern room, ready to be lit up. My heart is in my damn throat with the plan I fully intend to execute the second Evie crosses the threshold of the room.

The last rays of the day pour through the glass top of the lighthouse, shattering as they meet the lamp in the center, casting a brilliant golden-tinged rainbow around the room, at my feet, and passing over my face like molasses in winter as the suns sinks further.

A soft knock comes at the right time.

Sucking in a fortifying breath, I stand in front of the door, blocking her view of the room as I open it.

"Close your eyes, baby girl."

She huffs a nervous breath and her eyelids close. She holds out a hand. "Did you sweep out the glass?"

"Maybe. You'll see."

"What are you up to, McCreary?"

McCreary. I can't wait for that name to be hers, too.

For us to be officially inseparable.

Nonnegotiable. On paper.

It's a nice thought.

I lead her into the lantern room, checking her eyes are, in fact, sealed shut.

"Where's Reese?" she asks.

"In the shack. Shhhh."

Her brows rise in tandem, and I smile at the prettiest little face she's ever pulled. I move her toward the new Fresnel and stop her in front of the control panel. The internal lever that turns the power on. The one that is only ever turned on once, and then the auto-system takes over. It's on the inside, so I take her hand and send it into the apparatus until her fingertips are touching it.

"Now, do not open your eyes when you push this lever down, okay?"

She gasps.

She's got it.

"Cal! When?"

"While you and Iris were busy lunching yesterday."

"Oh my god. I want to open my eyes. Please?"

"You can when I say so."

"Fine." She smiles around the word.

"Push the lever down, mo ghràdh."

She pushes it down, and the queen flickers to life, her dazzling beam shooting through the glass walls that keep her, piercing through the pale violet sky around us. Evie's hands explore the glass lamp above the lever.

"Oh," she cries.

I move her where she stands to face the eastern wall, safely with her back to the lamp. "Open your eyes, Evie baby."

Her eyes fly open, and she stares with wonder capturing her face as the light behind us swings around, leaving her glittering glow across the lantern room. The small box on the ledge glows with every pass and it takes a little while for her to notice it.

"What is that?" she asks, taking a step toward it.

She reaches the east wall, and I flick the lever up and kill the Fresnel. She picks up the box and spins back round. I hit the floor on one knee.

Her face slackens.

I've never been one for long speeches. So I get to the point.

"Evie Holland. Love of my damn life. Will you marry me?"

She looks down at the box in her hand.

"Open it," I rasp.

She simply stares at me, her face twisting with shock before she sinks to her knees, her hands wandering my face. As she huffs a strangled laugh that disintegrates into a sob, the box slips from her hand, still closed. "Where else would I be?"

"Baby, you're gonna have to spell it out for me," I rasp through my own swollen throat. I search her face desperately for what she means.

"Of course I will, Cal."

Tears slip from her eyes as her hands settle on my jaw, and she pulls my mouth down to hers.

Happiness is a man with the woman he will love for the rest of his life.

That's me. I'm that man.

"Cal," she whispers as she pulls away. "Turn the lamp back on."

I chuckle, knowing what she means. Remembering the last time we were up here, tangled in each other. I flick the lever up and the Fresnel bursts to life. Like my heart just did when Evie agreed to be mine, and me hers.

I rock back on my heels, and she climbs onto my lap. I reach past her and flip the velvet box open, sliding the ring onto her elegant finger, and her face breaks. Her other hand covers her mouth as I lace my fingers through hers. Her bejeweled ring finger sparkles insanely every time the light swings around.

Ring forgotten, her fingers tug at my beard, her mouth parting.

She rocks on my lap, eyes darkening by the second.

Her mouth finds mine again . . .

My little woman is fucking starving.

"That's new." Reese shovels a mouthful of cereal into his face.

The look on my face ought to be warning enough.

Evie simply smiles and says, "It is."

"Congrats?" Reese drawls.

"I have work to do." Evie plucks up her half-finished bowl and takes it to the sink.

When she's safely upstairs, I glower at him.

"What?" The most innocent look washes over his face.

I would ask him if his mother didn't love him enough, but we both know the answer to that one. "One more syllable, bud, and you're out."

"Yeah, yeah, I know."

He leans back, running his hands through his hair. In

a T-shirt and sweats, his frame is so similar to mine. Stretching out on the chair, he looks around. "How much do they pay you for living like a hermit?"

"Enough."

His gaze drops. "I didn't mean any—"

"I mean they pay me enough."

"Oh, okay. How'd you land this gig?"

"It was my father's before me."

"Oh shit, then I guess then it's mine in, what, twenty years?"

That pulls a chuckle from me. He's a smart ass, but he's witty, I'll give him that. "Maybe, but I would recommend just about anything else if you want a life."

"Nah, people are overrated."

"Sometimes they are." I take my bowl to the sink and rinse it out. "Why aren't you at college?"

"Not my thing."

"Not your thing, or you didn't get in?"

He snaps his focus to me now, his face hard.

Like I said, a mirror.

"You have to do something with your life. Living here isn't a life."

"It's yours."

"Yeah. Because the life I had before this was destroyed."

Too much?

"Another thing Ava's pride has ruined," he says,

rubbing his hands over his face. "I have no idea what I want to do, that's the problem, and low-paying jobs don't do it for me."

"Sometimes, you take what you can. At least until something better comes along."

"Yeah, maybe . . ."

I walk past, patting him on the shoulder. "You'll figure it out, bud."

He shrugs my hand away, and I chuckle as I climb the stairs. He's just too easy to rile up. But I'm deadly serious about this island, it's no place for a young man. This is an old man's game. He deserves a life, and I will make sure he gets one.

Even if he hates me for it.

Waiting for Evie, I walk the distance between Iris's and the library where I dropped her this morning. We're staying the night while Reese keeps an eye on the lighthouse. I gave him a thorough rundown. Besides, the lamp itself is automated. He only needs to radio the watchhouse if something goes wrong. I pray to the heavens the old girl behaves.

We haven't told Em or Iris about the engagement yet.

Evie called her parents this morning. That went over as well as a fart in church since they've never met me . . . And I'm not a great deal younger than them. She was disappointed to say the least, so I'm hoping Iris's excitement can mend that hurt a little.

The doors to the library whoosh open, and Evie walks out, waving her goodbyes to a trio of young girls holding copies of her books. When she turns to focus on where she's going, her gaze lands on me.

"Oh, hey. I could have met you at the café . . . But I'm glad I didn't have to." Her arms slide around my neck automatically, and I wrap her in my hold.

"Hungry, my famous, beautiful girl?"

"What, no Gaelic?" She smiles.

The three girls are all but plastered to the glass window at the front of the library, watching their favorite author.

"You have an audience," I breathe.

"I do?" She turns back and gives the girls another little wave. "We should get to Iris's before dark."

"We should. When does the library close?"

"Around seven, I think. It stays open later Friday night for book club."

"What a way to spend a Friday night," I drawl.

She slaps my arm, and I chuckle.

"Come on, Irry's waiting. I can't wait to see her explode when she discovers the rock on your hand."

"Such a loving big brother."

"Hey, I've got decades of torment from that girl. This might wipe a few years clean."

"Happy to be of service," she whispers into my ear, lacing her fingers through mine.

We make it to the café in good time. It's all but cleared out tonight, with people mostly frequenting restaurants and pubs for their Friday night fun. As we approach, the last few people leave through the front door, and Iris turns the *Open* sign to *Closed*.

We meet the door as she goes to turn the lock. "Oh, where'd you two come from?" Her face lights up.

I tilt my head, giving her a deadpan look. "Let us in, Irry."

She narrows her eyes and rubs her chin comically like she's thinking it over. "Fine." She beams as she opens the door, and we slip inside.

"You're just in time to see Em, he'll be here in a few."

"Got another sofa to move?" I tease.

Iris's eyes narrow. "You'll be on it tonight if you keep that up, Cal."

"You kicking me outta bed, baby girl?" I ask Evie.

She tamps down her amusement as she shakes her head. "Nope."

Iris studies the two of us for a moment before heading behind the counter and disappearing into her living space. We follow. I have to run back to the boat and grab our overnight bag, but I'm sure Evie can keep our secret a little longer. "Be back in a minute. I'll go grab the bag."

I peck a kiss to her cheek, and she releases my hand. "Okay. I'll be here."

I wink at her, and she rolls her eyes playfully.

Out on the sidewalk, I make quick time to cross the road and parking lot and skip down the stairs to the marina. Firefly bobs in her slip, and I step over the side and into the cabin. The overnighter is under the bench seat. I pluck it up and turn back to leave. Something white on the console catches my eye.

I spin back and snatch it up.

A letter.

Addressed to Evie.

I look around the boat, as if whoever left it could still be here. Dropping the bag, I open it.

The messy handwriting is all aggressive strokes and impatient cursive. Like someone wrote this angry.

My eyes fly down the page.

My heart races faster with every sentence.

At the bottom, it's signed with one letter.

T.

I flick my focus to the top of the page . . .

He called her Butterfly.

Butterfly.

I crumple the page in my fist.

"Hello?" Em's voice drifts in from the dock. I pluck up the overnight bag and disembark.

Without a word, I hand the note to Em.

Em looks up after reading the note, his face tight with worry. "He's back?"

"He steps one foot on our island and—"

"We have to take this to the police, Cal. The longer we wait, the longer she's in danger. And so are you."

He holds the note out. "They have her abduction on record; this is all they would need to put them away. He's basically threatened to kill the both of you."

I can't tell Evie about this now. Tonight's supposed to be about us. About our enga—

"Here goes." Em nods at two figures walking toward us in the half dark, dressed like trouble with dark jeans and hoodies. I drop the bag and brace on a widened stance. Em's built, like a Corps officer should be. We may be older, but we're formidable.

Em folds his arms over his chest, putting on his harbormaster's voice. "You boys lost? This gangway is for boat owners. You're trespassing."

Technically they're not, but it's my guess Em hopes they don't know that.

They don't respond and Emmett monitors them as they stride past, like nobody spoke to them.

I strain to see the faces under the hoodies. I can't see anything clearly. And as much as I would love to get my hands on the low-life piece of shit who hurt Evie, now is not the time. Emmett in uniform is not the right time. He would be fired for assaulting a civilian.

No.

I'll handle this on the island when the time comes.

The note still clutched in Emmett's hand tells me that day isn't too far away.

Twenty-Nine

EVIE

Cal smiles at me as he and Emmett walk through the doorway from the café to Iris's space. The space that right now smells incredible. The aroma of whatever she's cooking is delectable. Em's still in his uniform, but a backpack is slung over his shoulder. "Evening, Miss Evie."

"Hey, Em." I can barely contain my excitement. For now, I've thumbed the engagement ring around my finger so the dazzling diamond my heart gave me is not on display. Iris is upstairs changing. I heard the water start, but this new sofa is too good to leave. So I stayed here, my Kindle in hand.

Cal drops beside me, dotting a kiss on my temple.

"I'm going to head upstairs and change out of these blues." Em takes the stairs two at a time.

You go, Emmett. I'm sure the shower is big enough for two.

I look back to Cal. "You were gone a while."

He pulls me into his side. "Yeah, found Em down there."

I chuckle and rest my head on his shoulder. "You two are something else, you know."

"Yeah, not too many friendships last as long as ours. But when you go through that much, you know." He sighs and closes his eyes as his head falls to mine.

We are like an Evie-and-Cal burrito, all wrapped up in each other. Now I wish we'd stayed home, tangled in the sheets to celebrate. But we'd have had to come out of the bedroom sooner or later. Besides, Reese is at home, which makes our usual intimate life harder to pull off.

No more tables, sofas, getting tied to chairs . . .

"You okay? Your breathing kicked up." He breaks away, his gaze falling to my face under a frown.

"I'm good . . . thinking about you."

He raises a brow. "Oh yeah? What kind of thoughts were you having, mo ghràdh?"

"Well, there was this one time a grumpy lighthouse keeper tied me to a chair."

"Fuck, baby girl." He runs a hand through his hair, blowing out a breath.

Things escalate between us so fast—

"Christ, now you've done it." He groans as he sinks his face into my neck, engulfed by my hair.

"That all it takes, sweet man?" I whisper.

"That's fucking all."

My hand reaches for his jawline as heat blooms in my center.

Heavens above. That really is all it takes for us.

He slides a hand over my belly. "How long's Iris been upstairs?" His voice is low, rough.

"A couple minutes."

His hand slips under my dress.

"What about Em?" I ask.

"I guess he'll need a shower, too. Maybe we've got five minutes?"

His finger slips under the band of my panties, brushing over my aching center. I grab his head, turning it, and capture his mouth with mine. His thumb swirls around my clit as two fingers sink into me. "Oh, god, Cal."

"Shhh. You're going to have to swallow those pretty noises this time."

"I can't."

"You want me to stop?"

I shake my head violently. "No, please . . ."

He curls his fingers forward, and I almost buck off the sofa.

Iris's new sofa.

Shit.

"We should stop," I pant.

"When you're done, we will."

"I—"

His thumb flicks my clit, over and over. My back arches, shoulders digging in as I climb up the back of the sofa. One hand on his jaw, one white-knuckling the arm of the couch. "Please, I'm going t—"

My mouth gapes on a silent cry as release finds me.

"Good girl. Fuck, I love watching you come."

He nips my earlobe before scraping his teeth over my neck.

Thunderous footsteps tumble down the stairs.

Emmett.

Cal removes his hand, sliding his fingers into his mouth. I readjust my dress and suck in long, slow, calming breaths. My face is flushed, my breathing far too erratic for someone who's been reading on the sofa. Em walks past, freshly showered and in a polo and jeans. Corded forearms and bulging biceps have his shirt straining. His hair is still damp and a little messy.

Good lord, Iris must be freaking blind.

"Want a beer, Cal?" Em calls from the refrigerator that's now open.

"Sure, bud."

Cal tilts my chin with his hand and kisses my lips. "Be right back, mo ghràdh."

He moves toward the half bath downstairs, and I readjust my now-soaked underwear. We did not think this through. Then I remember the overnight bag we packed—I have spare panties.

I push from the sofa and grab the bag, heading up the stairs.

The shower in Iris's room is still on.

That means . . .

My jaw drops. I scoff an amused, impressed sound. The water stops.

Shit.

I duck into the spare room and dump the bag on the bed. Unzipping it, I hunt through the mix of clothes until I find another pair of panties. Pulling the ruined ones down, I don the fresh ones. As I bundle up the dirty ones and slip them into the side pocket, a knock comes on the door.

Iris appears in a towel. "Remember pajamas this time?" The smile on her face looks similar to the one that was on mine, and I . . .

I clamp my mouth shut.

If Iris doesn't want anyone to know, I'm not going to be the one to spill her secrets. Besides, Cal adores both her and Em. They should be the ones to tell him.

"Yeah, brought it all this time."

"Good. Give me a hand in the kitchen in a sec?"

"Of course. Meet you down there."

She pushes off the doorframe, padding down the hallway in the direction of her room.

I zip the bag back up and walk out, pulling the door closed behind me. Something feels grainy in my right eye. Damn contacts. Padding to the main bathroom, I slip in and lean into the mirror. Sure enough, the contact has shifted. I wash my hands and set it right.

It's then I realize the mirror is framed with condensation. Steam still lingers below the ceiling.

I turn to find the shower wet.

My excitement and hope for Em and Iris deflates.

How did I get that wrong? I was certain Iris looked like she just . . .

A little confused and disappointed for them, I head downstairs. The boys are watching some ball game on the television when I make it to the sofa. Sliding my arms around Cal's neck and down his chest, I lean over the back of the sofa. The ring glints in the light of the television in the darker space.

Em doesn't notice.

At least, he doesn't say anything if he does.

When I hear Iris walk down the stairs, I move my mouth to Cal's ear. "I'm going to help Iris, okay?"

He turns his head, pecking my cheek before turning back to the game.

"Come on!" Em shouts. "The hell, *man*."

Cal chuckles. "Sucks to be on the losing team, bud."

I shake my head and walk to the kitchen. Iris is already plating up something that's been bubbling away on the stove in large bowls. I suspect that's the amazing smell we were hit with when we first arrived. She hands me a plate, and I take it with my right hand. "What is this?"

"Ah, this is the legendary McCreary stew. We start making it when fall starts to show its face."

"That's now?"

She chuckles. "That's this week sometime, I think. Cal's the weatherman."

I can't help but smile.

"Here, take these out and come back for the bread, will you?"

"Of course." I take the bowls to the table and head back for the bread.

As I reach the kitchen, Iris is rifling through the cupboard, trying to find something. Two empty bowls sit by the large pot on the stove. "You want these two filled up?"

"Sure," she says, her head still stuck in the cupboard.

I take the ladle in my left hand and pour a generous amount in each bowl. When I set the ladle on the spoon rest, Iris is by my side with a jar of something in her hand.

I place the full bowl on the counter beside her.

She blinks, her gaze following my hand. My ring-clad hand. Hesitating, she stares at me. "Evie!"

"Yeah?" Happiness stretches my face.

"Holy shit!" The jar crashes to the floor. Iris jumps up and down, her hand covering her mouth. "You—are Cal and y—" She squeals and jumps on the spot again. Her face breaks, positively exploding with joy. "Evie—oh my god!"

I slide the plates onto the countertop when Iris looks set to burst. She flies at me, arms folding around me in the tightest squeeze.

I chuckle.

"Emmett! Get in here!" Iris calls as she releases me. I can't take my eyes off her ecstatic face, and I absolutely didn't miss that the first person she wants to talk to is Em. My work here is done.

I chuckle under a huffy breath when Em flies into the room, his hand gripping the doorframe, worry scrunching his face. "Irry, what is it?"

She crosses the couple of feet to where he stands and grabs his shirt at its opening. With Emmett standing in front of me, Iris snatches up my left hand and holds it under his nose. "Look!"

Suspense claims her pretty features, her bottom lip pulled through her teeth.

"Shouldn't we wait for Cal?" I interject softly.

"I'm here," he says, his low voice coming from by the

door. I find him leaning on the doorway, happiness beaming all over his gorgeous face.

Emmett folds me into his arms. "Congratulations, Miss Evie. Told you he'd find his way back. And then some."

Now emotion floods my senses, burning behind my eyes. "Thank you."

Without Em, there is a high chance neither Cal nor I would be here.

"Anytime." He releases me to Iris. "Welcome to the family."

He gives me a Cheshire cat grin with crazy eyes, and Iris slaps his arm as she rolls her eyes at him. "Ignore him, we McCrearys are the essence of good people, and we are honored to call you one of our own. Besides, I always wanted a sister."

Now Cal huffs a laugh and pushes from the frame. "If you're all done with the squealing, I'm hungry."

He folds himself around me from behind and drops his face into my neck with a low groan.

"Me Cal. Me hungry. Me eat Evie . . ." Em winks at me.

"You'll keep, bud," Cal mutters, rising his head to glare at his best friend.

Iris gives Em a hard look as she walks past with two bowls, heading for the dining table. "Come on, you dunderheid."

Em springs into action, following Iris as she sashays toward the table. God, those two are killing me.

"Em's not wrong. I could eat you right now, baby girl."

"But I'm so hungry." I lean my head back, running a hand behind his neck and into his hair. "And it smells so good."

"Hmmmm. Yeah, you do."

I chuckle and he nips my neck before resting his hands on my shoulders and guiding me to the dining table. We sit across from Iris and Em in our places, and Iris was right—we feel like a family.

firefly

Thirty

CALLUM

Try eating dinner with your sister staring at you half the night while you try to fend off a boner from the woman beside you whose slightest touch sets you craving. The craving is so damn bad, I could toss the food from the table, haul her onto it, and devour her right here and now. Audience be damned.

Instead, I inhale my favorite stew like a man starved.

Hilarious, because I am.

Just not for my little sister's stew.

I don't know whether it's from fooling around on the couch or Em's offhand comment, but I'm strung out tonight. Finally, when everyone's finished, I stand and pluck up the bowls and head for the kitchen like it's a goddamn race.

A moment later, Em files in behind me with the cutlery and a shit-eating grin on his face. "Someone has plans tonight."

"Fuck off, bud."

He chuckles, dropping the cutlery into the sink, and starts washing up. "It's all good, Cal. I haven't seen Iris this happy since the day we found her . . ."

Evie. Since the day Em plucked Evie from the water, after those fuckers . . .

That sucks the joy right out of the fucking room.

"Shit. Sorry, man," Em says, eyes tight as he pulls a bowl from the sink and sets it to rest on the drying rack. I tug the tea towel from the oven door handle and grab the bowl, wiping it down with more force than necessary.

"You going to take that letter to the station?" Emmett says quietly.

"Yeah, just not with Evie. She's finally got some stability. She's carried this burden long enough. I'll handle it."

Em gives me a proud look. "She's the best thing that's happened to us three in a long time."

"Three?" I raise an eyebrow.

"Yeah. Irry needed someone as much as you did. Sister-type, you know. And . . ." His face turns serious, like he wants to say something but is having a hard time putting it together. "Seeing a smile on your grumpy-ass face—I'm happy for you, Cal. It's been far too fucking long."

I clear my throat, the one that's too thick to respond.

"Don't fuck it up, you hear?" Em grins at me now.

Like I ever would.

I've been that guy, and I lived through the consequences. Never again.

"Need a hand?" Evie says from the door. I turn back to find her holding a wine glass. Iris must have opened the red already.

"Nah, we're good. You girls go enjoy the game." Em winks at her.

She shakes her head and sips her wine. "Not likely, Emmett. How about a movie?"

"What did you have in mind?" I ask.

She contemplates this for a moment, then says, "*One Small Hitch*. Or maybe *Happiness for Beginners*?"

They sound like romance movies. I guess we did watch an action flick last time. Em tilts his head, then opens his mouth like he's about to object.

"Either sound okay," I say. "What does Iris want?"

Em clears his throat, and a second later, a bowl crashes into the drying rack. Then another. What's got his goat?

"That's a good question. Maybe I'll ask her." Evie gives me a coy smile I don't understand as she walks from the kitchen, heading for the living room.

We finish up the washing and drying and make our way to the living room to find the girls still scrolling through the romance options. I don't mind watching romance, but something with a little subplot would be great. If I fall asleep in the first half, I'll never live it down.

I drop onto the couch on one end by Evie. Em sinks down on the other next to Iris. These seem to be our regular spots now. It's cozy. The fact that Iris uses Em as a big-brother pillow cracks me up. Poor guy, last time he had to stay wedged into the end of the sofa after she fell asleep at the movie's midpoint.

He doesn't seem to mind, though.

Iris would have his balls if he made a move. That sister of mine knows her mind, and if she had a mind for Emmett, he would have been out of the friend zone years ago.

I shake my head at the ridiculous thought.

Like hell.

That's how friendships are ruined. Families torn apart.

Ain't going to happen.

The movie is decided on and the girls snuggle in. Evie huddles closer, her head dropping to my arm as the credits roll. I run a hand down the arm of the sofa and rest my head back when I see it's one I've watched before.

Happiness for Beginners.

Solid film. Not sure how much I'm going to get through . . .

Like clockwork, my eyes start to heavy around twenty minutes in. Evie glances up when my body relaxes around hers. She runs her fingertips through my beard, sending her hand past my temple and into my hair.

Fuck.

Now I'm awake.

I drop my head, my lips almost brushing her ear. "Baby girl, you keep doing that, we're going to need to go upstairs."

Her fingers run through my hair again, the tips massaging my scalp. I almost don't remember to tamp down the groan rattling its way up. She's playing with me.

Eyes glued to the screen, she continues to explore my hair, neck, and beard.

Her touch is addictive.

Huddled into me, she is all I can smell.

My cock stretches my jeans, and I try desperately to focus on the movie in front of us. Evie doesn't stop. She simply huddles closer, leaning into me as her other hand rests on my thigh. Her finger traces patterns on my jeans, slowly moving toward my now-bulging crotch.

I glance at Em and Irry. They sit perfectly relaxed, side by side, watching the movie.

"Bedtime." Evie angles her head up, her lips almost brushing my earlobe.

"Why don't we go for a walk?" I rumble back on a threadbare breath.

She smiles up at me. "I could catch some air."

Thank *fuck*.

It's not that I don't want to devour her—I am dying to do just that. But with Em and Iris awake downstairs, it feels . . .

"Come on, old man, let's take a turn of the town square." She squeezes my leg.

I clear my throat. "We're going for a walk."

Em looks up with a frown. "You want company?"

"No, we're good," Evie chirps.

Understanding claims Em's face, and he grins before turning back to the movie.

"Oh," Iris says, pausing the movie. "Can you grab ice cream on the way back?"

"Sure." Evie grabs my hand, leading me away. I slide my wallet from the kitchen counter where I dropped it earlier and shove it into my back pocket. We weave through the café and make the sidewalk as she bursts out laughing.

I pin her to the front door as it closes. A huffy breath tumbles from those pretty fucking lips.

"God, Cal. All I could think of the entire thirty minutes

on the couch was straddling your lap." She tugs on my collar, now wrapped in her fingers, and I drop my mouth to hers. I run my tongue along the seam of her lips, wanting in. She opens automatically, the way she always does for me. I claim every part of her she willingly surrenders.

Fine fingers wander into my hair. I grab her wrists, shoving them against the door above her head. The bell jingles as the door rattles with our movement.

Fuck.

Not wanting my sister to walk out and ruin the moment, I haul Evie to my waist and start for the marina. Kisses dot all over my face and down my neck as her hands turn to fists in my hair. As I take the first step heading down to the docks, she pops her head up. "No. I want to see Pearl."

"You want to see a useless old relic in dry dock?"

"Uh huh." Deep browns study my face. "Please."

"Alright. But don't get your hopes up. She's a damn wreck."

"They're the best ones . . ."

Emotion sees me clench my jaw shut tight. I turn on my heel and head for the dry dock on the other side of the watchhouse. Evie's eyes study me the entire way, as if she can pull whatever information from my head with one look. Her scanning eyes have probably seen the entire Callum McCreary User Manual by the time we reach the large diamond-mesh metal gates to the dry dock yard.

"Put me down," she says, twisting back.

I set her on her feet, and she tugs at the gate. The chain around it, locked, rattles but doesn't budge.

I wrap my arms around her waist, hugging her from behind. "Errol has the key."

"Looks like we're breaking and entering, then."

She reaches for the top of the gate and hauls herself up the mesh. I assist with my hands on her gorgeous ass. She tips over the top and jumps down, landing on her feet. I follow, less elegantly than Evie. Inside, we wander through the small allotments home to a variety of vessels. Some are seaworthy but not in use, some are busted. Some lots are empty.

We finally reach the far back corner where she stands on her tripods, in the spot Em and I left her years ago, tucked up with hole-ridden, weathered covers. One has slipped off completely, and the paint is peeled on the exposed front of the boat. Evie walks around Pearl as if discovering a new treasure for the first time, running her hand along the side of the old boat, over the cloth keeping the boat's true form a secret.

I pull the covers from her as I walk around, sending years of dust and mildew up into the air. Waving a hand to clear the murky cloud, I toss the covers to the ground as I go.

Evie comes to my side. "She's wonderful, Cal."

I huff a laugh. "She's going to need a lot of work."

Evie's face lights up. "So we're doing this, then?"

"Between the bike and the boat, we're not going to have much free time . . ."

"Does it matter, if we're together?"

"Em's going to have to help, baby. This is going to take a hell of a lot of skill."

"Okay . . ."

I wrap her into my hold. "You want to go aboard?"

"Can I?"

"Should be safe. Just take it easy." I steady the ladder as she climbs aboard. The old boat moves a little with her weight but stays put. When she's safely aboard, I climb up. Evie pads around the deck slowly, running her hands over every surface she goes past, bending her neck to look up the half a mast that's left.

"How long will it take?" she asks, spinning back to me.

"Maybe eighteen months. Longer, if we get busy."

"What are you busy with?" She narrows her gaze.

I can't help the smile stretching my face. "You, baby girl."

"How will I keep you busy, mo ghràdh?"

I close the distance between us. *Mo ghràdh.* That's the first time she's used the phrase. I love the way it rolls off her tongue. How I would love to take this woman around the world. Experience everything life has to offer, just her and me. I cup her face in my hands, tilting her mouth up.

"With your insatiable need, your research . . . That will take up days."

"My research does take hours, and I can only get the best results with you."

Her fine fingers travel my chest as I fist her hair, nipping her neck. Wanting her fucking bare already.

Wanting to be balls-deep inside this little woman, giving her my soul. Making sure she's so satisfied, so thoroughly fucked, you'd never be able to wipe the sweet little smile she gives me in the afterglow every time from her face.

Harried hands pull at the hem of my polo shirt.

This old tub is filthy. But the night sky overhead is magnificent. The moon is hidden behind the northern trees, giving us the most incredible blanket of stars.

"Wait, I'll be right back." I break away, dotting a kiss to her nose before making my way down the ladder to the nearest, newest boat up on stilts I can find. Stealing two of its covers, I bundle them up and scale Pearl's ladder again.

Laying the covers out, I leave one folded at the side. Just in case.

The old rust-spotted rail trimming the deck sends up a speckled glint. The night breeze whips Evie's hair around. It's now I realize her breaths are choppy, her eyes desperate. I cross the deck that spans between us and palm her face, sinking my mouth to hers.

A pretty little whimper rises, and I take it.

Breathless, I break away, double-checking the yard is empty as I rest my forehead to hers.

"Fuck me, mo ghràdh. My heart is yours, Evie."

"Mine to protect."

I groan through a huffy sound. "If anything happened to you—"

"I will not leave you. I promise you that."

I want to tell her I would die for her. I would use my last breath to keep her safe from those fucking low-life pieces of shit. But I'm not ruining this moment. Instead, I channel the desperate need for her safety into affection. "That's the only promise I will ever hold you to, Evie."

"Good," she breathes. "Now, fuck me like it's the last time you'll ever touch me."

Christ almighty.

I grind my molars. Just the thought alone is enough to take this man down. It takes everything I have to not crumble and beg her to make sure that never ever happens. I won't. I won't yield to my insecurities. Not this time. Never again.

That's the difference twenty years makes. The difference between a boy and a man.

With a low growl, I tug her T-shirt down. The material gives way, ripping a little at the center. Sliding two fingers behind her lacy black bra, I expose one perfect tit. It bounces in my rough hand, and I clamp my lips around her hard peak, rolling my tongue around it.

Hands sink into my hair instantly, and a sweet little moan breathes into my neck as her head drops. "Cal."

I'm hard as a rock, stretching these jeans to the point of agony.

It's not enough.

I want her under me, over me. Wrapped fucking around me.

I want her soaked pussy in my face. My name tumbling out on every breathy cry I can pull from her.

I haul her shirt from her body. It hits the deck. Removing her black bra, I stand back, taking her in.

"Fuck, look at you, baby. Bare under the stars."

"Not yet I'm not . . ."

I move to fix that, but she holds up a hand, saying, "My turn."

Her finger releases the button on her jeans.

Christ.

She holds my gaze as she pushes those tight jeans over her hips. The black lacy panties are all she stands in on the moonlit deck as the moon pokes its way over the trees now. Illuminated and backlit, she's stunning. She pulls her hair around her shoulders, and the ends fall over her chest, tickling her nipples.

"No touching, Callum. Only watching."

I swallow past the stone in my throat. "Okay."

She slides the panties down. They hit the deck. She tosses them aside with her foot.

"Now, you need to do as I ask, *fear milis*."

Sweet man. In fucking Gaelic. This woman . . .

"Shirt off, now."

I tug the shirt from my back and toss it away.

"Thank you," she says, running a hand over her left breast. Her lips part as her fingers find her nipple.

The breath in my lungs evaporates.

"More, please. The jeans next."

I flick the button open and shove the zipper down. Rough hands push the jeans from my legs. I stand in my boxers, my rock-hard cock tenting them.

"Hmmm, I like that."

Elegantly, she sinks to her seat. Leaning forward, spreading her legs, she pulls her knees up as she caresses my cock through the silk boxers.

Christ, woman.

I pant a groan, my restraint harder to hold by the second.

Evie strokes me like she's exploring something precious. It throbs, and now the air in my lungs burns on each too-short inhale.

Hands hanging by my sides as I stand over her, she looks up at me with those big brown eyes. With one hand, she drags her hair around her neck, letting it settle over her shoulder. Her breasts now fully exposed, she leans back, knuckles grazing over her pussy.

"I'm soaked, Cal."

I lick my lips. Fucking parched.

Bracing herself with one hand behind her, she leans back further. Her hand unfurls, and she slips a finger over her clit.

"Show me, Evie baby."

"No touching, remember?"

I nod, and it's a shallow movement.

On a huffy breath, she sinks one finger inside herself. I grind my jaw shut, tamping down the growl wanting out. Tensing every damn muscle to root myself to the spot.

To not touch her.

Thirty-One

EVIE

The sound that leaves my lips is pure tortured bliss. Cal shifts on his feet, his face feral as I pump one digit in and out of my aching center. I want him to witness. Not to touch. This moment, once spoiled, must belong to him. I can barely control the sounds slipping past my lips.

I pull my finger out and slide it between my lips, and he flinches.

His control is almost broken.

I know how hard this is for him.

Not touching.

Knowing what I'm recreating.

But that hideous memory will be replaced by one so spectacular, it will be erased from time forever.

Needing to move, I spread my legs wide, I look back up at my starving lighthouse keeper.

"No touching, remember. Not until I say so."

He grunts at me. His breaths are so fast his chest is heaving, snapping down and back up again.

"I want you to watch me come on my fingers. Then take the spoils."

His jaw feathers.

I roll my nipples through my fingers, laying my head back. The boat rocks a little, and I snap my head back up to see Cal fall to his knees a solid foot from where I sit, his face twisting with emotion.

His boxers are straining, and I can't resist. My hands wander over the ridge before tugging the band down. His hard length springs from the silky confines, and my mouth immediately waters.

Oh god.

"Still no touching, sweet man."

He makes a sound I don't recognize as he gives me the world's most subtle nod. I grip his cock, sliding him into my mouth. I can't help the moan that captures his warm, velvety tip. My clit throbs, my breath disappears and doesn't return.

Cal's hands turn to fists before flexing open. I sink him deep into my throat and suck hard all the way up, slowly, as he trembles. He tastes incredible. I couldn't resist, but that's all I give him.

Cruel, I know, but this is about taking things to the breaking point, and my gut tells me we are close.

I release him and lean back on one hand again, circling my clit. His face twists as he struggles to haul in enough air.

Sinking two fingers inside my wet center, I slide them back out.

"I want to come. I want you to be the one to see me fall apart," I pant.

He swallows hard, gaze fixed on my hand, my fingers moving in and out of my dripping pussy.

"Then I'm yours to devour."

"You're killing me," he rasps. His jaw flexes.

"I'm so close." I swirl my thumb over my clit as I curl my fingers forward and quicken my pace. "Oh, Cal . . ."

"Come on. Fuck, Evie," he growls.

Bliss barrels through me as I tighten around my fingers. I arch on the deck, riding my hand through the orgasm.

"Enough," he grunts out.

I'm hauled forward. Cal drops beside me, lying down, and rough hands manhandle me until I'm straddling his face. His grip on my hips is harsh. His first sweep through my aching center is hot and aggressive. "Ride my fucking face. Give me another one."

He laps at my entrance, diving his tongue deep inside me before suckling my clit. He devours my pussy, working over my throbbing clit with every other stroke. My hands wander to my breasts, kneading them, pinching my hard nipples before rolling them to ease the sting.

Cal takes me like a man starved.

His tongue rips over my clit.

He rocks my hips over his mouth.

Teeth close around my aching nub, and I cry out. His hand lands on my ass, hard. I jerk, my aching nub tugging between his teeth.

"Fuck, Cal. Fuck."

"This memory will burn so fucking bright, you won't be able to see back to the things that dead man ever did. And believe me when I say it, Evie baby—he is a dead man. He just doesn't know it yet. I promised you once, whatever was haunting you wouldn't take a second breath if it ever stepped on our island. I fucking mean it. Now, give me another one."

His hand meets my ass again as he sucks down hard on my clit. I explode. Rolling my hips over his mouth, I come so fucking hard I can't breathe.

My body trembles as every inch of me floods with ecstasy.

Cal's grip reaffirms as I falter a little.

Like the rag doll I am after the world's most incredible orgasm, he flips me over, hauling my hips up to his.

"These are the only memories worth having, mo ghràdh."

He slams into me.

The stretch takes the small parcel of air I only just managed to catch. I cry out.

Pulling out, so slow, he leans over and slides one hand up my belly, between my breasts, and circles my throat. "I'm the only man who will ever touch you. You're mine."

His grip closes around my throat.

My clit throbs.

My lips part.

He slams into me. I arch from the deck.

"Fuck, Evie, you are so fucking precious." Emotion tugs at his face, thinning out his words.

"I—"

"My turn. You want this boat, this life. The island and the man that comes with it. Then I'll give you every damn thing you've ever wanted."

The boat rocks as he thrusts into me. The stars overhead shimmer like our own personal brilliant little universe. For this moment, it feels like we are the only people to ever exist.

"I—" I breathe through the sob rising in my throat. "I'll give you everything you ever ask for."

"No, don't. Because I'll take it all, mo ghràdh."

I sob, and my face splits with a strained smile. "Good."

Cal leans down, his hands sliding under my shoulders. He rocks back on his heels and buries his head in my chest. I take up the rhythm between us. His head leans back, eyes closed as he groans. "Fuck, baby. Hell."

I rise as slow as I can until his tip rims my entrance. My mouth gapes as I inch back down. Cal's face breaks. His hands slap to my hips. "Stop. Have to stop."

I stay motionless for as long as I can. When his eyes don't open, I cup his jaw, fingers tangling in his short beard. "I love you, Callum McCreary. It would be impossible not to."

He smiles gently, eyes studying my face. "You—"

A flashlight sweeps over the yard.

"Shit." Cal lies down, pulling the sheet over us. Hovering over him, I lower my body to his. Footsteps close in and we huddle tight. The sound of someone muttering about bored kids has me tamping a giggle. Cal slides a hand over my mouth. I turn my head, sucking a finger into my mouth. His head leans back, his throat working. Under the blanket, I can make out his angles. I drown in his masculine smell, breathing him in, and it sends my core aching.

The footsteps round the boat and we both freeze. I hold my breath.

They fade before disappearing and I release the air.

I toss the cloth off and straddle Cal's hips. He sits up as I rock.

My breasts bounce with every move, and he clamps his teeth around a nipple.

Rising on my knees, I cant my ass, pulling up until he only just breaches my entrance. I hover there, soaking up the delicious stretch. Now wanting my fill, I drop down, letting my chest jostle.

Cal groans. "Fuck this, baby girl." He pushes up to his knees and then hugs me to his hard angles as he stands and pads to the front of the cabin. Pulling out, he spins me around and bends me over the weathered surface. Tugging my hips back, he nudges my swollen entrance with his cock before pushing my left leg up. Balancing on one foot, I look back as he slides inside me.

My clit aches.

I send a hand down to rub it, needing to ease the agony.

"Nope. Mine."

"What's mine?" I pin him with a heated glare.

"Anything else."

His hand slides around my hip, sinking to my front before his thumb swirls over my bundle of nerves. "This pussy is mine."

With every hard, blissful stroke, the stilted boat rocks. Each perfect inch Cal gives me is the sweetest kind of torture. Pleasure builds in my core, and I tighten.

He groans.

"Fuck, Evie."

I need to be closer. I rise from the cabin, and a hand catches me, guiding me upward until my back meets his chest. Cupping my breast, he sinks his face into my neck, sending thrusts so hard they steal the last control I have. I explode around him. My hand slides into his hair. He bites down on my neck, fingers rolling my nipple. He thunders into me with messy, wild strokes, as a low growl rumbles from his throat.

"Tha gaol agam ort," I breathe.

I love you.

In the most intimate language we share . . .

His.

"Christ, baby girl, where have you been all my damn life." The words are ragged, too thick to be any more than a whisper.

"I'm here now, sweet man."

He folds me into his chest, dipping his head to my shoulder. I wrap my arms around his head, turning mine to press a kiss to his temple. Reluctant to unravel from our moment of bliss, I stay in his arms as long as he is willing. Knowing there will be things that will test us. But those things will not steal our happiness right now.

"I don't want to let you go," Cal mutters.

"You don't have to. Besides, this time I won't let you, you stubborn ass."

He chuckles. Pulling away, he spins me around. "Imagine how many times we could do that in this very spot if we were sailing around the world?" he says with the happiest smile.

"The world will never be big enough . . ." I cup his face in my hands. "I like this plan."

"You want to stay here or head back?"

"Maybe we could stare at the stars for a little while?"

"Sure thing."

I take his hand and lead him back to the deck where our clothes are scattered over the wooden floor. I lie on the cloth and hold a hand up to him. He sinks to the deck, putting out an arm. I snuggle close, my head on his arm. He rests his to the side. "I could lie here all night counting stars with you."

"You'd be snoring in no time, old man."

He chuckles. "Well, let's not fall asleep here tonight. This old man needs his bed."

"We won't." I tilt my head up, kissing his jaw.

Watching the stars shift overhead, we whisper our thoughts as the world turns around us. The night's cool air sends an ache through my muscles on the hard wooden deck, and I roll over. "Bedtime, my love."

"Think Irry and Em finished the movie?"

I study him for a minute. He really has no clue . . . "Most likely."

"Irry's probably asleep by now."

I push up onto my elbow and trace the angles of his face. "Sleep sounds so good."

"Yes, it does."

After covering up the Pearl as much as we can, we head back through the yard and scale the gates again. Ten minutes later, without the ice cream, we push through the café front door, careful not to jingle the bells. Locking it behind us, Cal grabs my hand, leading me up the stairs to the spare room.

Safely inside, we strip out of our clothes and climb under the covers. The tiny bed has us wrapped around each other a moment later. I press my hand to Cal's chest, over his heart. It's faster than usual, and I glance up.

"What is it?"

He looks down, his jaw flexing.

"I can't lose you, Evie."

Crawling up the bed the best I can on my side, I cup his face and tilt it down so his eyes are level with my own. "That's not going to happen, okay?"

He nods, his Adam's apple working as he tugs me close, so tight my mind is wild with worry. For whatever he's thinking. For whatever could happen next that I can't control.

Sucking in a raw, deep breath, he whispers, "Tha gaol agam ort."

firefly

Thirty-Two

CALLUM

The officer at the Bay Shore station stares at me like I have five heads.

"What do you mean, the case is closed?" I snap.

"No further evidence was brought forward, so the case was closed out."

"You mean, you let them get off without bothering to chase it up. Find the assholes who did this to her."

"Sir, we have limited resources and too many cases of women being *assaulted* . . ." He sighs, like I'm the waste of time. "If anything *substantial* arises, report it to the officer on duty."

"I'm giving you this." I hand him the note that was left on Firefly's console. "This is further evidence."

"It's a note. Not exactly hard evidence of a serious crime."

The officer bites into his sandwich, which is obviously more important than the life of the woman I love. "I want to talk to your supervisor. Now."

"He's away for a training for the rest of the week."

"Maybe you should have gone with." I snatch up the letter and stalk from the police station. *Useless motherfuckers.*

I'll handle this bullshit myself.

If these clowns think they are getting anywhere near Evie, they're fucking delusional. And their lifespan just got a hell of a lot shorter.

I march my way back to the docks to find Em and Evie by Firefly. Em's in uniform, arms crossed, chatting away about god knows what. He's done a great job of occupying her while I paid the police a visit, as much of a waste of time as it was.

"Errands all done?" she asks with the sweetest smile.

"Yep, all done. Shouldn't you be working, bud?" I say to Em.

He rolls his eyes at me and slaps me on the shoulder as he starts to head back to the watchhouse. "See you later, Miss Evie." He waves at her.

"Bye, Em." She returns the wave, and we board Firefly. The sooner we make it home, the better.

"Can I drive?" Evie says.

I'm taken by surprise. She's never asked to captain the boat before. But she should learn and get her license if she's going to be staying. The last thing I want is for her to feel trapped or dependent.

"If you want." I haul in the mooring lines and head for the cabin.

"So, ropes off. Then engine check?"

"Lines, but you got it."

She looks damn excited.

Who would have figured . . .

"Throttle down and guide her in by the jetty. I'll dump the fenders." I leave the cabin, tossing the long, soft tubes over the side to keep Firefly from crashing into the rickety old structure. The engine dies down to a low idle as we come in close to the jetty. Back in the cabin, Evie checks the dials of the console like we spoke about on the way home before killing the engine.

She's a natural.

"Pretty good for a first-timer," I say.

She grins at me, and I sweep her up in my arms, depositing her on my waist.

"Can I drive next time?"

"Absolutely, baby girl."

"Good."

"Wonder what we'll find in the house?" I grumble as she studies my face that's not holding the excitement hers is.

She drops to her feet. "I'm sure everything is fine."

Only one way to find out, I guess. We head up the jetty, and I shoulder the overnight bag. Everything is quiet and just the way we left it from the outside.

Evie goes first, and I brace for a mess.

She pushes the door open, and her face falls.

Our house is trashed.

Furniture tossed, books scattered. The sofa's been sliced up, its shredded fabric moving in the breeze.

"No," she utters, stepping over the threshold. "Oh no."

"Reese!" I stalk through the rubble, half expecting him to wander over from the shack, or down from upstairs. "Reese, where the hell are you?"

"Cal . . ." Evie's voice is too quiet. I turn back. She's standing by the refrigerator, her back to me. She raises her hand to touch something sticking out of the fridge.

A knife.

A knife is stabbed *into* the appliance. Something flaps in the breeze against its piercing hold.

Evie rips the paper from the blade and reads it. "Oh god." Her hand slides over her mouth.

I round the counter and take the note from her hands.

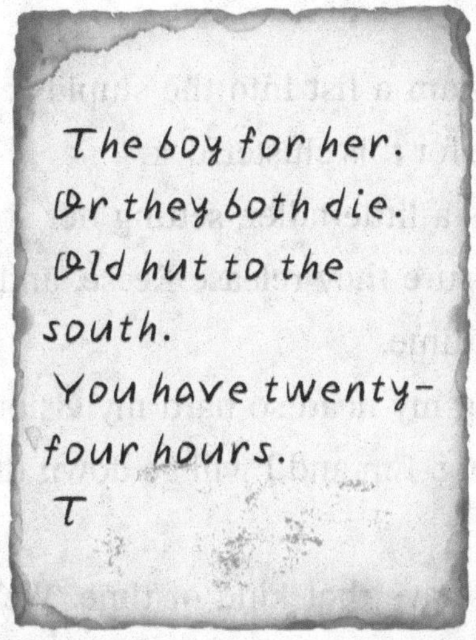

"For fuck's sake, don't these low-life pieces of shit ever give up." I crumple the note in my fist, stalking through the living room, kicking debris from my path.

Evie's staring at the floor, her face distraught. "Time's almost up."

"What?" I halt my pacing.

"Time. It's almost up. I can be there in under an hour."

I fly back to where she stands, grabbing her face. "No, you're not going anywhere near them."

Fire lances through my chest, flooding my veins as anger commandeers my senses.

"You can't lose him, Cal. You just found him."

"I just found you, too!"

I can't help the volume of my voice. I can't help the sick feeling in my gut that comes with having to fucking choose.

"Fuck!" I slam a fist into the stupid refrigerator like it's responsible for this clusterfuck.

Evie stands a little taller, setting her shoulders back. "I'll go, make sure they release Reese, and Em can pick me up like last time."

I'm shaking my head so hard my vision blurs. "That is *not* happening. Em and I will go down there and bring him back."

"You don't have that kind of time. We've been gone for a day and a night already. That's already twenty-four hours. We—"

"We have till tonight, sunset at the latest." I slump against the counter and shove my head in my hands.

"What are you talking about?"

I pull the note from my back pocket and pass it to her.

She stares at it for too long before sliding it from my fingers. Opening it, she tilts her head, her jaw clenching.

She knows exactly what the note is before she reads a word.

Her breaths shorten as her eyes track across the page and back again. With every line, her face tightens further.

"Where did you find this?" she finally says, setting the paper on the counter like it could explode and take us both out at any second.

"On the console of Firefly last night, when I went to grab the overnight bag."

"Why didn't you tell me then? We could have come home." Her inhale is staccato. Her hands wring around themselves. "We would have had better options. And Ree—"

I take her arms in my hands. "We couldn't have known. I didn't know they would take him. I thought they were in Bay Shore."

She shrugs my hold off and paces around the living room. Her hand flies up to her mouth but a scream rips past her trembling fingers. Padding to the sofa, she grips it with white knuckles.

"I'm so sick of this! The torment. The manipulation . . . I'm done. I'm. Done."

She stalks to the fridge and tugs the knife from the door. "I'm done being a side character in my own story."

"Evie, *no*."

"Stay here, Cal. I won't risk you again. Never again. I'll bring him back, I promise."

I fly at her. "No fucking way. You go, I go."

"*You* find Emmett," she says. Now her voice is too calm. "Meet me at the southern tip in an hour and a half."

"Evie, *please*, don't do this."

She slides the knife into her back pocket before cupping my face. Her wobbly smile breaks as she searches my expression. "You changed my life, Callum McCreary."

Tears swell in those brown eyes.

"Please stop," I rasp, sobs spiraling up my throat. I can't let her go by herself.

I won't.

But I can't fight this battle for her, or she'll always be looking over her shoulder.

Fucking Christ.

I stand frozen to the spot, torn in utter fucking half.

We have no time to wait for the police. Hell, getting Em here in time will be a stretch.

Lips crashing to mine, she kisses me like I'm her last meal. Her hands slip from my face as she whispers, "Tha gaol agam ort."

I slam my jaw shut, molars aching with the grinding I need to do to keep my damn mouth shut. To let her fight her own battle. To leave.

Opening the door, she hesitates, looking back, and I fall back against the counter. The sweetest smile blooms over her face. A moment later, the door closes, and she's gone.

I shove my hands through my hair, loosing a roar that would see the dead wake and see them roll over in their goddamn graves.

Feeling as helpless as a man can get, I stumble to the radio.

"Fi—Fire Island to watchhouse."

Come on, Em.

Static mocks me with its siren squeal.

"Fire Island to watchhouse. Respond!"

The radio whines as it crackles. "Watchhouse to Fire Island. Calm your farm, McCreary."

Errol.

For fuck's sake.

I slide my forearm over my forehead and hang my head. Slamming a fist into the old desk, I curse him and his entire bloodline before responding, "Errol, I need Emmett. Over here. NOW."

"Well, you don't make the orders, command does. Unless there's an emerg—"

The radio squeals and goes dead.

Thirty-Three

EVIE

I sprint through the forest, brush snapping at my legs. The knife tucked into the back of my jeans moves with every stride. I pray to god I don't lose it like I lost my belongings last time I was running hell-for-leather through these old trees. Arms out in front of me, I smack the low-hanging branches and fronds out of my way. Every minute counts.

I truly believe that.

I half expected Cal to close in, thundering through the shrubs behind me. But in true Callum McCreary style, he's respected my wishes, letting me fight my own battles. A gift I am sure is costing him the last of his sanity as I plunder through the wilderness toward uncertainty.

Toward his only child.

His son.

I will not let Reese pay the price for my cowardice.

That is not how this story is going to end.

In the next two hours, the last six years will be done with. I will have reclaimed my life. I brought this mess with me, and I intend on cleaning it up and taking out the trash.

Permanently.

I reach the waterhole before too long. Halfway. I take a small break, walking a tight circle like my heroines do mid-battle. Turning up breathless and exhausted is how you get dead. So a minute of rest is essential.

The burn in my lungs fades, and I take off again for the fishing hut. The closer I get, the more I scan my surroundings. I'm not naive enough to think they won't have prepared for my arrival. I slow my pace when I feel I'm getting close. Picking my way through the under-growth, I stay as quiet as I can. I pull my shirt out at the back and cover the knife.

I need the element of surprise.

I need stealth.

I nee—

A twig cracks underfoot.

I still.

I crouch and close my eyes, listening.

I'm about to push to my feet after hearing nothing when a chuckle echoes through the trees.

Glancing around, I walk, hunched over, trying to creep closer to the hut. Deciding to come around on them from the back to assess the situation, I take each step one at a time, making sure to stay as quiet as I can in the littered undergrowth.

I make the back of the hut without incident and lean up against the weathered wood, peering in through the grimy window. Three figures inside. Two move about like shadows while the third sits. I'm guessing that's Reese tied to a chair.

Their voices are dulled through the wood, and I strain to hear.

"I'm nothing to her. Fuck, man, you have to believe me. You want someone she'll actually come for, you should have nabbed the old man."

The little fucker.

"He'll never let her come, she's his frigging pet. He ain't going to swap her for me, so just let me go."

He's deflecting, disconnecting from the primary target . . . Smart boy.

Guy, I guess.

Reese is no more a boy than I'm a girl.

His ruse couldn't be further from the truth. Cal will do anything to protect his family, and Reese is family. Whether he likes it or not.

"Shut it!" The larger of the men lashes out, kicking his chair.

Big guy.

Great.

The chair topples over, and Reese grunts as he meets the floor. If I could break him free of the chair, it would be two against two. Not this two-against-one situation I find myself in. Even numbers mean much better odds.

To do that, I'm going to need a distraction . . .

Something to draw them out of the hut for a few minutes.

Something like . . .

A decoy.

My gut flips with the idea that surfaces.

If they see me, get a fleeting glance, and make chase, I can circle back. Free Reese. Run like hell for the southern tip. And pray Em and Cal are waiting.

Simple, really, when you think about it.

It's the execution that has my nerve up. Adrenaline flooding my veins.

"Maybe we dispose of you, anyway. If you're really no use to us . . ." one of the men says.

Timothy.

His voice will be burned into my memory until the day I die.

Which hopefully won't be today.

Fingers crossed.

"No! Please, I'll do anything you wan—"

I take off at a run for the east side of the cabin,

making sure to give the hut a large enough berth so I'm not easily heard or seen. I find a half-shrouded position, half hidden by bushes, and haul in a lungful that stretches my chest.

"Hello?!"

Hand brushing over the small of my back, I double-check my knife is securely where I left it.

It is.

Timothy flies through the hut's weathered door. His usual black sweats and T-shirt hang on his reedy frame. But it's when the second man appears that my fear spikes. He's much larger. Last time, I was half blind without my glasses. Now, wearing contacts, I see how muscular he is.

Shit.

They finally see me amongst the brush, and I take off toward the north . . .

. . . and they make chase.

Both of them.

I pump my arms, putting forest between us. I may be smaller, but I know the island better. And I'm more nimble.

And I have more to lose.

I sprint for the waterhole, ignoring the lancing heat consuming my lungs.

Legs flying over the earthy debris, my crashing echoes through the trees as the wind tangles my hair behind me. Time seems to slow a little. Before I know it, the waterhole comes into sight.

Glancing back, I see the trees moving. I slow to a halt.

They're yelling.

They're harried.

They're right where I want them.

On quiet feet, I slip into the water. Careful not to make large ripples, I move slowly until I'm in up to my waist. I turn to face the forest, and when I hear them closing in, I sink. Drawing in a long, deep breath, I submerge. Hands moving like molasses through the dark liquid, I wrangle my hair around my neck.

I close my eyes, every inch of my body doused.

Their shouting, albeit muted, drifts over my watery hiding place. My lungs begin to shrink, the air turning to ash in between my ribs, so I count.

One Mississippi.

Completely still, I listen over my heartbeat, now thundering through my head.

Two Mississippi.

Their yelling fades, like it's moving away.

Three Mississippi.

The ash ignites, and I wince, clenching my jaw to stave off the heat. To stop myself from moving.

Four Mississippi.

My heartbeat rattles my skull. My limbs tingle in the coolness, and I don't dare move.

Five Mississippi . . .

I strain to hear above the water over my mutinous body. But between each heartbeat is now silence. The only sound I can make out is the waterfall behind me, filling its glittering pool endlessly.

Six Mississippi.

Feet pushing into the muddy ground beneath me, I rise. The slow, precise movement takes a moment. As water cascades from my body, I scan my surroundings with one hand behind my back, fingers brushing the handle of the blade. I can make out the men shouting and crashing through the trees to the north.

I glide to the shoreline with steady movements.

Each step up the bank, water runs from my body and my soaked jeans. My T-shirt clings to my skin. My hair I twist and sweep to one side, letting it dangle over my chest.

Assessing the distance between us and their direction of travel, I glance back south.

My wet jeans are restrictive. Not like the second skin I need to be able to move freely and silently through the forest. Toeing my shoes off, I slip out of the jeans and lay them over a fallen tree. Making quick work of hacking back and forth, I cut them off to shorts.

Better.

I slip them back on and slide my shoes onto my feet. Tucking the knife back into my waistband at my back, I swiftly run through the trees. Thanks to my light feet and delicate placement, I make next to no noise as I close in on the hut.

I slow before entering the small, weathered structure. Reese lies on the floor, still tied to the rickety chair, his wrists straining at the ropes he's bound with. I squat by him as he mutters something to himself. His eyes are closed, his jaw clenched, like he's about to . . .

I touch his arm. "Reese, I'm here."

His eyes fly open. Shock floods his face but then anger fills it just as fast.

"Fuck! No, you shouldn't have come, Evie. God, what the hell?"

"I'm not going to let them hurt you. Or me. We're getting out of here."

I lean over and pluck the knife from my back. I cut the ropes on his wrists, and he scrambles to his feet.

"I don't know where they went, but they'll be back," he says, his gaze darting around the cabin before settling on the doorway.

"I know. We need to get to the southern tip. Cal will be waiting, hopefully."

"He let you come?" His face twists with disgust.

"He doesn't *let* me do anything, Reese. I make my

own decisions, and this is one of them. So don't let me regret it."

He waves a hand at the door. "After you, MacGyver."

I huff a laugh, surprised he knows who that is. Didn't take him for a *MacGyver* fan.

"Let's go." I slide the knife into my waistband and turn back for the door.

Mid-step toward the threshold, I catch a syllable. The low tone is one I recognize.

Fuck.

I hold a hand up.

Sure enough, they are crashing through the trees, closing in on the hut. We can't go through the front door; we'll end up right in front of them.

"Window," I breathe.

Reese rushes the window, shoving it open. It takes a few hits to budge it.

"Go!" I hiss.

His brows lower as he shakes his head, wasting damn time. I all but shove him into the window and he clambers up and out of it in a tumble of long legs, landing with a thud.

Dammit.

I pull myself up the wall and drape my body over the sill. Reese stands, turning back as he reaches for me. The second his expression changes, I know I'm done for.

A rough hand closes around my thigh.

"Where do you think you're going, *Butterfly*?"

firefly

Thirty-Four

CALLUM

The radio dangles in my hand, the air leaving my lungs. I stare at the floor.

"Cal, you good?"

Emmett.

Thank fuck.

"No, bud. So far from fine, it may as well be in fucking space."

"I'm coming."

"Southern end, Em. As soon as you can."

Snatching up my radio and phone, I sprint for Firefly. Evie may have taken the most direct path to the hut, but I'm taking the fastest one. I toss off the mooring lines and pull the fenders in like the fucking jetty's on fire. I crank her over, and the engine roars to life as I shove the throttle forward, not waiting for the old girl to warm up.

Water churns behind us, and I send her south. Fast.

"Firefly to Coast Guard."

"Coast Guard, responding. Over."

"I'm leaving dock now. Anchor out of sight, Em."

"Ten-four. Over and out."

Not for the first time in my life, I'm so grateful for the only brother I've ever known. Emmett has my back. He has all of our backs. Always.

Fuck, we'd be lost without him.

Every chop Firefly buffets over sends my nerves closer and closer to the edge. To the tipping point that I've stayed away from for decades. A dangerous man is the one who is about to lose the only thing he cares about. Having nothing to lose is a privilege I no longer have. I have everything to lose.

My entire world.

She is my entire world.

And I will tear this one apart to keep her safe.

If I make it in time . . .

The southern tip comes into view a few minutes after I've radioed Em. His big-ass boat will no doubt be thundering its way over the water toward our position.

He can take these fuckers in.

If I don't end them first.

When the rocky outcrop that protects the little strip of beach I use for hunting is close enough, I kill the engine and glide Firefly in, sending her bow south. The lapping water pushes her toward the rocks, and I can step off from here and run up the beach if I have to. The wind travels to the west, so any engine noise should have drifted over the water and not the island.

"Come on, baby girl."

I pocket the radio and phone, then pull open the cabinet under the console, searching for binoculars. Finding an old set, I rip them from the pouch and stalk to the gunwale to see what I can. The island is quiet. The forest shrouds its inhabitants well, keeping prying eyes from seeing inside her emerald paradise.

"Evie McCreary." Emotion closes my throat, my hands tightening around the binoculars. "Show your face, beautiful."

As if she can hear me, I keep talking. Keep telling her I'm coming in to bring her out if she doesn't show. Convincing myself I did the right thing, letting her go by herself. But hell, this feels anything but right. I should be with her. I should be sorting out those fucking animals. They should cease to exist for the torment they have created.

Antsy, I pace the deck, focus never leaving the beach as Firefly rocks with the waves. I toss the fenders over in case we contact the rocky ridge. Honestly, I couldn't care less. I'd swim the ocean to get to her.

Every man has his limit, and I'm coming up on mine. Fast.

Of all the ways she could stretch my heart, this one is the worst.

The fire lancing my veins grows hotter with every minute that passes and the beach remains empty.

Desperate, I stalk back to the cabin and grab the binoculars. A blur of green fills the lenses when I press them to my eyes. Focusing with the tiny wheel on the top, the blur fades as the forest sharpens.

Still, all I can see is trees, brush.

Nothing else.

"Dammit!"

I toss them to the storage box at the stern. Running my hands through my hair, I take to pacing.

"Come on, mo ghràdh." The growl leaving with the words rattles me.

When the low tone doesn't fade, I look over my shoulder.

The Coast Guard boat races toward my position, its bow plowing over the choppy water like it doesn't exist.

"Coast Guard to Firefly, we have a visual."

I pluck the radio from my hip. "Firefly, copy. Hold position. Over."

"Holding, bud." Emmett's voice is strained. Evie is like a little sister to him. This must be all too familiar after the last time he had to come to her rescue.

Movement from the forest line catches my attention.

I squint to make out—

Reese breaks through the trees, stumbling when his feet hit dense sand. I wait for Evie to burst from the thick green brush right after him.

Reese looks up and down the beach, as if hunting for someone. His gaze sticks on Firefly and he picks up the pace, flying across the sand.

I jump the gunwale and pick my way along the rocky ridge, heading for the beach. Slipping on the sharp rock I slow a little. Bracing, I jump down into the shallow water and wade toward my son.

His face is wrecked.

My heart stops in my fucking chest.

"Reese!" I break free from the water, running over the damp sand.

We collide, and I pull him into my arms. He's breathless, groaning as he sags against me.

"You're okay, bud. You're safe." I cup the back of his neck in a tight hold.

A beat passes, and he pushes away, shaking his head violently. "No, no."

"Where is she?"

Thirty-Five

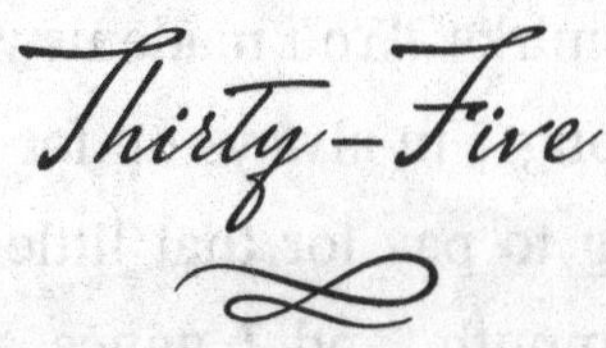

EVIE

My own stupid knife presses against my throat, my back pushed up against Timothy's chest, my wrists burning in his hold as he restrains me. Warmth trickles down my neck as the sting sets in. The big guy closes the small distance that's left between us, eyes searching my face.

"This a game to you, Butterfly?" the big guy says.

"Don't call me that," I hiss, straining in the grip holding me.

Timothy sneers, his hot breath hitting my ear. "We can call you whatever we want, whore. Nobody's coming for you. You're all ours."

I struggle in my confines but don't react other than to say, "I never have been, nor will I ever be, yours."

"You look pretty much ours at the moment," the big

guy says, tracing a filthy finger over my jaw. It hooks over my bottom lip.

My gut churns.

Chest heaving, I hold my composure . . . just.

The big guy smirks. "You made us work for it, angel. Don't get me wrong, I'm always up for a good hunt, but now you're going to pay for that little chase." His foul breath hits my mouth, and I wince, pressing my lips closed and turning my head to the side.

His fingers pinch my chin, snapping my face back to him as he towers over me.

"*Now*, you don't leave this little island. You don't get to ease into this. You take us both, right here, right now."

"Get your depraved fucking hands off me!"

"Not this time, little one," he whispers.

Heat licks my spine as fear seeps through my body. My airway all but closes over. Trembling, I groan, trying one last time to pull away. The knife disappears from my throat as it hangs in his hand. His gaze travels down my body, slow and heated, his pale-blue eyes darkening as his expression changes.

When it comes back up, the tip of the knife pushes the neck of my T-shirt down. The material slices under the sharp blade. Crimson soaks into my T-shirt.

"I like that, you bleeding. Me taking what I want, *Butterfly*."

"Please . . ." I sob. "Please don't do this."

My heroine is long since gone.

My bravery left along with my last chance to escape, scurrying after Reese as he fled.

Like I told him to.

Because the heroine doesn't throw lives down for protection. She stands her damn ground.

She. Stands. Her. Damn. Ground.

Still trembling, I set my shoulders back.

It's not fear, it's adrenaline.

It's not fear, it's adrenaline.

It's not fear, it's adrenaline.

No fear.

One long breath in. I fix my attention on the man towering over me. The blade, my knife, in his filthy fucking hand.

This is *my* story.

You are side characters, just begging to be killed off.

I write this ending.

I have the control. Like every underestimated woman who came before me.

Feigning a sob, I bend my head. I wait until Timothy's hold gives just a little . . .

One swift, manic thrust of my head backward, my skull slams into his face.

My bonds split instantly as he doubles over, grabbing at his face. Blood pours from his nose.

I step sideways, putting both men to my side.

The big guy advances with the knife. I dance past him, alternating my gaze between the two men. Skirting the room until I come to the cupboard.

Kicking the door open, I sweep down and swipe up the two small blunt knives I left behind last time.

Now the fight's a little more even.

Big guy chuckles, but his face tightens.

They don't like it when prey fights back.

That I already know.

I figure he is my biggest threat now. Not Timothy. The size difference alone makes him more formidable. He's wiping at his face with the back of his hand, his glare burning into me now. "I will stab you, bitch, I have no problem fucking you unconscious."

Christ.

Timothy lunges at me. I sidestep him. As he tries to circle back, I twist my wrist, sending my blades backward. Spinning toward him, too quick for him to move out of the way, I slice the top of his arm.

"Fuck!" He cowers, grabbing his wounded arm. Blood seeps through his fingers. "You fucking cut me."

"Want another one?" My voice is low, foreign.

Each breath sears from my lungs before they barely inflate again. My head is vacant except for a singular focus.

Hurting them both.

I wait for one to advance. For them to realize I won't

go down without a fight. My rusty blades and I are committed. In this for the long haul. To the end.

The very end.

Not giving the adrenaline pumping through my harried veins a chance to settle, I close in on Timothy.

He's my bait.

My target, the bigger threat.

Timothy backs away as I stalk toward him, head bent, my gaze boring into him. My labored breathing fills the hut with no other sounds bar the few raspy breaths from either side of me that I intend on snuffing out.

"Stand still," the big guy barks at Timothy. "She's bluffing. She ain't going to hurt us."

My weeks of torture and years of torment would disagree.

Still, the big guy holds his position. I slide one knife under Timothy's throat. Keeping the big guy in my peripheral, I hiss, "I ought to spill your blood all over this damn floor. For every month you sent me letters. Revenge for every butterfly that died at your sadistic hands. For the years of freedom you stole from me."

He tries to huff a dismissive laugh, his gaze flicking to his buddy, and I shove the blade against his throat harder.

"Nothing about this is funny. And yes, this is *all* your fault."

"You don't have a clue. Get the fuck off me, you stupid bitch," he rasps.

I lean in, close. His sweat-clad skin is caked with dirt and filth. "Said the mouse to the lioness," I growl.

Movement rushes at my side.

I spin to face him. A wall of sweaty man hits me. I stumble, and he shoves me to the ground. I scramble backward, but he grips my legs, crawling over me until his hand closes around my wrist, the other sinking into my hair and making a fist. "Looks like we're doing this the hard way."

He leans down, licking my neck with a groan. "Good, I like a little fight in them."

Timothy steps toward us.

"Fuck off! She's mine, you pathetic excuse."

I send my free hand into his side, sinking the rusted blade between his ribs.

He roars, face twisting with pain. The knife lodges, and I can't pull it back. It's stuck.

No!

He pants through the pain, spittle hitting my face. "Fuck!"

The hand closed around my hair pulls up, and the back of my skull hits the ground. Hard.

Stars pop into my vision, and I whimper. I grip my last weapon with every bit of remaining strength I have. Bucking underneath him, I scream out, "I will kill you!"

He seethes, leaning down. "Not if I kill you first, little one."

I snap my head up, smashing into his nose. He groans, swaying a little before he sits back, pinning me under him. With a deep breath, he tugs the knife from his ribs and tosses it through the front door. His fingers around my wrist, he slams my hand into the floor until my grip falters and the blade falls.

No . . .

No!

"You can't win this game, Eve. So don't bother trying." His eyes study my face.

Eve.

He called me by my name.

Was T his sidekick all this time? Is he the bigger wolf, lying in wait to sweep in and take the spoils?

"Wha—what did you call me?"

"Your name, precious girl." The last two words are almost a snarl.

I glance at Timothy, and he looks as deflated as I do, surprised.

"What kind of man lets his girl get away?" the man over me whispers, his lips brushing my ear.

My heart flings against my ribs, bruising the air right out of my lungs.

He is the stalker?

What?

"My useless cousin over there is about as good at operating a semitruck as he is abducting a meek little woman."

"You still owe me a new fender," Timothy whines.

The man straddling my hips gives him a dirty look that registers as a *not now* expression.

"I like to watch my prey being played with, Eve. He's good for that, but I'm done waiting."

That explains why Timothy drugged me but never . . .

"Please, stop. You can have me willingly, if you j-just let me go! Please!"

I'll trade an unwanted encounter for my life any day.

"I don't want you willing." He tugs at my shirt, and I slap at him with both hands. "Hold her!"

Timothy takes a tentative step toward me.

His nervous gaze flicks from us to the door, like he's about to make a run for it. Something snaps on the ground outside, and Timothy shakes his head, fleeing the hut.

"Fucking coward," the man hovering over me says.

"Who are you?" I ask, half wanting to know, half wanting to buy myself time.

"Need a name to scream?" He runs his knuckles down my cheek, and I wince, snapping my head to the side. "You can scream Thorin while I fuck the life right out of you."

My mouth gapes.

Reaching over, he takes my knife from the floor and holds it up while inspecting it.

My heart rate kicks up. I squirm beneath him, wanting out. Now.

His gaze falls from the blade to my face.

"How about I mess you up before the good part?"

The knife comes down, the tip aiming for my chest.

His piercing eyes find mine.

I slam them shut. He won't get the satisfaction of seeing my fear.

Hauling a long, slow, stretching lungful, I wait for the piercing pain of the blade, the tang of crimson and the burn of death to find me . . .

firefly

Thirty-Six

CALLUM

Reese spins back on the sand, a hand rubbing over the back of his neck. "They caught her, they—"

"Who and where."

"That old hut, and there's two of them."

I take off for the forest.

The world around me blurs as time grinds to a halt. The air in my lungs stalls out, never to return. Branches whip my face, neck, and shoulders. I thunder through, not feeling a thing. It doesn't take long before I come across a guy in black sweats and a black T-shirt running through the forest toward the south. I slide to a halt, crouching behind a tree as he closes in on my position.

The second he's close enough, I jump out, tackling him to the ground.

"What the hell!" he screeches. "Get off me."

I pin him to the ground with my forearm sunk into his throat. "Who the fuck are you?"

He chokes under my weight, hands pulling at my arm to no avail.

"I promised her she would be safe on this island. That the thing haunting her would not draw a second breath if it ever stepped foot on this floating fucking rock. Guess that means you."

"Plea—"

I slam a fist into his face. His head lolls to one side. He's out cold.

Well, fuck. That was too damn easy.

Footsteps crash toward me, rustling the forest alive as they approach. Reese bursts through a layer of bushes, breathing heavily.

Hell.

"You should have stayed on the beach. Waited for Em." I push to my feet as his gaze drops to the scrawny unconscious guy at my feet. "He ain't dead yet. Watch him. I'm going to find Evie."

"We'll be right here," Reese says, stepping closer to the limp body on the ground.

I make my way to the fishing hut. The small rustic structure my family spent happy, sunshine filled days in. The point our school holidays orbited around as kids.

Now it's been reduced to this tarnished scenario by some fucker who doesn't belong here.

The hut comes into view. I hesitate, leaning on a tree to listen.

The sounds I can hear I can't make out.

I move closer, watching every step I take. Evie's whimpers drift through the forest and into my ears, and I file my molars down. Hands flexing into fists, I shift for a better view, and heat spills through my veins at what I see.

Lying on the filthy floor, she trembles. The guy pinning her there sends a blade over one breast, a fine line of blood welling up behind it.

The ringing in my ears drowns out every one of my senses.

That limit, the one every man has when it comes to the people he loves—I just smashed right the way through it. The fucking wrecking ball is still swinging, crashing into my sense of self-preservation . . .

My world, mere feet away.

My *everything* to lose.

Unable to control another thing, I rush to the hut, flying through the doorway.

He looks up, knife still on her chest.

I tackle him, sending him toppling backward, slamming into the floor. One knee sunk into his gut, I slam my fist into his face. His round moon face jerks as my knuckles crash down, strike after strike.

A small little sob spills from behind me.

I glance back. Evie is sitting up, wrapping her ripped shirt around her body. Tears streak her face. I hold her gaze for a moment, letting my heart see she's okay.

"Cal!"

My shoulder burns, bursting with pain. Something thuds up the side of my head. Stars flood my vision. I turn back, but it's too late. He grabs my throat. Dropping my gaze to the knife stuck in my shoulder, I growl, the sound squeezing through his grip.

His face is bloodied, his nose leaks, and his left eye is busted. The scowl on his face cracks his injuries further, and blood flows freely. "You know what happens to fucking heroes?" He seethes.

I hang in his grip as he rises to his feet. My hands hang by my sides.

I feel the floor behind me, hoping to find the knife.

Soft fingers meet mine, placing the knife in my hand as she moves closer in my peripheral. I fling the weapon round, aiming for his thigh.

He kicks the knife from my hand.

His knee slams into my chest.

Air flies through my lips, leaving my lungs vacant.

I hunch over, gasping, unable to catch a decent parcel of air.

"Heroes die, fucker." He leans down, plucking up the knife that fell from my hand.

On my knees in front of the man who cost *mo nighean* six fucking years of her life, I can only wonder what drives a man to do such a thing. To take a life as easily as this.

"Now you die, on your knees, while she watches."

"Go on, boy. Do your worst," I spit.

"No, Cal. Please, stop this. I surrender . . ." Evie moves to my side. "I surrender!"

"Too late, Butterfly. Besides, you're already mine."

"Never."

The guy chuckles like she just told some witty joke.

His hand grips my throat, closing off my airway, as his gaze hovers across her body with a sickening expression.

My gut sinks at his lurid gesture. I can't breathe, and I groan before gasping out, "No . . . Plea—my life for hers. T-take mine . . . let her go."

There is no way I'm living without this woman. No way I'm letting her wear this consequence. That's a fresh hell I can't take. I don't give two fucking shits who started this, I'm finishing it.

His attention shifts back to me, his hand raising across his chest diagonally, ready to strike. The hand around my throat crawls into my hair, tugging my head back.

Evie moves in my periphery.

It's then I notice her left hand behind her back.

His arm slashes toward my exposed throat.

"I said *no*," Evie breathes, lunging forward.

Her hand flings up and around. The small blade in her grip finds its mark. His knife-wielding fist strays, thumping into my jaw, the blade missing by inches.

Knife sunk deep into his carotid, Evie twists her wrist, stepping closer. Then a little closer again.

Shock floods his widened eyes. His grip falls from my hair, the knife in his hand clattering to the floor. He fumbles for her wrists. His face breaks. "Butte—"

He hits his knees.

She bends, following his movements as she holds his gaze. "This is how this story ends. Your life for Joshua's. Now we are even."

Evie jerks back, the knife dislodging from his neck. Gripped in her hand, it drips crimson dots to the floor at her feet.

Blood spurts from his neck with every heartbeat.

Suffocating on the gurgling red spilling from his mouth, he falls onto the floor.

Evie drops the knife, her body trembling as she stares at her bloodied hand for a beat. With a wobbly cry, she turns back, falling on her knees.

"Oh my god." Her hands claim my face. "Cal, are you alright?"

I wrap my hands around her fingers and press my forehead to hers. "I'm alright, mo ghràdh." I tug the blade from my shoulder and blood seeps through, soaking my sleeve. It's not as bad as I thought.

"Did you find Reese?" she says, leaning back.

"I did. He's standing sentry over the other guy."

She huffs a strangled cry of relief, and I rise to my feet. "Come on, Em will be waiting."

She holds a hand up as her face crumples, her body still shaking.

"I just—" She turns to the side, losing her stomach to the floor.

Shock is setting in, and she's taken a beating. Bloody cuts litter her chest and neck and shoulders. Christ, I should revive the asshole just to kill him all over again.

But I didn't kill him.

I'm not the hero in this story.

Evie is.

Lord knows she's saved me more times than I can count. In ways nobody's been able to for the last twenty years. I lean down and scoop her into my arms, wincing as the wound in my shoulder burns. But I don't care. "No arguing, baby girl. This is how you're leaving this old hut. Safe and in my arms. And the second we cross that threshold"—I nod to the weathered front door—"that's exactly where you're going to stay."

Fine hands sink into my beard, pulling my mouth down to hers. Hovering, not quite touching. "Sounds like a promise, Callum McCreary."

"Hell." I sink my face into her hair and groan. Breathing her in for a heartbeat, I lift my head to find her searching eyes. "It's the only one I'm ever going to make you keep."

We cross the threshold, not bothering to look back. As we near the spot where I left Reese, Evie wriggles in my arms. "Can I borrow a shirt?"

I let her down, pulling my shirt from my back. She slips it on, buttoning up a few buttons in the center. Her fingers still coated in red, she studies them briefly.

"Let's get you cleaned up," I say softly, taking those fine little writer's hands in my own. They may be small, but they are formidable. Infallible. It's no wonder that, between her incredible mind and these pretty little digits, she's an author who reaches hearts and minds. "I'm so fucking proud of you, Evie baby."

I hold her to my chest, kissing the crown of her head as the first tears fall.

All choked up, I stay holding her until the emotion clears and her body wrapped around mine is all that registers.

"You two need a room?" A lilt-lined voice reaches us.

Reese.

I chuckle into her hair, and we put space between us.

Reese reaches the area we stand in, dragging the still unconscious guy behind him with both hands. "Was wondering how long you were going to be. Don't tell me you had an unnecessary pit stop while I was on guard duty."

I double-check the guy is still breathing.

Fuck, that's the last thing I need, another tortured soul on my hands.

I lean around Reese to see the rise and fall of the guy's chest.

Still breathing.

Thank fuck.

"No pit stops, but I do need to wash up a little," Evie says.

"There's a waterhole a little way to the north," Reese offers, waving a hand in that direction, like this is our first time on our own damn island.

"Take that fucker to the beach and meet Em." I pull the radio, still miraculously attached to my hip by its metal clasp, off and hand it to him. "We'll meet you there in a bit."

"Sure. Come on, fucker." He slides the radio into his back pocket and walks south, dragging the guy behind him.

He's going to have a sore head when he comes to.

I turn back to Evie, sweeping her into my arms. I walk for the waterhole, and her arms slide around my neck.

"You know, Mr. McCreary, this kind of feels like riding off into the sunset."

A hearty laugh escapes me that echoes through the trees. "Only your mind could connect those two."

When we reach the waterhole, I don't bother slowing, don't release her.

I walk into the water, wading into the cool, cleansing waters like both our lives depend on it.

Like our souls do.

The water laps my back and soaks Evie's shorts through, and I let her down.

"Arms up," I rasp.

She obeys, lifting her arms over her head.

I slide my shirt and her cut-up one over her head, tossing them in the water. I tug my T-shirt from my back and push it into the water. Bringing it back out, I wring it out before dabbing it over her chest to clean off the blood. She hisses when it sweeps over her cuts. And when she is clean of a dead man's blood and her own, I dot kisses above each wound as if it'll accelerate the healing.

"Cal?" Her voice is too soft. Her hands wander up my neck, resting on my jaw.

I look up to beautiful browns that have darkened since we left the hut.

All the adrenaline has her body in a frenzy. I can tell by the way she scans my face and her hands wander my body. Pressing against me, she closes in.

"Close your eyes, fear milis."

My eyes slide shut, the blood that's been racing through my body plunging south, heat building with only the touch of her fingertips as they skitter over my shoulders. Then . . . she disappears, and the loss of her touch is cold.

"Keep them closed," she mutters. The water moves. Sloshing. I hear drips and then something slapping to the water's surface. Warm legs wrap around my waist.

"Open," she breathes.

Eyes widening, I find her brown eyes burning as she nips my mouth. Only when her tongue slides over mine do her eyes close.

Hands sliding down her spine, I knead her bare ass.

Fuck me, mo ghràdh.

This is going to take longer than we thought.

Thirty-Seven

EVIE

Em's throat works as I cross the sand and fall into his arms. I swear to god, this man is my brother from another mother. I know now why Cal is so protective of Em's place in his life. The man is one hell of a guy, and my heart aches with the knowledge Iris may never—

"Hell, you scared us, Miss Evie." His hug tightens around me.

I wrap my arms around his bulky frame and sag against the rock we call Emmett.

With a rough, playful hand, he messes up my already filthy, tangled hair. "Before McCreary takes me out, you got to know how fucking brave you are. Iris is going to be so damn pumped over this. She'll be talking about it for weeks."

I chuckle, but it disintegrates into a breathy sob.

His hand runs over my hair. "You're okay."

Yes, yes, I am.

Timothy is in custody on the Coast Guard boat. Thorin is . . .

Sleepin' with the fishes.

I chuckle a laugh into Em's chest.

A throat clears behind me, and I turn back to find Cal.

"I'm taking her home, Em. The police can come take our statements or whatever tomorrow."

"I'll call it in. The crew will secure the hut." He slaps Cal on the shoulder and gives Reese a nod as he walks back toward the small inflatable powerboat he made shore with. "Be checking in tomorrow. Iris won't let me come alone."

Cal waves him off, and Reese picks his way along the rocky ledge toward Firefly. Taking my hand, Cal leads me back toward the boat. Once over the jagged, slippery rocks, I step up Firefly, never more grateful for her waiting here for us than now.

"Watch your step, baby girl," Cal says, guiding me into the boat.

Reese leans on the doorframe to the cabin, his arms crossed as he watches us board. Of course he does. Apparently, the McCrearys' comfort zone is leaning against a doorframe. His eyebrow raises with the name

Cal uses for me. "We're going to need to change that name."

Cal looks at his son. "Would you prefer mom?"

I freeze, laughter flying upward and crashing into my pursed lips.

"Urgh, no . . . Whatever." He rolls off the doorframe and drops onto the bench seat.

"Not one syllable, remember?" Cal warns.

"*Fine*, whatever."

"Then, my son," Cal says, ruffling his hair as he walks past and to the console. "I'll call my wife whatever the hell I choose to."

My wife.

My focus alternates between father and son. Reese slouches in the chair, acting more like a moody teenager than the young twentysomething he is.

Good lord, the McCreary words are sinking their hooks in early.

I smile at the two of them.

Never before have I been so exhausted and so damn happy all in the length of one heartbeat.

The lighthouse comes into view mere minutes later.

Home.

Although, to be fair, Callum is my home. And he always will be.

He was willing to die for me.

From the day I stepped foot on this island, my grumpy, stoic, kindhearted lighthouse keeper's been taking care of me. Livvy sent me here to heal. I didn't only do that, I came full circle. I reconnected my heart and soul in the most magnificent reunion ever.

Through a sunset in a dead-engine floating boat, through a storm, through hunting and gathering, through a festival, through losing us to retrograde amnesia, through rerouting my career, through people coming back from the dead . . .

Now, after the rise and fall of the one thing, the one man, who haunted me for years, I am free.

Happy.

Free.

Home.

". . . sweet home, baby," a low rasp sinks by my ear. I find myself wrapped in warm arms, huddled with my back against his chest, the boat stationary by the jetty. I look up to find Reese already almost to the lighthouse.

I spin in Cal's embrace and lean back on the console, resting a hand over his heart. "This right here is my home."

His jaw feathers. "Then I will endeavor to outlive

mine." His palm presses over my own heart. "So you never spend another day alone or scared ever again."

"That's a long, long life, old man."

He smiles, cupping my face with both hands, and breathes, "Good."

Iris practically runs from the jetty, flying at me with red hair trailing behind her like some fantasy film. "Heavens above, Evie, thank the stars." She crashes into me, arms holding me tight. Em strolls up the jetty behind her, a content smile on his handsome face.

Iris unravels her hold on me, spinning to my right. "And you!" She pins Cal with a finger pushed into his chest. "You daft bastard. Don't you *ever* do that again."

Fire fills her eyes. But despite her fluster of an entrance, she crashes into his embrace, muttering curses.

Cal swallows. "Sorry, Irry. But I'm going to protect my family the only way I know how, and it was the best choice at the time."

Emotion nails a burn behind my eyes, and I clench my jaw tight to stave off the huffy sob trying to squeeze its way out. Iris pushes away and turns back to Em. I scrunch my face up and lean into Cal.

"What did the police say?" Em asks.

"Took our statements, including Reese's. They collected the body yesterday before dark. Since it was self-defense, it seems like an open-and-shut case."

"We also provided a statement. Turns out both guys have a rap sheet. The dead guy's is a mile long and in multiple jurisdictions."

Em's looking at me now. Like this information is what I need.

But my closure was sealed the moment I opened Thorin's artery.

Urgh, I should probably see someone about that . . . Who knows how it might come back to bite me later on if I don't.

"I could use a beer," Iris says with a sigh. "It's been one hell of a few months."

Cal chuckles. "Make that two."

"Three," Em adds.

"Think I'll take a bottle of wine," I drawl. Laughter drifts over the island as we head for the house.

Reese mills about in the shack. When we all head for the fire pit, the chatter flowing, he walks outside.

"Sit, nephew of mine." Iris pats the chair by her.

Reese leans on the shack but studies each of us in turn. "Nah, I'm good. Not into small talk when it's with the olds."

Iris turns in her seat, her eyes narrowing. "Who you calling old, you dunderheid?"

Reese tries to flatten a smile and fails. His dark hair flops over his face, and he brushes it back. In this violet light that's fast turning dark, I'm gifted a momentary glance of Callum McCreary twenty years ago.

And he was stunning.

With that image safely stored away, I wedge the cork out of a new bottle of red and let the dark maroon liquid glug into the glass balancing precariously on my Adirondack chair.

Iris raises her beer. "To family. To the people we love, and to loving them back, hard. To the ones who have been there since forever and the ones who found us when it was time." She looks at me, then back to Reese, raising her drink.

Reese chuckles, still leaning on the shack, picking at a stalk of grass.

"To family," Em says, tapping the neck of his bottle to hers.

"To family," I say around the stone in my throat. Iris clinks her beer to my glass.

Every gaze settles on Cal. He studies all of us in turn. Like father, like son. His attention homes in on me as he lifts his beer. "To ending up right where you're meant to be."

I smile.

The sentiment warms my heart. I'm right where I need to be. This is my home.

He is my home.

I have absolutely no intention of ever wandering so far I lose my way back.

Besides, if I wander, he will wander with me.

Our one nonnegotiable promise neither of us could break, even if we tried—

"Yeah, so I'm out of here." Reese rolls off the shack and heads into the house, no doubt to raid the fridge again. The fridge door opens, and Cal snaps his head up, gaze shooting at the kitchen window. "Don't you waste that hard-earned food, boy!"

I chuckle. Some things never change.

A constant, like the stars or the horizon. Always there. Stoic and permanent, like our old lighthouse. Like the McCreary legacy on Fire Island. And, if I have anything to do with it, the legacy will live on for decades after us.

"Damn hollow legs, that lad," Cal grumbles, leaning back in his chair, sipping his beer. I rise from the chair and drop to his lap, wine in hand. "What would you fill your days with if you didn't have us to take care of, fear milis?"

The delight lighting Iris's face reminds me she shares our language, too.

Without a word, she sips her beer, glancing at Emmett.

I wonder how long it will take until the elegant language of her heritage starts to slip out around Em the way Cal's did around me. When she's going to let her wall down, brave the particular storm that is her brother, and let the floodgates open on what torturously dangles between her and Em.

Lord knows they have waited long enough.

firefly

Thirty-Eight

CALLUM

The Indian stands on the grass in the midday sunshine.

She's done.

Weeks of hard work, cursing, and one incredible fucking memory of Evie on this bike, and it's ready to go. There's only one last finishing touch until I can kick out the stand and fire her up. And I won't find it on this island.

I roll the bike toward the jetty.

Reese waits by Firefly at the ramp we rigged up to transfer the bike onto the boat and across to the mainland. Back to Bay Shore, where I intend on surprising Evie when she gets back from her meeting with Livvy for her new manuscript. She's been gone a whole two days, and I'm antsy as hell without her.

"She looks good," Reese says, running a hand over the black leather seat when I roll her to a stop before the ramp. "If you two are going to go and ruin this sweet leather seat, I'm never touching this relic ever again."

Lucky for me, I have Reese to keep me grounded. I swear to god, the shit that flies out of this boy's mouth.

Christ.

I give him a hard stare, a subtle reminder of the boundaries we agreed on.

His gaze drops back to where his hand brushes over the polished chrome, the new black paint. His fingers track to the fuel cap before he looks up. "What do you think she's worth?"

"We still talking about the bike?"

He chuckles. "Yeah."

"Not as much as the girl I'm about to bring happiness to with just one ride around the coastline."

Reese rolls his eyes. "Yeah, that sappy shit's gotta stop."

"That's what he said, bud."

"Whatever." He runs a hand through his hair, his biceps flexing under his T-shirt.

"You'll find out soon enough," I say with a chuckle.

"Fuck, no. No woman is going to have me"—he waves a hand at me—"like this." He's shaking his head, and it's all I can do to not laugh at him outright.

Poor boy, he has no fucking clue.

"Right, time waits for no man, and neither does the New York bus line."

I push the handlebars as Reese pushes the rear. We get her onto Firefly, and I roll her up the deck by the cabin and kick the stand down. She really is a beauty.

Restored, re-loved.

"You be alright here for a few days by yourself?"

I wait, studying his face. The last time we left him here alone . . .

"I'm good."

"Don't forget the lamp. The harvest needs to be done every couple days or things turn. Close up downstairs every night in case a storm rolls in."

"Yeah, yeah, I got it. Get the hell out of here." He plucks up my overnighter and tosses it at me. I catch it and slide it under the bike before tying both to the side of the cabin in case we hit choppy water.

"Thanks, bud. See you in a few."

Reese waves and wanders up the jetty.

I fire up Firefly and throttle her out into the water. We aim for the east shoreline, and my excitement grows. I have missed my little woman every single minute she's been gone. And I intend on making sure she knows just how much.

How much she is loved.

Every mile we cover today and the next is the start of

our new life together. Here's hoping all went well with Livvy.

Twenty minutes later, I glide the old fishing boat into our slip, where Emmett awaits with bated breath. This is the first time he's seen the bike in almost twenty years. Somehow, everything feels like it's come full circle. Our lives, our loves. Our past catching up as we forge ahead and make anew on old promises and heal old wounds.

I let the mooring lines fly from my hands, and Em catches them, securing them to the dock. I slide the ramps into place and her bumpers over the gunwale, running a hand over the Indian.

"She came up great, bud," Em says.

"Sure did." I untie the bike, flicking the kickstand up with my foot. He takes one side, I take the other. We roll the big old girl up and over one ramp and down the other. Safely on the dock, Em slides the ramps back onto Firefly's deck.

"Better be going. The bus is notorious for being early." He nods toward the road.

I grab my jacket and an extra helmet from the cabin before swinging my leg over the Indian. Em beams at me.

I flick the kickstand back, and my gut flips.

It's been almost twenty years . . .

Sucking in a long, lung-stretching, heart-pounding breath, I fire her up.

And . . .

She *roars* to life.

Em pumps his fist in the air like a compete dolt. I can't wipe the fucking smile from my face. I twist the throttle on the right handle, and the loud, heavy sound echoes over the marina.

Happiness weaves its warmth through my chest.

Now there's only one piece of this puzzle missing. And her bus is about to roll in. I shift the Indian into gear and give the gas hell. Like a shot in the dark, we leave Em behind, flying over the old dock boards past boats in their slips. I take a left up the ramp by the watchhouse and stick it to her, hoping like hell Errol is mid-nap at the damn desk like usual.

I chuckle and turn onto the street.

With a not-so-subtle rev, I pass the café and wave at Irry. She looks up, her mouth agape as I ride by. Reaching Main Street, I open her up.

Here's hoping I make the bus station before Evie does.

The New York line is late.

And I couldn't be happier.

I sit on the parked Indian, one leg bent on the seat, helmet in my hands outside the terminal doors. God, it's been decades since I waited on a girl, perched on this small leather seat.

I study the ground, thinking of all the ways this thing could have turned out and counting my lucky stars they turned out the way they did. A slow whoosh has my head snap up. People wander through the doors in a messy, crowded formation.

No Evie.

I shift on the seat, running the edge of the helmet through my fingers. When the doors close and she hasn't appeared, I hold my breath. The finest sliver of panic tangles with my senses.

The doors whoosh open again.

She pads toward me. "I thought that looked like my grumpy recluse."

Christ, baby girl, you damn well scared me.

I push from the bike and drop the helmet to the ground as she flies into my arms, legs wrapping around my waist. Her belongings forgotten to the ground, she dots strings of kisses over my face.

This is where she goddamn belongs.

"Hell, mo ghràdh, I missed you."

Evie leans back, her hands cupping my face. "And I you, fear milis."

Lord above.

"You rode the Indian," she breathes.

"And you're about to."

She worries her bottom lip through her teeth. "I've never been on a motorbike before, Cal. I mean, while it's moving."

I smile at her. "That changes today."

"What about my bag?"

"We can leave it behind the counter and come back for it later."

I wave to the guy at the front desk, and he slips out, taking her bag back behind the counter like he agreed to when I asked earlier.

"Later? Where are we going?"

I lower her to her feet and hop on the bike, firing her up. "Anywhere you want." Clasping my helmet on securely, I hand Evie hers. She pulls it on and snaps the buckle closed. Stepping closer, she throws one leg over and slides forward, wrapping her arms around my waist, resting her chin on my shoulder. "Take me anywhere, sweet man."

We roll from the parking lot and onto the small street. After an age of the confines of our small coastal town, we find the highway.

"Hold on, mo ghràdh."

She tightens around me.

I open the Indian up, full throttle.

We fly forward, and Evie squeals. We cruise over the

winding coastal highway, stuck on each other as the wind whips past.

The woman I love is wrapped around me.

Every milestone in this life of mine has been marked by hardship. Now, by my own choosing, I will only count the good things in life.

Evie gave me that.

I've been living under one of the world's brightest lights for two decades, and it wasn't until this timid, kind, bighearted woman cracked me wide open that I stepped out of the shadows.

I slow the bike when the state forest sign comes up. Turning into the park, we roll into the secluded parking area, and I kill the engine.

Unclipping the chin strap, I tug my helmet off and hang it on the handlebar. Evie steps from the bike and hands me hers. "That was incredible!"

Her face is lit up, stuffing my heart even fuller with happiness. I slide back on the seat and pat the front of it. She moves onto the bike, her legs draped over my thighs. I clasp her face in my hands and sink my mouth over hers. Breathless, we part, and she gives me a shy little look.

"What?" I ask.

"So, I've been bursting to tell you this . . . Livvy loved my—our—story."

"She did?"

"Yes, but—"

I tilt my head and frown. "Do I need to send a strong-worded email to my cousin?"

She chuckles, and it almost sounds a little nervous. "No, nothing like that. It's just that my name is attached to my fantasy series. So she said I needed a pen name. She suggested one, but I'm not sure it will work . . ."

"What is it?"

Her hand brushes my jaw as she breathes, "Evie McCreary."

The grin stretching my face is ridiculous.

"Well, that figures, since you said yes, baby."

"I did. I do." She hangs her head. "But my parents—"

"You saw them this trip?"

"Yeah. They were less than supportive because of . . ."

"The old man you're engaged to?"

"It's mostly my father."

I slide my hands along her jaw, holding her gaze with mine. "We'll figure it out, I promise."

"No more of those, remember?"

"Alright," I say, tucking a stray wave of hair behind her ear. "On a more productive note, Em and I started the refurb on Pearl while you were away."

"You did!?" Her face lights up instantly.

I chuckle and nod.

"That's amazing . . . Almost as amazing as this gorgeous bike." She leans back on the handlebars, her hands sliding along them as she tosses her head back with a giggle.

"Keep doing that and you'll be getting more than just a joyride, Evie baby."

Her brown eyes rise, and I swear they're a hell of a lot darker than they were a moment ago when she says, "Good."

Leaning over her as she lies along the chrome-finished Indian, I pluck a nipple into my teeth through her shirt. "Hold on, mo ghràdh."

firefly

Thirty-Nine

CALLUM

Apparently, the chat Reese and I had last week about focusing on keeping his head down and finding honest work didn't take. Before Reese moved back to the Bay to start the job hunt, we hashed out what was okay in this tiny little seaside town and what was not.

But now, I stand outside Iris's café with an irate Errol. Iris stands behind the counter, pretending to dry up shake glasses as she peers at us.

"Keep your good-for-nothing kid away from my granddaughter, you hear?" Errol spits.

I lean back on my heels, trying my best to avoid his spray. *Say it, don't spray it, old man.* His finger points at my chest.

"This is history fucking repeating itself. That's what this is. You nip this shit in the bud, McCreary."

"Calm down. The boy lives here, Errol. He's not stalking your granddaughter."

Doesn't that phrase take a whole new meaning now.

He scoffs. "Lives here? Now that isn't going to end well, and you know it."

"I don't know, maybe he's a generous tipper . . ." I chuckle. I can't resist stirring the old prick up. I swear, a smile tries its damn hardest to tug that shriveled mouth of his upward.

He glares at me.

Nope. Must have imagined it.

"You about done? I've got somewhere to be," I say with a sigh.

I don't think our families will ever get on, despite Ava's reappearance and Paige working—happily, I might add—for Iris.

"You watch that boy like a hawk, or I swear to god." Errol stalks off in the direction of the watchhouse.

Some things never change.

Em bursts through the café door. "Geez, Cal. We got to get going, or Iris is going to serve my balls to the next paying customer."

"Right, I'm ready when you are."

Time to head up to Rockland and pick up our suits. Not that I had any intention of wearing a full suit to a beach wedding. But what makes my girl happy, I do. Em fires up his truck, and I climb in. "Oh, I have to run an errand up there after we grab the suits."

"What you got going on?" he asks.

"Ordered in Evie's wedding present."

"Let me guess, a cargo shipment of books?"

"Nah, something a little lighter." I smile at him, and he frowns over the grin stretching his face, confusion lining his eyes.

"You'll see. Hopefully," I add.

"Hopefully?" Now his brow raises as the truck pulls away from the curb.

"Yup. The timing has to be right, and we've been monitoring the progress for days."

Em's gaze alternates between me and the road. "Now I need to know . . ."

All I can do is smile at him as I give him the rundown on the gift I've been wanting to give Evie since the day she told me about T and his dead-insect-laden letters.

The sun sets behind me as the officiant beams at me.

Em stands to my right. Iris at my left.

My family.

Which is about to go from a party of four to five.

A lone fellow Scot stands on the dune where the grassy island meets the shore, bagpipes at the ready. The first note he plays whines through the air, and we all turn in unison.

Evie walks past the older man who plays "Caledonia" in traditional highland dress, his kilt waving in the late afternoon breeze. Holding a cluster of flowers from the greenhouse, Evie passes the island's boundary where land meets sea, padding down the sand toward us. Her dress sweeps over the sand, its silken material fitted to her elegant curves. The sweetheart neckline is held in place with two fine lacy-capped straps.

Em and Iris take a step back, Iris sliding her arm through Em's, her elegant frame leaning into his side as her green dress tangles around her legs.

Brown eyes find mine when I turn back.

My arms, previously crossed over my body, fall to my side before I clasp my hands together. Grinding my jaw shut, I tamp down the emotion currently closing over my throat.

A trio of people I don't fully recognize, escorted by Reese, walk across the grassy area following behind at a distance. *Better late than never.* Reese brought them over on Firefly. The boy has taken to the sea like a duck to water. A little something Iris arranged for Evie's wedding gift.

And I can't wait to meet them. Evie comes to stand in front of me, turning and handing her flowers to Iris. It's then she catches the people crossing the island casually. Like they're not about to wreck my girl's heart in the best way possible.

"Oh! What?!" Her face breaks. Hovering, she searches my face. "Cal?"

"That was all Iris, baby girl."

She looks to Iris with a sob before hitching up her long dress and flying back up the sand to her parents and who I assume is Allie.

"Thought they couldn't make it?" Em whispers, leaning over to where I stand.

"Yeah, it took a few video chats to get her old man to come around."

"You're her old man now." Iris snickers.

"Goddamn, Irry," I growl.

"The hell?" Em says at the same time.

The moment is like a catalyst of joy as laughter splits the air around us.

"Daddy, this is Cal," Evie says, dragging her father behind her. He's tall and lithe like his daughter. You can see where she gets her dark features from.

"Pleasure to finally meet you in person," Carl says.

"In person?" Evie's mouth gapes.

"We did that online chat thing a few times," Carl offers.

"Video call?" Evie asks, her face looking like she could die from embarrassment at any second.

"Yeah, that one." I wind my arm around her waist and plant a kiss to her temple.

"Cal," Vanessa says, "thank you for taking care of our little girl." She holds her arms out, and Iris all but shoves me into them. Evie's mother squeezes me tight, and now I feel like a damn kid.

"Mrs. Holland, you are going to suffocate the poor man," a new voice says.

As I'm finally released, I find Evie holding her hand, bumping shoulders like long-lost friends.

"Allie?" I ask.

"You got it, grumpy lighthouse man." She grins and thumps a fist into my shoulder and weaves on the spot, beaming. I shake my head at her. The girl's a goof.

"Well, we getting these two married, or what?" Em says as Reese comes to my side; he cleans up nice in a shirt and tie.

"Yes, most definitely." Carl chuckles.

"Thank you, Daddy." Evie kisses his cheek and comes to stand in front of me again. Everyone takes their place and the officiant, who's been waiting patiently, clears her throat.

"We are gathered here today . . ."

Iris and Em took the wedding party back to the café to prepare our little wedding soiree. But we have one more stop before we board Firefly for the first time as Mr. and Mrs. McCreary and cross that span of water. Dancing our way over the grass to the tune of the sounds of the forest, the sea, and the twilight breeze as stars pop overhead, we head for the house.

"You going to carry me over the threshold, Mr. McCreary?"

I spin her around, her gorgeous dark waves billowing around her shoulders as those browns light up even more.

"Nonnegotiable, Mrs. McCreary."

My face hurts from smiling. My grump-fueled self is not equipped for this much damn happiness. I sweep her from her feet on the next twirl and stop. Her laughter fades, and I dot a kiss to her forehead.

Fucking *mine*.

Always was. Always will be.

"Ready?" I breathe.

Worrying her bottom lip playfully through her teeth, she simply nods.

I pad for the front door and kick it open.

Her head hangs over my arm as she cackles.

I step over the threshold.

And we're home. To be fair, my home is this incredible woman. Where she goes, I go, from this day forward.

I don't want to put her down.

Not having her in my arms isn't how I would have planned on spending the rest of the day. But we can't keep our family waiting, so I set her down.

"We could just go upstairs and stay there. No one will miss us, husband," she coos.

Christ, the sound of that steals my breath and leaves me hard all in a heartbeat. I tug her into my chest, dropping my lips to her ear. "They absolutely will. So we better make this quick."

"Make what quick?" She angles her head, a quizzical expression taking over her face.

"Your gift from me is upstairs." I spin her around. "On the bed."

"I think I know what it is," she breathes.

"Nope, not this time."

"Okay, *now* I need to see it."

"Aye aye," I say, sweeping her into my arms.

She throws her head back with a laugh that fills my heart so full. One step at a time, her laughter peters out. As I cross the bedroom threshold, I lower her on her feet and turn her to face the bed. "Deep breath, baby. Be brave one more time, mo ghràdh," I whisper, the words brushing past her ear.

She steps toward the bed. I lean back and close the door, double-checking the windows are shut.

The large white box is wrapped up in a wide silver bow. She slips the small envelope out from under the ribbon. Sliding a finger under the flap, she glances back as she opens it.

I wrap around her from behind and read it for her, wanting my voice to carry the words for this moment.

"Evie, what can a man say to the woman who patched him back together, saw him for who he truly is, and stood by while he relearned it all for himself? I don't think a word exists for it. But if it did, *mine* sounds like the perfect syllable. We have come so far and never even left this little island. Open your present, baby girl. See how far you've come, my *Fire Heart*. Callum."

Her hand trembles around the paper. She turns, planting a kiss on my jaw. Tears streak her beautiful face.

"Go on, open it," I rasp, emotion turning my expression gravelly.

"What is it?"

"*Victory*, Fire Heart." I let my tongue roll on each R to emphasize the importance of the moment.

She stares at me for a beat before tugging at the ribbon. The two flaps of the lid are only half closed by a small strip of tape, and she peels it back. I drop my head to her shoulder, kissing her neck before I whisper, "Tha gaol agam ort."

Fine fingers pry the lid panels open.

On the prettiest gasp a man's ever heard, her breath stops.

Hundreds of orange monarch butterflies soar from their confines. The fluttering cloud surrounds us in our small bedroom. Evie raises her head, turning it as wonder fills her face. Her hands cover her mouth and nose.

The fluttering calms a little as some settle, landing on furniture around our bedroom, while others circle the room, free and wild. The potted flowers I have around the room brighten the space. A few nectar trays lie on top of the wardrobe to keep them fed and happy.

"They're magnificent," she breathes and turns back, sliding her arms around my neck. "I love them. Do we really have to go to the party?"

"It's our party. And your wee winged friends will be here when you come home. You have a whole two weeks with them."

She huffs a breath and lifts her head to behold them as they flurry about our room. One lands on her head before another comes to rest on my shoulder. Retracting her arm carefully, she holds her finger beside it. I regard her with absolute awe as the tiny little insect steps onto her finger.

And my girl smiles.

Her fear now well and truly replaced by adoration.

The darkness that once shrouded Evie obliterated by her light.

This little woman, *my* fucking woman, outshines this old lighthouse. And it just so happens I am the luckiest man alive, because she chose to shine her light on me.

firefly

Forty

CALLUM

Firefly is decorated with tin cans on strings floating in the water behind her. Shaving cream and white streamers adorn the cabin. Evie carries her shoes, our fingers laced as we stroll down the jetty. Stars shimmer overhead as we board this old fishing boat that's bared witness to our first meeting as well as to our first day as man and wife.

Tossing the fenders over to the deck, I release the lines before holding Evie's hand again as she navigates the gunwale in her long, stunning dress. When she's safely on board, I climb up and make for the cabin. One of the kitchen chairs sits beside the bench seat in the small space.

"What's with the chair?" I ask.

"You'll see." My wife pecks my cheek with a chaste

kiss.

Letting Firefly idle for a beat, I crowd her against the console and claim her mouth. She leans back, away from my touch. My brows drop, a low raw noise rattling up my throat. "Evie?"

"I'm driving, husband." She smiles. Spinning in my hold, her hands settle on the wheel and throttle. Firefly pulls away from the jetty under the careful direction of her new captain. Once free of the shallows, Evie sends the throttle forward, and we cruise over the water. I fold myself around her, sinking my head into her hair. But as I close my eyes, breathing her in, the engine quiets.

Raising my head, I check the gauges.

The revs are down.

The throttle is still in her grip as she kills the engine.

"What's going on?"

Without a word, she slips away from the console and disappears from the cabin with the chair. Curious, I follow. I find her standing behind it, a line from the stern storage box in her hands.

Brown eyes burn into mine. "Sit."

With a smile, I close the distance, stopping short at the chair. "Alright," I say with a chuckle.

I sit and fine fingers take my wrists, moving them behind the back and tying them together. She pads round, coming to face me.

The knot loosens. I keep my hands where she left

them, focusing on the most magnificent woman I've ever known. "Are y—"

A finger presses over my lips, and she shakes her head. That finger drags its way to the opening of my shirt. She moves closer and I spread my legs, letting her into my space. Deft hands make quick work of the buttons, and my shirt hits the floor. Next the belt goes. Then the pants. Until I'm left in boxers and socks.

Tied to a fucking chair.

Evie sinks to her knees.

I clench my jaw, blood rushing its harried way through my body before plummeting south. She curls her hair around her hand, sweeping it to one side before looking up at me. Big brown eyes take me in, darker than the night sky. But now, there's a fire that took her months to find. Then months more to get back, after . . .

And that fire currently burns for me.

Her lips part on a pant, hands walking up my thighs until they find their target, and my cock springs free. Elegant fingers curl around the base of it, and I let out a low moan, wishing my hands were free to fist her hair, to sink my swollen length to the back of her throat.

She studies me with darkened eyes before sliding me onto her tongue.

And . . . *fuck.*

Tongue swirling around my tip, she grazes her teeth

over the sensitive skin before plunging me deep. My breaths heave in short choppy waves that sear.

Sucking her way back up, she trains her eyes to my face.

Fucking Christ.

My legs tremble.

Desperate to be free, to touch her, I tug at the rope binding my wrists together. It loosens, slipping from one wrist and dangling from the other.

Evie stills, as if she wants this moment of having me subdued on the chair to last.

So I stay put.

Closing my eyes, I grind my molars, my only salvation from the overwhelming need to haul her to her feet, spread those pretty thighs, and sink balls-deep into my incredible fucking wife.

I don't move.

She grips me harder, ratcheting up the suction as a pretty little mewl slips around my damn cock.

Heat floods my body and I groan, every inch of me vibrating with soul-crushing need.

Another stroke upward, and I'm reeling.

I couldn't catch a breath if I tried.

The throb in my cock has disintegrated into a painful ache.

She releases me with a pop, her sweet little tongue poking out to lick her lips.

FUCK.

She stands, slipping the straps of her dress over her shoulders, tugging the neckline down to expose her perfect tits.

That's it . . . *I'm done.*

Ripping the line from my wrist, I fly from the chair. My hand is around her throat, sending her backward a heartbeat later. Her back meets the wall of Firefly's cabin. I hoist her up to my hips, pushing her dress up until my hand finds—

No goddamn panties.

"Hell, mo ghràdh," I growl.

Running a digit through her soaked center, I close my mouth over one gorgeous, pert nipple. She writhes against the cabin wall.

"Going to the party with no panties, baby girl?"

"Overnight bag," she breathes.

I chuckle. This is all for me.

Mine . . . My wife.

Her hands sink into my hair. "Please, Cal."

"No panties and begging, wife. So fucking needy."

She dots kisses down my neck, teeth grazing the sensitive skin below my ear.

I nudge her entrance with my tip, a hand moving into her hair and fisting as I tug her head to one side. "Mine, mo ghràdh. All fucking mine."

"Yours," she breathes. "Now, stop procrastinating, fear milis."

I slam up into her. Slapping a hand on the wall over her head, I thrust into her so deep, Firefly rocks. Evie's hands fly up to press against the wall behind her, climbing higher and higher with every thrust.

Every single one is a testament to my love for her.

The way we become one in so many ways.

The pleasure she gives me that I wish to return a thousand times over.

She tightens around me, her whimpers turning to cries, and I peel her from the wall and stride to the chair. The wooden seat hits my bare ass, and she cups my face, taking up the desperate rhythm we have created. The one between me and her that hums along with a life of its own.

Rising, she hovers at the point where we are only just joined.

Her favorite fucking spot.

"Down," I grind out.

Her mouth finds mine. I open, like the lovesick pup I am.

Slowly, ever so damn slowly, she descends. The second she's fully seated, she milks my cock. Her head falls back, hair dangling over her back, those perfect tits presented to me. I close my teeth around a nipple, tugging it before sucking away the sting that would have spread through the tender skin.

She rocks, releasing wave after wave, sending me insane.

Before her orgasm is over, I rise from the chair, spinning it around with one hand as I set her to her feet. We part for only a second as I cup the back of her neck and cover her mouth with a searing kiss. Hand in her hair, I bend her over the back of the chair and flip her dress over her ass.

I don't let her settle before sinking balls-deep into my damn wife. She teeters for a heartbeat before bending lower, bracing with her hands. I knead her ass with my hands, thundering into her. With a harsh slap, I'm rewarded with a delicious jerk along my cock as she cries out.

"Come for me, wife."

Her legs tremble, and she tightens again. Sending a hand along her spine, I grip her neck, leaning over her. "Was this what you had in mind?"

Her head turns to the side, brown eyes burning. "Better." Her hand slides over mine on her hip. "Fuck, Cal."

She rocks, every tight milking wave wringing my cock. Heat blooms low in my spine, my balls tightening as I thrust into her in sloppy, desperate moves.

With a roar, I spill into her in erratic surges, every

rope of release sinking deeper than the last. "Fuck, mo ghràdh. Always mine."

"I'm yours. Until my light goes out."

The air leaves my lungs, not returning. I haul her up off the chair, wrap my body around hers, and whisper, "Until my light goes out."

I barely have the last word out before my throat closes over.

Her hands wind backward around my neck. I drop my mouth to hers as she turns her head. The ocean breeze tangles in her hair, sending it over my face. She lets loose a huffy laugh as she brushes it away. The night sky overhead glimmers over the glistening moonlit waters as a shooting star streaks across the night sky.

"Time for a party?" I whisper.

Lord knows what Iris has got in store for us.

"It's time," she breathes.

All Evie needs now is dancing shoes and some goddamn panties.

Epilogue

EVIE

Two years later . . .

It's hard to believe it's been two whole years since our quiet little affair with an officiant and our family. On the beach, under the watchful eye of the lighthouse, Cal and I made our only promise official. At sunset, of course. Because why not?

Since then, Pearl had her glow-up, and we have embarked on our round-the-world tour.

Cal and Evie style.

Sunny days, lazy mornings, and more boat sex than you could fit into the smuttiest smut book.

And . . . today's my birthday.

Thirty.

Urgh, I feel old.

Heavens knows how blessed I am. How many thirty-year-olds have the career of their dreams, can literally sail around the world, and have the man their heart called for?

I do. I can.

Heavens, I will never forget how stinking lucky I am.

Without this man, I'd still be hovering somewhere in the dank shadows of a life of fear.

Or worse.

Now, sunshine soaks into my bones every morning out on deck. I get to watch the best man I've ever met in his happy place. The smile he gives me every day the sun sets on another one of our days at sea . . . I'll take with me into the next life, I'm sure.

Sitting on the deck on calm waters, I type out my latest romance, one I've been dying to tell for the past six months. Another one close to home. I guess I'll have to change the names. Maybe call them Emerson and Isla.

Too obvious?

I chuckle at myself as Cal walks up the companionway, two coffees in hand.

"Thank you, my love." I tilt my face to the sun and Cal's kiss presses down on my lips, the warm mug slides into my waiting hands.

"Happy birthday, baby girl."

"Thank you." I sip the coffee, gaze drifting to the glistening light blue waters of the Pacific Ocean. Swallowing, I wince. The coffee tastes odd. Cal disappears below deck for a moment, returning with a large box in his hands. The one I thought was full of non-perishable rations is now wrapped in a navy ribbon ending in an oversized bow. He sets it at my feet and sinks to the bench seat cushion. "Open it."

"What on earth did you haul all the way from the last port for my birthday? How are you this organized, Callum McCreary?"

"This one's special. Go on, open it." He nods to the box.

I slip from the bench seat to sit by the box as I tug the ribbon undone and slide it away. The last box like this had hundreds of butterflies. But that wouldn't be the case now, with the open skies above us.

I glance to Cal. The softest, most handsome smile lights his face.

I open the lid, and when nothing flies out to greet me, I push to my knees and peer inside.

"I figured since you like old things, you'll love *this* old thing."

I pluck the tissue paper from the top, tossing it to the deck. My mouth gapes when I see the retro keys. The pale-blue painted metal.

"Oh Cal," I breathe.

He stands and leans down, lifting the old-school type-writer from the box. "He's a heavy little git." His forearms flex as he squats and places the typewriter in front of me. I sink to my seat and run a hand over the pearlescent finish, then the black keys. The chrome return handle gives easily as I try it out, sending the roller round a little.

"You two need a moment?" Cal chuckles, dotting a kiss to the crown of my head.

I look up at him, still stunned. "It's beautiful, thank you. It's too much."

My gut flips as he leans down, tilting my chin up so my eyes level with his. "For you, my love, nothing will ever be enough."

I tug my bottom lip through my teeth before it slips out on a smile.

"Lunch will be ready in a couple of hours. Get some words in, hey?"

Lunch . . .

"I will," I reply softly, feeling the remnants of something like nausea at the mention of food.

Returning my focus to the typewriter, I rip a blank page from my journal and wind it through the machine.

I decide to try out a few working titles for my next book.

Tapping the keys, the thrill of them falling away under my fingers as the letters smash against the page . . .

Urgh, perfect.

The sound of the clickety clack—pure addiction.

My mouth waters, and not in a good way.

I shift on my seat, stretching, hoping a few deep breaths will stave off the discomfort.

It doesn't.

I retch, slapping my hand to my mouth.

Shit.

My stomach revolts, and I scramble to my feet and make the yacht's railing. I lose my coffee to the sea.

Footsteps thunder up the companionway. Cal crosses the deck, face tight. Those blue eyes that hold my heart are flooded with worry.

I straighten and think back.

Surely . . .

It's only after a moment of rough calculations I realize how much time has passed since—

"Oh my god." I retch and lean over the rail again. A large, warm hand rubs my back.

"Coffee no good?" he asks.

I breathe through the next wave of nausea and turn back. "Cal, I don't think it's the coffee . . ."

His face tilts a little before it falls with shock. "You—you're?"

"I think so."

His hands cup my face a second later. I press mine to his chest. I just threw up, twice.

Pressing his forehead to my own, his jaw feathers. "We having a wee bairn, mo ghràdh?"

"We are," I breathe.

Tears swell, pooling beneath the blue I adore. I weave my fingers through his beard and smile a wobbly smile, despite the nausea clawing at my insides.

"Well, baby, looks like we're heading home." He sounds so damn happy.

"No, it's our first trip. It's too soon." I force myself upright.

"How long do we have?"

"A good five or six months, at a guess."

"Well, let's make them count, baby girl."

Let's make them count.

Cal & Evie's journey has one last surprise, get the extended epilogue here.

Need more Fire Island romance?

Get **Emmett & Iris's story**.

FIRE ISLAND SERIES

Book 3

ALEXANDRA BANKS

firefly

Scot's Gaelic

AS USED BY CAL (AND SOMETIMES EVIE)

Just in case you need it . . .

mo ghràdh ~ my love

mo nighean ~ my girl

nighean bhrèagha ~ beautiful girl

fear milis ~ sweet man

cailín luachmhor ~ precious girl

Beannachd leat, a nighean milis ~ goodbye, sweet girl

Tha gaol agam ort ~ I love you

Acknowledgments

Evie & Cal (and Iris & Emmett) have been with me for a long time. So when it was time to write their story, I was so stinking excited!! I hope that I have done it well enough that they shine. Grump and people pleasing aside, these two are incredible. And I hope you think so too.

As always, *thanks to my editors, Lindsey and Zainab.* Your input and guidance is always wanted and appreciated.

To every **ARC reader** who volunteered to read this book, thank you!!

And lastly, but most certainly not least, my family for putting up with the endless playlists that I made them endure during the writing process to get into the zone. Sorry... ;)

Alex xx

About the Author

Alexandra Banks is a romantic at heart, and an optimist down to her very bones. Her love for everything romance sees her writing HEAs all day long.

But don't be fooled, there will be angst along the way, possibly heartbreak. But her fierce heroines can handle just about anything!

For more heartwarming reads, follow her on socials and join the mailing list so you never miss another heart throb!

9 781764 194938